SPIRIT OF THE CENTURY™
PRESENTS

KHAN
OF MARS

BY
STEPHEN
BLACKMOORE

EVIL HAT
PRODUCTIONS

An Evil Hat Productions Publication
www.evilhat.com • feedback@evilhat.com

First published in 2013 by Evil Hat Productions

Editor: John Adamus • Proofreading: Amanda Valentine
Art: Christian N. St. Pierre• Design: Fred Hicks
Branding: Chris Hanrahan

Hardcover ISBN: 978-1-61317-037-3
Softcover ISBN: 978-1-61317-018-2
Kindle ISBN: 978-1-61317-039-7
ePub ISBN: 978-1-61317-038-0

Printed in the USA

OTHER TITLES AVAILABLE OR COMING SOON FROM SPIRIT OF THE CENTURY™ PRESENTS:

THIS BOOK WAS MADE POSSIBLE WITH THE SUPPORT OF...

Michael Bowman *and a cast of hundreds, including*
"The Cap'n" Wayne Coburn, "The Professor" Eric Smailys, @aroberts72, @syntheticbrain, A. David Pinilla, Aaron Jones, Aaron Jurkis, Adam & Jayce Roberts, Adam B. Ross, Adam Rajski, Adan Tejada, AJ Medder, AJT, Alan Bellingham, Alan Hyde, Alan Winterrowd, Alex, Alien Zookeeper, Alisha "hostilecrayon" Miller, Alosia Sellers, Amy Collins, Amy Lambzilla Hamilton, Andrew Beirne, Andrew Byers, Andrew Guerr, Andrew Jensen, Andrew M. Kelly, Andrew Nicolle, Andrew Watson, Andy Blanchard, Andy Eaton, Angela Korra'ti, Anonymous Fan, Anthony Laffan, Anthony R. Cardno, April Fowler, Arck Perra, Ariel Pereira, Arnaud Walraevens, Arthur Santos Jr, Ashkai Sinclair, Autumn and Sean Stickney, Axisor, Bailey Shoemaker Richards, Barac Wiley, Barbara Hasebe, Barrett Bishop, Bartimeus, Beena Gohil, Ben Ames, Ben Barnett, Ben Bement, Ben Bryan, Bill Dodds, Bill Harting, Bill Segulin, Blackcoat, Bo Saxon, Bo Williams, Bob Bretz, Brandon H. Mila, Bret S. Moore, Esq., Brian Allred, Brian E. Williams, Brian Engard, Brian Isikoff, Brian Kelsay @ripcrd, Brian Nisbet, Brian Scott Walker, Brian Waite, Brian White, Bryan Sims, Bryce Perry, C.K. "Velocitycurve" Lee, Calum Watterson, Cameron Harris, Candlemark & Gleam, Carl Rigney, Carol Darnell, Carolyn Butler, Carolyn White, Casey & Adam Moeller, Catherine Mooney, CE Murphy, Centurion Eric Brenders, Charles Paradis, Chase Bolen, Cheers, Chip & Katie, Chris Bekofske, Chris Callahan, Chris Ellison, Chris Hatty, Chris Heilman, Chris Matosky, Chris Newton, Chris Norwood, Chris Perrin, Christian Lindke, Christina Lee, Christine Lorang, Christine Swendseid, Christopher Gronlund, Chrystin, Clark & Amanda Valentine, Clay Robeson, Corey Davidson, Corinne Erwin, Craig Maloney, Crazy J, Cyrano Jones, Dan Conley, Dan N, Dan Yarrington, Daniel C. Hutchison, Daniel Laloggia, Danielle Ingber, Darcy Casselman, Darren Davis, Darrin Shimer, Daryl Weir, Dave BW, Dave Steiger, David & Nyk, David Hines, David M., David Patri, Declan Feeney, Deepone, Demelza Beckly, Derrick Eaves, Dimitrios Lakoumentas, DJ Williams, DL Thurston, Doug Cornelius, Dover Whitecliff, Drew, drgnldy71, DU8, Dusty Swede, Dylan McIntosh, Ed Kowalczewski, edchuk, Edouard "Francesco", Edward J Smola III, Eleanor-Rose Begg, Eli "Ace" Katz, Ellie Reese, Elly & Andres, Emily Poole, Eric Asher, Eric Duncan, Eric Henson, Eric Lytle, Eric Paquette, Eric Smith, Eric Tilton, Eric B Vogel, Ernie Sawyer, Eva, Evan Denbaum, Evan Grummell, Ewen Albright, Explody, Eyal Teler, Fabrice Breau, Fade Manley, Fidel Jiron Jr., Frank "Grayhawk" Huminski, Frank Jarome, Frank Wuerbach, Frazer Porritt, Galen, Gareth-Michael Skarka, Garry Jenkins, Gary Hoggatt, Gary McBride, Gavran, Gemma Tapscott, Glenn, Greg Matyola, Greg Roy, Gregory Frank, Gregory G. Gieger, Gus Golden, Herefox, HPLustcraft, Hugh J. O'Donnell, Ian Llywelyn Brown, Ian Loo, Inder Rottger, Itamar Friedman, J. Layne Nelson, J.B. Mannon, J.C. Hutchins, Jack Gulick, Jake Reid, James "discord_inc" Fletcher, James Alley, James Ballard, James Champlin, James Husum, James Melzer, Jami Nord, Jared Leisner, Jarrod Coad, Jason Brezinski, Jason Kirk Butkans, Jason Kramer, Jason Leinbach, Jason Maltzen, Jayna Pavlin, Jayson VanBeusichem, Jean Acheson, Jeff Eaton, Jeff Macfee, Jeff Xilon, Jeff Zahnen, Jeffrey Allen Arnett, Jen Watkins, Jenevieve DeFer, Jenica Rogers, jennielf, Jennifer Steen, Jeremiah Robert Craig Shepersky, Jeremy Kostiew, Jeremy Tidwell, Jesse Pudewell, Jessica and Andrew Qualls, JF Paradis, Jill Hughes, Jill Valuet, Jim "Citizen Simian" Henley, Jim & Paula Kirk, Jim Burke in VT, Jim Waters, JLR, Joanne B, Jody Kline, Joe "Gasoline" Czyz, Joe Kavanagh, John Beattie, John Bogart, John Cmar, John D. Burnham, John Geyer/Wulfenbahr Arts, John Idlor, John Lambert, John Rogers, John Sureck, John Tanzer, John-Paul Holubek, Jon Nadeau, Jon Rosebaugh, Jonathan Howard, Jonathan Perrine, Jonathan S. Chance, José Luis Nunes Porfírio, Jose Ramon Vidal,

Joseph Blomquist, Josh Nolan, Josh Thomson, Joshua K. Martin, Joshua Little, JouleLee Perl Ruby Jade, Joy Jakubaitis, JP Sugarbroad, Jukka Koivisto, Justin Yeo, K. Malycha, Kai Nikulainen, Kairam Ahmed Hamdan, Kal Powell, Karen J. Grant, Kat & Jason Romero, Kate Kirby, Kate Malloy, Kathy Rogers, Katrina Lehto, Kaz, Keaton Bauman, Keith West, Kelly (rissatoo) Barnes, Kelly E, Ken Finlayson, Ken Wallo, Keri Orstad, Kevin Chauncey, Kevin Mayz, Kierabot, Kris Deters, Kristin (My Bookish Ways Reviews), Kristina VanHeeswijk, Kurt Ellison, Lady Kayla, Larry Garetto, Laura Kramarsky, Lily Katherine Underwood, Lisa & M3 Sweatt, Lisa Padol, litabeetle, Lord Max Moraes, Lorri-Lynne Brown, Lucas MFZB White, Lutz Ohl, Lyndon Riggall, M. Sean Molley, Maggie G., Manda Collis & Nick Peterson, Marcia Dougherty, Marcus McBolton (Salsa), Marguerite Kenner and Alasdair Stuart, Mark "Buzz" Delsing, Mark Cook, Mark Dwerlkotte, Mark MedievaMonkey, Mark O'Shea, Mark Truman of Magpie Games, Mark Widner, Marshall Vaughan, Martin Joyce, Mary Spila, Matt Barker, Matt Troedson, Matt Zitron & Family, Matthew Scoppetta, Max Temkin, Maxwell A Giesecke, May Claxton, MCpl Doug Hall, Meri and Allan Samuelson, Michael Erb, Michael Godesky, Michael Hill, Michael M. Jones, Michael May, michael orr, Michael Richards, Michael Thompson, Michael Tousignant, Michael Wolfe, Miguel Reyes, Mike "Mortagole" Gorgone, Mike Grace (The Root Of All Evil), Mike Kowalski, Mike Sherwood, Mike 'txMaddog' Jacobs, Mike Wickliff, Mikhail McMahon, Miranda "Giggles" Horner, Mitch A. Williams, Mitchell Young, Morgan Ellis, Mur Lafferty, Nancy Feldman, Nathan Alexander, Nathan Blumenfeld, Nestor D. Rodriguez, Nick Bate, Odysseas "Arxonti" Votsis, Owen "Sanguinist" Thompson, Pam Blome, Pamela Shaw, Paolo Carnevali, Pat Knuth, Patricia Bullington-McGuire, Paul A. Tayloe, Paul MacAlpine, Paul Weimer, Peggy Carpenter, Pete Baginski, Pete Sellers, Peter Oberley, Peter Sturdee, Phil Adler, Philip Reed, Philippe "Sanctaphrax" Saner, Poppy Arakelian, Priscilla Spencer, ProducerPaul, Quentin "Q" Hudspeth, Quinn Murphy, Rachel Coleman Finch, Rachel Narow, Ranger Dave Ross, Raymond Terada, Rebecca Woolford, Rhel ná DecVandé, Rich "Safari Jack Tallon" Thomas, Rich Panek, Richard "Cap'n Redshanks" McLean, Richard Monson-Haefel, Rick Jones, Rick Neal, Rick Smith, Rob and Rachel, Robert "Gundato" Pavel, Robert M. Everson, Robert Towell (Ndreare), Ross C. Hardy!, Rowan Cota, Ryan & Beth Perrin, Ryan Del Savio Riley, Ryan E. Mitchell, Ryan Hyland, Ryan Jassil, Ryan Patrick Dull, Ryan Worrell, S. L. Gray, Sabrina Ogden, Sal Manzo, Sally Qwill Janin, Sam Heymans, Sandro Tomasetti, Sarah Brooks, Saxony, Scott Acker, Scott E., Scott Russell Griffith, Sean Fadden, Sean Nittner, Sean O'Brien, Sean R. Jensen, Sean T. DeLap, Sean W, Sean Zimmermann, Sebastian Grey, Seth Swanson, Shai Norton, Shaun D. Burton, Shaun Dignan, Shawna Hogan, Shel Kennon, Sherry Menton, Shervyn, Shoshana Kessock, Simon "Tech Support" Strauss, Simone G. Abigail C. GameRageLive, Stacey Chancellor, Stephen Cheney, Stephen Figgins, Sterling Brucks, Steve Holder, Steve Sturm, Steven K. Watkins, Steven McGowan, Steven Rattelsdorfer, Steven Vest, T I Hely, Tantris Hernandez, Taylor "The Snarky Avenger" Kent, Team Milian, Teesa, Temoore Baber, Tess Snider, Tevel Drinkwater, The Amazing Enigma, The Axelrods, The fastest man wearing a jetpack, thank you, The Gollub Family, The Hayworths, The NY Coopers, The Sotos, The Vockerys, Theron "Tyrone" Teter, Tim "Buzz" Isakson, Tim Pettigrew, Tim Rodriguez of Dice + Food + Lodging, TimTheTree, TJ Robotham, TK Read, Toby Rodgers, Todd Furler, Tom Cadorette, Tom J Allen Jr, Tony Pierson, Tracy Hall, Travis Casey, Travis Lindquist, Vernatia, Victor V., Vidal Bairos, W. Adam Rinehart, W. Schaeffer Tolliver, Warren Nelson, Wil Jordan, Will Ashworth, Will H., William Clucus Woods...yes, "Clucus", William Hammock, William Huggins, William Pepper, Willow "Dinosaurs and apocalypse? How could I NOT back it?" Wood, wufl, wwwisata, Wythe Marschall, Yurath, Zakharov "Zaksquatch" Sawyer, Zalabar, Zalen Moore, and Zuki.

CHAPTER ONE
MANTIS OF TERROR!

"Khaaan!"

Professor Khan loped down the Grand Hallway to the sound of Bulls-Eye's voice. There was a tremendous crash, a splintering of wood, the sound of shattering glass.

"Here," the professor yelled. The adrenaline pumped through him, making him feel powerful, alive. The sound of jungle drums thundered in his ears.

The great ape covered the distance quickly, his massive knuckles slamming into the marble floor like hammers, jungle blood thrumming in his ears. He doubled his efforts as he heard another crash.

He sincerely hoped Bulls-Eye was all right. The Texan was a recent addition to the Century Club and seemed to have little regard for his own safety. Khan wondered sometimes if he was suicidal, but the cowboy always seemed to come out of his many scrapes with nothing but bruises.

And now it sounded as though he was in the thick of whatever was making a mess of the London chapter house.

Khan rounded a corner and skidded to a stop. Bulls-Eye, Stetson hat somehow miraculously still atop his head was riding an enormous... Khan stared, his educated brain ticking through family, genus and species. Mantidae. Mantis. *M. Religiosa.*

A giant praying mantis.

"Oh my."

If anyone didn't belong in the London chapterhouse, with its sweeping English gardens, its majestic halls and exhibits, its history of erudite learning, it was Enrique "Bulls-Eye" Gutierrez. A lowly cowboy from Texas who nonetheless managed to impress the Centurion Benjamin Hu.

And when Bulls-Eye met Khan, the Texan didn't even bat an eyelash. As though a talking gorilla with an Oxford education was something he saw every day. If nothing else, that had won Khan over to the new arrival.

"Could use a hand here, Perfesser," Bulls-Eye yelled, riding the mantis like a bucking bronco, his hands firmly tucked in a space behind the giant insect's head to keep from flying off. "I got my eight seconds in, but I don't think I'm gonna hang on much longer."

"Yes, of course," Khan said, shaking himself out of his momentary fugue. He cinched up his kilt, straightened the lapels of his houndstooth coat and launched his 400-pound frame toward the mantis.

"Look out for the—" Bulls-Eye began, but was cut short as the giant insect heaved, swinging a foreleg that swatted Khan out of the air. Khan slammed against the wall, shaking the hallway as though it were made of balsa wood. The mantis bucked and threw Bulls-Eye into a portrait of an English hunting scene.

Khan still felt strange to find himself with the Centurions. There was a time not long back where Khan's connection to the Century Club was as an advisor, using his immense intellect to solve the unsolvable, and plan the unplannable.

But never execute. He was always left behind in his Oxford rooms to pore over dusty tomes and moldering scrolls. Not that he didn't enjoy that, of course. It was his life's pursuit, his *raison d'etre*. He was a genius and he could no more deny the workings of his mind than he could his animal nature.

Not that he didn't attempt to hide his animal nature, of course. Living in a world of men and trying to be one would do that to an ape. But try as he might he was still, as the saying goes, the 400-pound gorilla in the room.

It took a dinosaur invasion led by his genetic progenitor, Gorilla Khan, the Conqueror Ape, to change all that. And change it did.

Khan shook his head to clear it, the jungle drums in his mind blotting out all other sound. His rage took over. Khan let loose a mighty roar and took another leap at the mantis. He grasped a foreleg, barely avoiding the spikes dotting the massive insect's hide, and yanked down with both hands.

A crack loud as a gunshot echoed through the hallway and the mantis screamed an unearthly shriek that shattered the nearby windows. It flailed its ruined foreleg about, its now useless claw hanging from pulpy meat that shone through the shattered chitin. He forced his rage down as the mantis shrieked. It had been a cruel move, he realized, and he immediately regretted it. Though he'd done damage, this was merely a mindless beast. Frightened and frustrated more than angry, no doubt.

After the fight against Gorilla Khan and his Psychosaurs had been won, Khan was back to his studies, back to his classes. And it was, well, there was no other way to put it, dull.

A part of him longed for adventure. Hoped for a disaster in which he could use his skills practically, in the field, again. Not that he wanted another dinosaur invasion, of course.

Well, maybe a little one.

He was a full member of the Century Club now, and though he knew that he was welcomed as colleague rather than consultant there were still times, with his heavy tomes and esoteric lore, where his adventuring companions seemed to not quite see him.

He felt, more often than not, as though he didn't quite fit.

Much like a certain trick-riding cowboy in a posh, English manor house currently picking himself from the floor, Stetson hat still somehow firmly in place.

Khan took a moment to examine the beast flailing wildly before him. It wasn't truly a praying mantis. More some kind of Mega-Mantis. The raptorial forelegs weren't spiked quite right, the head was longer and narrower and it was mottled the color of rust, giving it an almost mechanical appearance.

And then, of course, there was its size.

It filled the hall, a good fifteen feet long and twelve high on legs that could easily double that height. It whipped its body around, slamming its legs into the marble flooring and leaving craters from the impacts, as if it were trying to—

"That's it," Khan said. He dove out of the way of a striking foreleg toward Bulls-Eye, who was shaking his head and still trying to stand. The man had taken quite a beating. Khan scooped him up and dove back the direction he had come. The Mega-Mantis scuttled forward to follow.

"Can you rope it?" Khan asked.

"Huh?" Bulls-Eye said, his eyes slowly clearing.

"Can you rope it? Get a leash on that infernal beast?"

"Perfesser, ain't nothin' on God's green earth I can't rope I got a long enough lariat. But my ropes ain't here. And why in tarnation you want to rope it, anyhow?"

"It can't go backwards," Khan said. "If we can lead it the way we want we can trap it."

"Well, heck, Perfesser, I'm in. I ain't never trapped a thing bigger'n a grizzly bear. Still ain't got no ropes, though."

"Leave that to me," Khan said. "There's a laboratory down here where Miss Slick has been experimenting with new forms of electricity," he said. "There are no ropes, but there are many long, stout cables. Will that do?"

Bulls-Eye looked over Khan's shoulder at the beast hot on their tails. "Thirty foot length oughtta do it. Let me off here and I'll distract it while you grab me them cables."

Khan paused. Perhaps the Texan had finally lost his sanity.

"Doc, I seen Miss Slick's workspace. I'm likely to get myself electrified I start yankin' on things."

"True, but—"

"And I got on that thing's head without so much as a bump on the noggin afore you came around. So go get me them cables. I'll keep that thing hoppin' around 'til it don't know if it's comin' or goin.'" Without another word, Bulls-Eye flipped himself over Khan's shoulder, and into the path of the oncoming monster.

"Try to lead it further down this hall!" Khan yelled after the bouncing cowboy and headed toward Sally Slick's laboratory.

Sally Slick was a wizard with technology. There didn't seem to be anything that woman couldn't fix, jerry-rig or whip up out of whole cloth. She usually worked out of the New York chapter house, but after the dinosaur invasion had razed so much of it in their attack on the city, she had set up a new shop here. She was back in New York now overseeing reconstruction, but some of her work was still in her London lab.

He hoped.

Khan allowed himself a quiet, if uncharacteristic swear as he searched for cables that would fit Bulls-Eye's needs. Perhaps the Texan's rough demeanor was rubbing off on him. He pulled sheets off of unused equipment, finding a pile of cables beneath a generator in the corner, grabbed a coil and headed back out.

True to his word Bulls-Eye was hopping around like a jackrabbit, staying just out of the Mega-Mantis' reach. Each strike of the forelegs left cracks in the floor and Khan hoped the Texan could keep it up until he could get to him.

"Toss me them cables, Doc, and come take my place," Bulls-Eye yelled over his shoulder. "Just gotta hop around like a jumpin' bean and you'll be right as rain."

Khan did as the cowboy said, throwing the coil of cables at him and leaping into his place to distract the beast. It was harder than it looked. Bulls-Eye was a born trick-rider with years of acrobatic experience. Khan had bulk on his side, strength, even speed. But maneuverability? He wasn't some annoying monkey hopping from branch to branch. His only advantage was that the Mega-Mantis had the same disadvantages. Moving that much mass took time.

"Boy, Doc, you couldn't a found me something more like rope? These things is stiffer than a polecat in heat."

"Sometimes we have to make do with what we have, my boy," Khan said, dodging another leg. One of the spikes on the femur caught his coat, ripping a gash along the back. "Please hurry. At this rate it will have me down to nothing but my bowtie in short order."

"Gotcha, Doc. Stand clear."

Khan leapt backward as Bulls-Eye threw his lariat expertly at the beast's head. The cowboy cinched it tight and held on as the Mega-Mantis yanked him up and almost off his feet.

"I gotcha yer bug, Doc. Now what? You wanna put it in a jar, or somethin'?"

"In a manner of speaking," Khan said, grabbing the cable from Bulls-Eye's grasp and heaving with all of his strength. Unable to leverage itself away from the sudden shift in its center of gravity, the Mega-Mantis' head crashed down into the floor, the rest of its body quickly following.

"There's no room for it turn around in the hallway," Khan said. "And it can't back up. If we can lead it to the back of the house there is a cage for large game available."

"Heck, Perfesser, we could'a just had it follow us for that."

"And risk it running into someone else who looks more appetizing? That would hardly do."

Khan yanked on the lariat, his massive muscles bulging. He dragged the Mega-Mantis down the hallway, its legs flailing, ripping great gouges in the dark, oak wall panels. But it came. It had little choice.

By now some of the Chapter House's staff finally came out to see the carnage. Non-combatants, Khan knew. They had no business trying to help. They knew it was best to let the Centurions handle things.

And right now there were only three Centurions in the house, Khan, Bulls-Eye and Edison Thomas, an inventor who had been pulled backward in time and had been working feverishly in a lab in the Chapter House for months on a way to get back to his own future.

Where was he? Surely he had heard the commotion.

"Where do ya think this thing came from, Doc?"

"First things first," Khan said. "We have to secure the beast and then we can determine where—"

An explosion sounded from the other side of the building, cutting off Khan's words. Edison Thomas' lab.

"Nevermind," Bulls-Eye said. "I can guess."

Securing the Mega-Mantis ended up being easier than either of them had expected. By the time they had dragged it down the hallway to the cage it was as if all the fight had left it.

"You think the cage'll hold?" Bulls-Eye said, coiling his impromptu lariat and running to keep up with Khan as the gorilla loped down the hall toward Thomas' laboratory.

"It should," Khan said. "It was designed to hold dinosaurs after Gorilla Khan was defeated. There was a certain amount of, how do you Americans say it, 'batting clean-up' to do. And, of course, the opportunity to study the psychosaurs was impossible to pass up."

Khan felt sorry for the beast. Wherever it had come from it wasn't from Earth. It must be confused, disoriented, frightened. And now, it lay exhausted in a cage of steel bars designed to hold dinosaurs.

Ripped from its home. Out of its element. Khan understood that. He understood that very well.

He wondered if Bulls-Eye ever felt that. The Texan was a gregarious, if hot-headed young man, given to brawling and drinking. For all that, he rarely seemed angry, as though taking a round-house punch in a tavern was grand fun.

Khan shook himself out of his thoughts. There were greater priorities. That explosion had clearly come from Thomas's lab and there was no telling what sort of danger he might be in.

Khan had to admit a grudging respect for the young inventor. A genius, certainly, but a genius from the future. Decades of invention and knowledge that Khan could only guess at. He had somehow opened a portal into the past and fallen through and in the last several months had been trying to recreate the portal in order to return to his own time.

Khan had spoken with the man several times, but even with Khan's superb understanding of theoretical physics Thomas left the Professor firmly in his dust. Though Khan had been through portals to other worlds, even travelling to Atlantis to stop Doctor Methuselah and Gorilla Khan, there were aspects of the underlying science that were still a mystery, even to his advanced intellect. But Thomas could pick apart the math so seamlessly it made Khan feel like a graduate student.

The trail to Thomas' lab was strewn with shattered glass, destroyed walls, cratered flooring. Clearly the Mega-Mantis originated there. But how?

As they approached the room Khan could hear strange noises. Sounds of electrical equipment, strange buzzings, an occasional loud pop. And when he and Bulls-Eye rounded the corner he saw it.

The lab was a disaster. Where there had once been a door, the entire front of the room was missing. It had exploded outward in a shower of splinters.

Only bits of framing remained. Inside was worse. Equipment overturned, holes punched through walls. Sparks burst from generators and blown fuses.

In the middle of the room was a large, gleaming device, all steel and brass with a strange green crystal glowing inside a glass container at its top and a nozzle that looked somewhere between a cannon barrel and the front of a vacuum cleaner. It buzzed in loud pulses in time to the pulsing of the crystal, the sound getting louder with each one.

"You see Doc Thomas, Perfesser?" Bulls-Eye said.

Khan leapt up and grabbed a pipe jutting high out of the blown-out wall to get a better view of the room. "There," he said. "Next to the device. He's unconscious, I think. Yes. Yes, he's breathing."

Khan swung from the pipe to another hanging from the ruined ceiling until he was just over the device. "Watch your step. There's quite a lot of broken equipment with sharp edges here. And chemicals. Some of this may be toxic."

Bulls-Eye picked his way through the debris. "Doc, I been wading through cow-patties since I was in diapers. Ain't nothin' more toxic than stepping in the leavings of a colicky steer, let me tell ya."

Khan dropped from the pipe and knealt next to Thomas. "I'm not sure if we should move him," Khan said. "I can't tell the extent of his injuries."

"Well, if another one of them bugs comes poppin' by we don't want him lying there to get snacked on."

"Excellent point," Khan said, eyeing the humming device. Was this the machine that Thomas had been working on to open a new portal through time?

"Let's get him moved and then—" Khan stopped as the device's pitch suddenly changed from a lowly pulsing buzz to a high-pitched wail. It was then that he realized that Bulls-Eye was standing right in front of the device's nozzle.

"Bulls-Eye, move!" Khan yelled, but it was too late. A jet of bright green light burst from the nozzle. Bulls-Eye was quicker than Khan had expected, jumping to one side as a portal onto an alien landscape opened up just past him.

A fierce wind blew through the opening, pulling papers and debris in through the hole. And Bulls-Eye. The cowboy was pulled off his feet and yanked through the hole. Khan leapt to the opening as Bulls-Eye's lariat snaked out, wrapping around Khan's massive forearm. Khan heaved against the pull of the portal. A few more feet and he'd have the man out.

He heard the device's pitch change again. It started to shake, rattling as though it were about to fly to pieces. Just another foot and he'd have the cowboy out. Just another foot and they could get away from this infernal device.

But before he could get so much as another inch, a terrible explosion rent through the lab. The device shattered into a dozen smoking pieces. Khan lost his footing as the blast propelled him through the portal.

The portal shimmered, destabilized, and with a crash of thunder ceased to exist.

With Khan and Bulls-Eye on the wrong side of it.

CHAPTER TWO
CAPTURED BY THE CYCLONE PRINCESS!

Khan woke with a spinning head and a mouth full of metallic tasting dirt. His body felt as though it had been stuffed into a taffy-pulling machine, stretched and yanked. He brought himself up onto his elbows with a groan.

The landscape was like nothing he had ever seen. A desert of red dirt and a hazy, yellowing sky. The sun was an emaciated blur above the horizon. In the distance he could see the wisps of dust devils as they churned up the endless sea of sand.

Bulls-Eye sat up beside him and spit out a clod of rust-colored dirt. Khan marveled again at how his hat seemed to never leave his head.

"Mister Gutierrez, how are you feeling?" Khan asked.

"Like I been passed through a rattlesnake's bunghole sideways." He groaned, and stood on wobbly legs.

Khan stood and brushed dust from his kilt and tweed. The tear in the fabric of his coat would need darning. He sighed. He had no skill with a needle. His fingers were simply too large for such delicate work.

"Colorful, but apt," Khan said. "I believe we have fallen victim to Doctor Thomas's experiment." He stretched his back and felt vertebrae pop.

Bulls-Eye squinted into the distance. "Well, if this is where that giant bug came from, I don't see none of 'em now."

"A spot of good fortune, then."

"Good news don't never travel without bad news close on its tail. So what's the bad?"

"No, I suppose it does not," Khan said. "The bad news, it would appear, is that we are not at the Chapter House."

"Ya don't say," Bulls-Eye said. "Ain't much out here but scrub brush and chaparral. I see some plants over yonder look like saguaro. Some Joshua, Manzanita maybe. Only they's got purple leaves. Huh."

Khan squinted into the distance but aside from some rock outcroppings could only make out hazy shapes. The cowboy's eyes were remarkably sharp to be able to pick out such detail. He peered into the sky and frowned.

"There's something wrong with the sun," he said.

"It's awful small," Bulls-Eye said. "Perfesser, you ever seen one of them giant bugs before?"

"I have not."

"And I suppose you ain't never seen the sun lookin' so small before, neither?"

"I fear this may be worse than simply being teleported away from the Chapter House," Khan said. "Do you see any signs of civilization?" Khan said.

"Nope, but if there's any out here it's gonna be where there's water. And that's our first order of business. Even if that sun ain't so big this is still a desert and when it gets high in the sky we're gonna be in a world of hurt." He began walking.

"Ah, yes," Khan said. Bulls-Eye was right. Survival was the first priority. The question of where they were would wait. Khan had experienced more scientific and mystical portals in the last year than he cared to remember, having traveled through so much time and space at this point he felt himself a veteran.

The two trudged through the desert in silence. The land was loose-packed dirt in most places, and deep sand in others, making the going difficult. As they continued on, though, Khan began to realize that the going should actually be harder. They were covering surprising distance.

"Bulls-Eye," Khan said. "How are you feeling?"

"Tired, thirsty, but— Hey Perfesser, do you feel, I dunno, lighter?"

Khan looked at their footsteps behind them and then checked his pocket watch. They had been travelling for almost three hours and had covered an incredible distance in that time. Though the desert heat was taking its toll Bulls-Eye was right. He did feel lighter.

"Interesting," Khan said. "I believe the gravity here must be less than on Earth, making our stamina much—"

The rest of Khan's words were cut off as a terrible thundering rose up from beneath their feet. The ground quaked and dirt and sand blew out in a ring around them. For a moment Khan feared they had stumbled onto a Mega-Mantis, or worse, a nest of them.

He readied himself for disaster as best he could, but the ground shook so hard and the dust blew so fast that he was blind, deaf and sprawled in the dust in moments. He covered his eyes with his arms, enveloped in the exploding dirt. When the cacophony ended and the air cleared enough for him to see, he was shocked. At least the Mega-Mantis was half expected, but not this.

Half a dozen massive spheres of brass and copper had burst out of the ground around them. Twice the size of any tank Khan had ever seen, the machines sported turrets with strange, spiked corkscrew devices sticking out in all directions, a fat central mast that towered a good twenty feet high with what appeared to be a giant cannon made of some glass-like material. Instead of tracks, giant screws dug deep into the sand.

"Well, leastwise they ain't giant bugs," Bulls-Eye said.

"Indeed," Khan said. That was the good news, but as the cowboy had pointed out, bad news often followed.

Strange sounds burst from a loudspeaker. It took a moment for Khan to realize it was language.

"I don't s'pose you caught any of that, Perfesser?"

"Not one whit," Khan said. Were they being commanded? Questioned? Greeted?

Khan stood, raised his arms in greeting. "Excuse me," he said. "I am Professor Khan of Earth and—"

His words were cut short as a bolt of green lightning shot from the glass cannon, knocking him back into the dirt. His head spun like a Tilt-A-Whirl. He couldn't move. He couldn't hear. His vision was fading around the edges.

He could see Bulls-Eye as though he were standing miles away, but soon even that faded and blackness took him.

Khan awoke to the mother of all headaches. He twitched an eye open. Closed it as light stabbed into his head. He let out a groan that was one part whimper, one part whine, and one part prayer to the Alimighty that he'd died and this was purgatory and not his final reward.

"Oh, don't make such a godawful ruckus, Perfesser," Bulls-eye said nearby, his voice a rough whisper. "Bad enough I can hear ya breathin' over there. I ain't had pain this bad since I won that tequila drinkin' contest in Abilene."

"For someone who can't handle noise," Khan croaked, "you talk an impressive amount."

"Brevity ain't never been my strong suit, Perfesser."

"Agreed." Khan hazarded another glimpse, blinking back tears. His head throbbed, lessening to a dull pounding once his eyes got used to the light.

When he could finally see, the first thing he noticed was the strange shackle on his left wrist. Silver and stamped with a design of lightning bolts. It was snug, but not tight. Khan could see one like it on Bulls-Eye's wrist as well.

He tugged at it, but though he could spin it around his wrist with some effort, it wasn't possible to pull it over his hand. Odd that their captors should have a shackle that could actually fit him. His wrist was far wider than any human's.

He turned his attention to their prison. The chamber looked like the inside of a boiler. Circular, a good twenty feet high and ten across, the entire room was made of brass with rivets the breadth of Khan's hand set every few feet apart. Recessed lights in the ceiling shone down through a cage of wire mesh. A single, large hatch was set in the wall.

Bulls-Eye sat up, squinting at the chamber. "Well, looks like we found us some people," he said.

"Indeed." Khan stood on wobbly legs and ambled to the hatch. His legs were more numb than sore, but feeling was beginning to return to them. Though shaped like a hatch on a ship, there didn't appear to be any mechanism on this side holding it in place.

Khan puzzled at it a bit. Ran his fingers along the edges. Rapped at it with a knuckle. It gave a dull, metallic thud.

He leaned an ear against the metal, could hear the humming of steam engines, the thrum of generators. Were they inside one of the infernal cannons that had captured them?

As he strained to listen, another sound reached his ears. Footsteps. A lot of them. He jerked back, pressed himself against the wall to the right of the door, motioned Bulls-Eye to do the same on the other side.

A moment later there was a loud thunk of metal, a hiss of escaping air and the door swung to one side. The barrel of a gun poked through the door. It had the same glass-like texture as the cannon that had stunned them earlier. It stayed there a moment, wavered back and forth. The guard stepped inside nervously.

He wore a silver helmet with sculpted lightning bolts where the ears should be. The face was covered in dark glass. The uniform appeared to be silver lame and sported a large red cyclone stitched to the front with lightning bolts of gold radiating out in all directions. A black belt with a large silver pouch at its side completed the ensemble.

Khan found himself examining the gun, wondering what it was made of and how it worked. Bulls-Eye, however, took a more immediate approach to things, reached over, and yanked it out of the surprised guard's hands.

"Not the face!" the guard cried just as Bulls-Eye slammed the butt of the rifle straight into his faceplate. The glass shattered and the guard dropped like a felled buffalo.

The two Centurions stared at him.

"Did he just say, 'Not the face'?" Bulls-Eye said.

"Indeed, he did," Khan said.

"I thought they were talkin' gobbledy-gook at us out there afore they shot us."

"They were. Interesting." Khan knelt and picked away the broken pieces of glass from the guard's face. Though humanoid, the guard clearly wasn't human. His skin was a light green with two stubby protrusions poking from either side of his forehead. Horns, perhaps, Khan thought. Or vestigial antennae?

He delicately pried one eyelid open. The eye was completely red. No iris, no pupil. Curiouser and curiouser.

The excitement of discovery began to hum in his brain. An alien species never before encountered. The possibilities of a new race of beings, contact with aliens!

"If you're done examinin' the patient, Perfesser, could ya maybe rifle his pockets and see if he's got anything useful could get us out of here? I don't think we got much time afore another one of them comes by, do you?"

"Hmm? Oh, yes. Yes, of course." The uniform had no pockets, but the belt pouch contained a series of metal cards with indentations drilled into them, keys, perhaps, and an identification card with the guard's photo.

Khan blinked. There was something odd about the card. The letters were all harsh slashes and blotches, totally unlike any language Khan had ever seen. And then, suddenly, they weren't.

"Can you read this?" Khan asked, handing the card to Bulls-Eye.

"It's all a buncha— Holy Jehosaphat, Perfesser, it's trick paper. And it says here his name's Willie."

"Probably the closest approximation to his name for us. No, I don't think it's trick paper." He fingered the bracelet around his wrist. "I think it might have something to do with these. But we can explore that at a more fortuitous time."

Khan closed the cell on the unconscious guard, the door clicking as the magnetic locks engaged. The hall outside was much like the cell, brass walls with rivets set at intervals, doors spaced every ten feet, with a grated floor and lights shining down from the ceiling through wire mesh cages.

"Which way, Perfesser?" Bulls-Eye said.

The sounds of marching footsteps echoed down the hall. "Away from that," Khan said, and headed in the opposite direction, Bulls-Eye close at his heels.

They passed closed doors and branching hallways, but avoided them when they heard conversations or approaching footfalls. A couple of tense moments passed as they hid in an alcove when uniformed guards marched past.

After passing through a series of open doorways, the hallway changed from merely utilitarian to a much more elegant design. Grated floors gave way to carpet, lighting became less harsh, the rivets disappeared behind wall panels decorated in the same cyclone and lightning motif that had been on the guard's uniform.

The hallway stopped at a carpeted staircase leading up to a pair of enormous brass doors also decorated with the cyclone and lightning motif. They had so far avoided closed doors, but there didn't seem to be anywhere else to go but up.

"Slow and sneaky or fast and hard?" Bulls-Eye said.

"I honestly don't know," Khan said. "I'm tempted to say stealth is the better option, but we won't know until we open that door."

"All this sneakin' around's makin' my head hurt," Bulls-Eye said. "So you know my vote."

"Noted." Khan climbed the steps to the door. The doors were too thick to hear anything through when he pressed an ear against them. Whatever they did, they would be going in blind.

Only one thing for it. He motioned Bulls-Eye to stand ready, and then pushed on one of the giant doors.

The door swung open smoothly, sending light stabbing into a darkened room. There was something wrong with the blackness that greeted them. Khan stood silently a moment to let his eyes adjust to the darkness, but they simply wouldn't. And there was no sound inside the room. No hum of machinery, no sounds of footsteps.

Whatever this was, it wasn't a simple lack of light.

He stepped forward gingerly, motioning Bulls-Eye to follow him and realized too late that it was a trap.

Sound and light burst in on them like an artillery shell and they found themselves in a room out of an Alphonse Mucha nightmare. Art deco panels covered the walls with the ever present cyclone and lightning bolts, couches lined the walls in garish colors clashing with the blood-red, marble floor.

The room was filled with all manner of beings. The green-skinned aliens, humanoid frogs, centaur-like creatures, men and women who Khan would mistake for human except for the giant bird wings sweeping behind them. Each decked out in clothing of the finest quality.

And the guards. Thirty at least, each armed with a raygun and wearing silver lamé uniforms, swarmed in from the sides to surround the two Centurions. They kept their distance, but every gun was carefully aimed.

Khan could feel Bulls-Eye tense behind him and hoped the brash young man wouldn't do anything stupid. He let out a breath as he heard Bulls-Eye put the weapon down.

"Perfesser," Bulls-Eye said quietly, a tremor in his voice. "Them folks look like frogs."

"Yes," Khan said. "And there appear to be centaurs and bird people as well."

"Yeah, but there's frogs."

Khan glanced at the young man and saw that he was sweating slightly. Khan was about to ask him what he was on about but was interrupted by a voice yelling from beyond the horde of guards.

"You dare to enter my kingdom, attack my people and then invade my throne?"

The guards parted to let through a tall, green-skinned, red-haired woman wearing a dress of silver and gold, with black and red designs of lightning bolts woven throughout and a cape with a high arched collar that swept up behind her head. Two short, horn-like antennae sprouted from the sides of her forehead and her eyes were a glowing, dull red. And atop her head she wore an impressive crown of swirling, silver filigree that sparked with arcs of electricity like a hundred tiny Jacob's Ladders.

But what really caught Khan's eye were the two blue furred gorillas shackled and in chains following behind her. They were smaller than he was, and had clearly been abused. One of them had a severe limp and the other was missing an eye. Both of them looked beaten down and hopeless.

"Madame, I—" Khan began but was cut off with a rifle butt to the gut. It was more shock than pain that caught him off guard.

"Silence, barbarian assassin!" the woman cried. "I will not have treason and sedition within my kingdom." She grabbed a hank of fur from Khan's neck. "Your failed attempts at murder here, in my own throne room, and your cheap attempts to undermine my rule with your false prophecy will be met with swift justice."

Khan withstood this tirade with total confusion. He had no idea what she was talking about. Prophecy? Barbarian assassins? Were the blue-furred gorillas members of this "barbarian" race she was talking about?

Dignity impugned, Khan batted her hand away from him. "I beg your pardon, madam, but I will not be spoken to in that manner."

The woman looked at him, stunned, and Khan realized that he had committed a major faux pas. She was clearly the ruler in this land and one does not simply swat away the hand of a reigning monarch.

"Oh, now you gone and done it, Perfesser," Bulls-Eye muttered behind him.

"Indeed."

The woman turned to the assemblage of alien races. "I, Princess Cyclone, Weather Witch and ruler of this world, pass judgment on these traitorous assassins. I condemn them to the Pits Of Despair beneath the palace!"

"That don't sound so bad, Perfesser," Bulls-Eye said.

"Where they shall be consumed by the Demon Dragon!"

"You were saying?" Khan asked.

"So is it declared," Princess Cyclone said, "So shall it be."

She turned on her heel and strode away, the two broken and battered gorillas in tow. Khan looked about for some indication of what had just happened, or some sign of help. In the back of the crowd he spied a younger, green-skinned woman looking aghast at the proceedings.

Well, at least not everyone agreed with the Princess. Cold comfort.

Fine. If they wanted a fight, then by God, he would give them one. The guards fidgeted. Yes, they had guns, but Khan was enormous. His massive simian muscles flexed beneath his houndstooth jacket. In the back of his mind he could hear distant jungle drums growing louder and louder.

Before he could do more, the floor shook beneath his feet and too late Khan realized the magnitude of their predicament. With a shuddering crash, the floor opened beneath them. Khan leapt for the edge of the trap-door, his fingers grasping the marble floor.

A guard slammed the butt of his rifle against Khan's fingers. As the guard came in for a second strike, Khan reached up with his other hand, grabbed the gun, and shoved, throwing the guard back into the crowd.

With one mighty heave, Khan pulled himself out of the pit. His roar filled the room, echoed off the walls. He swung his tree-trunk arms, knocking over guards like bowling pins. He threw one clear across the room, where he crashed into a group of frog people. Two more followed him.

Khan beat his chest, bared monstrous fangs. The jungle drums beat in his mind in a mad hammering of rage. He was the Conqueror Ape. He was King of The Jungle, the Avatar of Vengeance. How dare these insignificant beasts think that they could possibly subdue him!

He reared up on his legs and bellowed a challenge to the remaining guards. And then they shot him.

CHAPTER THREE
MEANWHILE...

As a boy, Edison Thomas dreamed of being a Centurion. He followed their careers with fanatic devotion, devoured tales of their exploits, pored over their research papers and histories. They were his heroes, his inspiration. One day, he knew, he would count himself among their numbers.

He dreamed of taking to the skies like Jet Black, uncovering ancient mysteries like the famous Benjamin Hu. But life had other plans.

A weakened constitution as a result of childhood fevers put the kibosh on that dream. He couldn't get into an airplane without becoming violently ill, couldn't spend much time outside without wheezing from asthma.

And then came the worst blow of all: Myotonic dystrophy.

He had always suspected that he had gotten the losing ticket in the genetic lottery, but never realized how badly his genes were betraying him. By the time he was fifteen one eye had already clouded over with a cataract that required surgery to correct. By the time he was nineteen he had lost so much muscle mass that he had to walk with a cane.

But as his body withered his mind soared.

His theories on quantum entanglement alone won him a Nobel prize in 1998, and the famous Burkholder experiment, the first successfully repeatable teleportation of a live animal across an entire continent in 2002, would never have gotten off the ground if it hadn't been for his mathematical formulae and elegant designs.

He was a genius among geniuses. A scientist unparalleled.

And so it was that in 2010, after years of hard work and study, that he was ready to try his hand at time travel.

His wasn't the first work in the field. The technology recovered by the Time Traveling Pirates who had been defeated by the Centurions in 1935 had formed the basis of his work. He studied their damaged machines, picked them apart and learned their secrets.

No one had been able to duplicate the machines' success. The devices had either been too far damaged or were too poorly understood. Even the greatest minds of the twentieth century couldn't crack their codes. But Edison Thomas was the greatest mind of the twenty-first century.

And he made it work.

"Thomas," said a voice. "Doctor Thomas, can you hear me?"

The voice snapped Thomas out of his reverie and he bolted upright, vertigo taking him. "Dear god, there's a giant bug in my laboratory!"

"It's all right, Doctor Thomas," Benjamin Hu said. The Chinese detective took hold of the scientist to keep him from falling over. "The monster is safely caged. Can you tell us what happened?"

Thomas looked at his ruined lab. The Quantum Dislocator, his latest attempt to reach home, had failed in a most spectacular manner. Instead of opening a portal back to 2010 it opened a portal to... somewhere else.

"I'm not entirely sure," he said. "I think the neutronium chamber overheated as it connected to the magnetic resonator in the quantum—"

"He meant in a broader sense, doctor," said Amelia Stone, stepping into the room and kneeling by Thomas' side. Thomas stared at her. He always stared at her.

Ever since he first read about the Centurions it was Amelia Stone, beautiful adventuress and aviatrix, who had enthralled him the most. Her dark skin and deep, brown eyes were so captivating in the photos, and when he came back to this time and finally met this woman he was even more awestruck.

"Doctor?" she said.

"Hmm? Oh. Oh, yes. Uh. My machine. My machine blew up."

"Yes," Benjamin said. "We had gathered that much. Perhaps a slightly less broad sense, then?"

"Ah. Well, um." Small words, he thought. Always use small words. "I was conducting an experiment with my quantum—with my time travel device. Instead of opening a small portal to 2010 like I had thought it would, it opened a huge portal to somewhere else."

"I see," Benjamin said. "And the caged giant insect? It came through?"

"Yes," Thomas said. "It destroyed the lab. And then it hit me. I don't remember anything after that." Only he did. Something tugged at the back of his mind, slid off his consciousness like water off a hot skillet. He shook his head, but the memory remained elusive.

"The staff said they saw Professor Khan and Bulls-Eye battling the beast," Benjamin said. "Do you know where they are now?"

Thomas thought furiously. Of course. Yes, that was it. A vague memory bubbled up in his consciousness. Khan and Bulls-Eye coming to check on him. His machine—

"Oh no," Thomas said, pulling himself to his feet. He ambled over to an overturned television screen with an attached typewriter. He hauled it upright, tapped keys until the device flickered to life. Green characters scrolled past.

"What is it?" Amelia said.

"The machine suffered an overload after the Professor and Bulls-Eye came into the lab. It opened one final portal before exploding." He scanned the numbers as they raced across the screen, his expression growing more grave with each second. "From these readings it looks like they were pulled into it before it closed."

"It sent them to the future?" Benjamin asked.

"No." He pointed to the series of numbers and letters blinking on the screen. "It sent them to Mars."

Thomas sifted through the wreckage of his lab with shaking hands. Everything had gone so wrong so fast. He wracked his brain trying to see where he had made his mistake. The hoses were secure, the coolant tanks were full. The magnetic resonator chamber had been secure and the quantum core had been painstakingly inspected a dozen times.

He picked up pieces of his device looking for the piece that caused the machine to fail so spectacularly. Each component he found proved to be largely intact. Then he found stumbled upon a broken piece of wreckage and it all made sense.

He knew it had been a bad idea. Knew he shouldn't have used it. But he needed the power and his attempts to use 1940's technology to generate the energy required to power the device simply weren't working.

"Did you find something, Doctor?" Benjamin said. He and Amelia were righting tables and lab equipment.

"I fear I did." He handed the remains of a small statue that was shattered about three inches up from its base to the detective. It glowed with an unearthly green.

"Is this the Atlantean Hand?" Benjamin said, aghast.

"It is. What's left of it. I had signed it out of the artifact room to conduct experiments last month. The power readings were off the chart so I decided to try it in the device. I think I know what went wrong. My connections couldn't handle the power output. If I used tungsten in the—well, that doesn't matter now."

"Excuse me, Doctor," Amelia said. "It very much does matter. If you can rebuild the device and make these improvements we can get Professor Khan and Mister Gutierrez back to Earth, can't we?"

"Well, yes, but—"

"But there is no other Atlantean device like this in the Century Club's collection," Benjamin finished.

"No, there isn't," Thomas said.

"There must be something," Amelia said.

Benjamin Hu tapped a finger against his chin in deep thought. "There may be," Benjamin said. "Start rebuilding your device, Doctor. Miss Stone, would you accompany me? We have some research to do."

CHAPTER FOUR
IN THE LAIR OF THE DEMON DRAGON

Khan fell.

His body reeled from the stun blasts of the guard's rayguns. Wind whistled past his face. Lights spaced at intervals along the walls of the shaft sped by.

Perhaps, Khan thought, plummet was a better word. It really was rather a long drop.

He began counting the seconds, calculating his velocity. At four-hundred pounds and assuming a gravity less than Earth's and... He shook his head to clear it and gave up on the math. It was hard to think through the waning effects of the stun blast. Regardless of the actual number, one thing was clear.

There was no way at this speed he was going to survive the landing. At this rate even water would have the consistency of concrete.

He imagined he would leave quite a crater.

A blast of sound and light burst out of the wall and he could feel himself slow. It happened again and again. Three more times until he hit the ground with no more force than falling out of a second story window.

Still, four-hundred pounds was four-hundred pounds. The impact knocked the air out of him and he lay there gasping like a fish.

"Perfesser," Bulls-Eye said, running up to him. "I was sure you was a goner when I heard them raygun blasts." He hefted the rifle he had entered the throne room with.

Of course he would have kept hold of his firearm, Khan thought. Even falling to certain doom the man was eminently practical.

"I seem to be little the worse for wear." Khan sat up, coughing. The cavern they had fallen into was immense. He looked up at the shaft and could barely make out the light from Cyclone's throne room. After a moment, it winked out into darkness.

"Fascinating," Khan said. "Do you suppose that it's some sort of gravity technology that slowed our fall? Magnetics, perhaps?"

"I don't think it matters none, Perfesser, if'n we don't get a move-on. You heard the crazy lady. There's supposed to be some Demon Dragon down here with us. I don't know about you, but I ain't looking forward to runnin' into it."

"A wise choice," said a voice behind them.

Bulls-Eye spun like lightning, the raygun aimed and pulled taut against his shoulder, ready to fire. A green-skinned woman with glowing red eyes stood a few feet away. She wore robes similar to the Princess, though her skirts were shorter and her shoes more practical.

It took Khan a moment to recognize her. "Wait," Khan said, placing a hand on the cowboy's shoulder. "You were the woman I saw in the throne room just before Cyclone dropped us into here."

She stepped further out of the shadows. "Yes. My name is Leandra. I am one of the Royal Prophets. A Priestess to the Weather Witches who rule over the Thavasians." She stepped forward, reached out to Khan.

"Whoa there, Missy," Bulls-Eye said, tapping her on the shoulder with the rifle. She stopped, and looked at the cowboy as though she was just seeing him for the first time.

"It's all right," Khan said. "I don't think she means us any harm."

"Indeed, I do not." She touched Khan's face. "Your black fur marks you for death. That is why you're here."

"Princess Cyclone said something about a prophecy," Khan said. "Is that what you mean?"

"The barbarians will find their champion in one such as they clad in all black," Leandra said. "And the red plains shall run green with the blood of our people. The Cyclone will be broken. And justice will be served."

Khan frowned as he pieced things together. The other apes he had seen, the barbarians, were blue, not black like Khan was. And clearly they were oppressed. How badly and for how long Khan could only guess, but it was a perfect environment for a prophecy to appear.

If another ape were to appear who fit the description of this barbarian messiah, it could be very dangerous indeed.

"I see," Khan said. He narrowed his eyes at the Priestess. "And how do you feel about this 'prophecy'?"

"The barbarians, the Inkidu, have suffered greatly for two generations. They are a proud people and do not deserve the terrors that have been rained down upon them. Princess Cyclone has ruled the kingdoms with an iron fist and when the Inkidu rose up to defy her, she broke them. My duty is not to Princess Cyclone. It is to truth. It is to the prophecy."

"And you think I'm this barbarian champion? This black clad warrior who will bring the downfall of your people? Clearly your Princess Cyclone does."

It was a ridiculous thought, of course. Prophecies were just stories. Fate was just a convenient collection of events and causation. But Khan knew that the weight of belief could drive people to do remarkable and sometimes terrible things.

"I do," she said. "And I can help you fulfill that destiny. I can take you to the Inkidu."

Khan tapped his brown in thought. "No," he said. "Bulls-Eye, I believe we have a Demon Dragon to defeat so that we can escape this prison. Shall we?"

"Always like beatin' on bigger things than me instead of the other way around. Which way you reckon, Perfesser?"

"Wait," Leandra said. "No? That's it? Just no?"

"I believe that is what I said. Mister Gutierrez, is that what I said?"

"Clear as dawn breakin' over a prairie full of cattle, Perfesser."

"That's what I thought. It seems that my colorful colleague and I are in agreement. I said no." He turned to survey the cavern. "Perhaps that tunnel there?"

"But the prophecy. Your destiny—"

"No, madame, not *my* destiny. I have far more pressing concerns than to be roped into some half-baked junta on the say-so of a green-skinned maiden I've only just now met in the bowels of an alien planet. I wish to get my colleague and I home. Where we belong. And so I say to you, good day."

"But—"

"I said, good day, madam."

Khan stared at the various openings leading out of the cavern. Very likely none of them were good. If they didn't all lead to Cyclone's Demon Dragon he would be very much surprised. There was, after all, little point in having a death trap if there was a convenient way out of it.

"I can get you home," Leandra said.

"Oh?" Khan said. "And how exactly do you propose to do that? Do you even know where we're from?"

"The third planet," she said. "Earth. That is what you call it, isn't it? We've been watching you for years."

That got Khan's attention. "Really? And which planet is this?"

"Thavas. The fourth planet," she said. "I think you call it Mars?"

Khan mulled this over. Mars. It made sense. The dim light of the sun, the thinner air, the lighter gravity. The rust red dirt of the plains.

"All right," he said. "You've piqued my interest. But how do you expect to get us home?"

"Our planet is made up of five races. The Alivons, the K'kir, the Monatu, the Inkidu and the Thavasians." Leandra touched her chest as she said that last.

"And you're Thavasian?" Bulls-Eye said.

"Yes. The Weather Witches are... were our royalty. There is only one left, Princess Cyclone. She is hated by everyone, even her own people. She crushes all who have opposed her and rules the other kingdoms with an iron fist."

"I believe I see where this is going," Khan said. "I imagine each of these kingdoms has been pursuing technologies in secret?"

"Not as well kept a secret as many of them think," Leandra said. "Cyclone allows a certain autonomy of her more loyal subjects. If any of them get too far advanced she takes their inventions and uses them for herself."

"And they ain't caught on to this?" Bulls-Eye said.

"They have from time to time, but when one is hopeless one will take any risk."

"Indeed. And you think one of these kingdoms might have developed something that could assist us?"

"I do."

"Let me guess," Bulls-Eye said, "them barbarians? The Inky-doos?"

"The Inkidu," she said. "That I can't say for certain. As I'm sure you noticed up above they are not welcome at court. Cyclone sends troops against them constantly in an effort to eradicate them. But somehow they survive the attacks and come back with devastating force using weapons no one has ever seen before. No one knows how they do it. They have no industry, they have no cities. They are barely hanging on, and yet they do."

"Cyclone keeps them as slaves," Khan said.

"She does. But they have secrets. They do considerable damage whenever Thavasian patrols enter the wasteland. And if they cannot help, one of the other kingdoms likely can. The K'kir have developed the technology that has allowed us to watch your planet. The Avilon rayguns are the best in the planet. The Monatu rocketships are unparalleled in construction. And everything uses K'kir technology somewhere in its construction. None of them have any love for Princess Cyclone."

"Whatta ya want to do, Perfesser?" Bulls-Eye asked. "Go our own way or get the Priestess' help? To be fair, I don't rightly trust her. Could be a trick."

Khan was thinking the same thing. "It could. But it is the best option we've had so far. All right, Priestess Leandra, I accept your offer of assistance. I will meet with the Inkidu, but I do not promise to be their messiah, or warrior or whatever your prophecy says. Agreed?"

She smiled and her face lit with delight. As humanoids went she really was very attractive. And judging from the look on Bulls-Eye's face that Khan caught out of the corner of his eye, the cowboy thought so, too.

"Then let us be off," Khan said. "Any thoughts on which way?"

"All of these tunnels lead to an exit, but they all pass through the dragon's chamber. If we're lucky it will be asleep."

"And if it ain't?" Bulls-Eye asked.

"Then your raygun will offer scant protection."

"Oh, I dunno. All depends on where you hit it. I once took down a rampaging bull with a Red Ryder BB Gun. Clocked it right in the nethers."

"I... don't know what that means," Leandra said.

Bulls-Eye sighted down the barrel. "Well, the nethers is—"

"I think we can forego the anatomy lesson for the moment, don't you?" Khan said.

Bulls-Eye suddenly turned beet red as he realized what he was about to describe to the Priestess. "Sure, Perfesser. Thanks."

"Now," Khan said, "it seems that all roads lead to certain death and possible salvation after. Mr. Gutierrez, would you mind leading the way?"

Bulls-Eye hefted the raygun, swallowed his embarrassment. "Happy to, Perfesser."

As they headed down one of the openings Khan turned to the Priestess. "How exactly did you get down here?" he asked.

"There are gravity chutes like the one you came down in each room of the palace. The Princess is... capricious."

"Gravity technology!" Khan said. "I knew it. Tell me, what other wonders do your people have?"

As he listened to Leandra tell him of the technology and history of Mars, Khan was struck with the fact that he was enjoying himself. The thrill of discovery, the adventure of being on an alien planet, the possibility of certain death. It was all rather thrilling.

"You two need to stop your jawin' back there," Bulls-Eye whispered. "We been moving two hours now and you ain't stopped talkin' once. We got a demon lizard to sneak past. Remember?"

"Dragon," Leandra corrected. "It's a Demon Dragon. It breathes fire and ice and has claws the size of a—"

"I don't care if it's another one of them twenty-foot cockroaches. Point is we're trying get past it without it tryin' to eat us."

"Yes, of course," Khan said. Bulls-Eye was right but the conversation with the Priestess had been fascinating. According to her, the races of Mars had been in constant conflict for generations before the Weather Witches had appeared.

The Witches' power was vast and terrible and was so named for a reason. They could call lightning and storms from the sky, lay waste to whole regions with the power of the Martian winds at their command.

Early in their days they brought peace to the planet. Unified the kingdoms under their central rule as benevolent despots. True, their power was terrible to behold and they exercised it with abandon, but they were less dictators than police force, holding the warring nations in check. Each learned to thrive under the Weather Witches' regime as they focused inward and not on bringing war to their neighbors.

It was a golden age of enlightenment and peace.

And then Princess Cyclone came along.

To hear Leandra tell it, Cyclone was Caligula and Genghis Khan rolled into one. She set her troops and powers onto the other races and, instead of unifying them in peace, she banded them together in fear. Those who questioned her authority soon found themselves under the headsman's axe.

Or under the palace to feed the Demon Dragon.

"You say it breathes fire and ice?" Khan asked, wondering at the physics of that. "At the same time?"

"So it is said. But I have never seen the beast."

Khan nodded. Understandable. After all, why would someone willingly enter the beast's domain. Khan had a thought.

"How long has the dragon been under the palace?"

"Since before Cyclone began her rule. A hundred years at least."

Interesting. "Perhaps this is all just a ruse," he said.

"Come again?" Bulls-Eye said.

"A ruse," Khan said, his step becoming more lively as he laid out his theory. "Think about it. A hundred years to feed and care for some demonic beast who lives in the dark? How do we know it's even alive? How do we know that Cyclone's victims don't just become frightened to death instead? Or become lost in this maze and die of starvation or thirst?"

His step came down on something sharp and brittle that snapped beneath his foot. The light was dim down here. There was enough to see the walls and the floor and little else. Bulls-Eye knelt down to inspect what the three of them had waded into. He pulled out a match and struck it alight off his tooth. It flared and guttered.

And Khan realized just how wrong his theory was.

The ground was littered for dozens of feet in bones. Simian bones, humanoid bones, bones of centaurs and amphibians and the hollow bones of the bird people. Piled high and scorched to nearly black.

"Oh dear."

A terrible roar rent the air, sending a shimmering of dust to cascade down from the ceiling. A thundering crash came from a side tunnel, followed by a gout of flame that illuminated the entire chamber in a deep, red glow.

The dragon burst out of the tunnel, powering forward on a dozen segmented legs. A nightmare blend of snake, lizard and centipede. Steady orange flames erupted from its nostrils and an icy cloud exuded from a thousand teeth filled mouths along its flanks. They chomped at the air, as though waiting for an itinerant meal to wander by. It spied the trio at the other side of its den, let out a mighty roar and charged.

Khan stood frozen, mouth agape. A mix of terror and fascination warring within his mind.

Bulls-Eye gave him a shove. "Get a move on, Perfesser. Get the Priestess to cover. I got this." With a holler and a whoop he hefted the raygun over his head and ran toward the beast like a maniac.

"He's going to get himself killed," the Priestess said, horror plain on her face.

"Knowing him, unlikely. His point is well taken, though, we need to find some cover." He lifted the Priestess in his arms and bounded down a smaller side passage, one he hoped the dragon would be too large to get into.

"Stay here," he said. "I need to go help him." Khan rushed out of the passage and into a scene of utter bafflement.

Every time the dragon bore down on Bulls-Eye he wasn't there. A split second before a gout of flame or a blast of icy breath would have killed him, he simply moved. It was as though the man was dancing and the dragon didn't know the moves.

Each time Bulls-Eye managed a quick pirouette, a jump off the dragon's snout or a quick dosey-do between the thing's claws, it only became more enraged. Bulls-Eye's feats with the Mega-Mantis had been nothing in comparison to this. The man seemed a force of nature, a ballet-dancer made of water and smoke.

And more, as Khan watched the dance unfold before him, he realized he had a plan. Each step twisted the beast's snake-like form in unsustainable loops while moving it toward a shelf of loose rock.

The dragon twisted one way, its jaws snapping and missing Bulls-Eye completely. It spun back around to try to catch him as he bounced in the opposite direction. And with a sudden, massive jerk of its body, and a very surprised look on its face, it seemed to realize that it had just tied itself into a knot.

The dragon was balled up in its midsection, legs tangled against each other. It scrabbled against itself in an effort to get free to no avail. It roared and whimpered, screamed in rage. In its struggles it totally forgot about Bulls-Eye. It thrashed and rolled, slamming against the floor, the walls and the shelf holding up the loose rocks.

Bulls-Eye calmly walked away from the beast to stand next to Khan. He raised the raygun to his shoulder, sighted along the barrel and let loose a long sustained blast that cracked the shelf of rock.

The wall of stone crumbled, dropping tons of Martian rock onto the mewling beast. It shuddered, sending waves of dirt and dust cascading through the air until, with a final quaking sigh, it lay still.

"Good show, old man," Khan said. "A knot? Ingenious." But Bulls-Eye looked sullen and upset.

It occurred to Khan, that Bulls-Eye had just killed a simple beast. One that had been operating on instinct. It wasn't evil. It wasn't cruel. It was just following its nature.

"I'm sorry," Khan said.

"Me, too," Bulls-Eye said, kicking a pebble aside as he walked past Khan to the passage where the Priestess was hidden. "I was trying for a bowline."

CHAPTER FIVE
CAPTURED BY CENTAURS!

Khan, Bulls-Eye and the Priestess Leandra stood at the mouth of the tunnels beneath the palace. Above them, atop the low mountain of rock that they had traveled through, Khan could see the walls of the city that Princess Cyclone called home.

Tall walls and taller spires bristling with massive raygun batteries towered above them. A hazy blue glow shimmered in the Martian night sky, extending upward from the walls and disappearing into the sky.

"What is that glow over the city?" Khan said.

"The city's shield," Leandra said. "It is our greatest defense against invasion. Nothing can get through it, and any force or fleet that comes close enough to try comes under fire by the city's guns. When we get further away from the walls, you'll be able to see it better."

Khan wasn't sure he wanted to see it at all. The gun batteries gave off an air of menace, their sleek black lines and chrome accents glinting in the starlight. They swept the skies with mechanical efficiency. Khan could not even imagine the terror those guns could rain down on an invader.

"It gives me the willies," Bulls-Eye said, his eyes steady on the horizon. The vast desert unfolded before them. Massive boulders were scattered across the plain, casting dark, blue shadows.

"Don't suppose you got yourself any horses or a truck or somethin' we could use?" he asked.

"I did not have time to secure transportation," Leandra said.

"Then I guess we better start walkin.'" He took a step forward and then stopped. He cocked his head to one side, listening. "Get down," he said, his voice a whisper.

"What is it," Khan said. He knelt in the dirt and pressed himself behind a boulder.

"Dunno," Bulls-Eye said.

A moment later Khan heard it as well. A low hum and the sounds of marching feet.

"It's a patrol," Leandra said. "They circle the area around the city. Usually four soldiers and a hovercraft. Sometimes there are more."

"Then we're in luck," Bulls-Eye said. "I'll be right back."

"Wait," Khan said, but it was too late. The cowboy disappeared into the darkness.

"Does he always do that?"

"Apparently, so," Khan said.

"I hope he doesn't die," she said. "He fought bravely to keep us alive."

"He's a good friend," Khan said. He paused, rolling that thought around in his mind. He *was* a good friend, wasn't he? The man never seemed to care, or even register, that Khan wasn't human.

And how had Khan repaid that friendship? So far, not well. The man went into the thick of battle with wild enthusiasm and Khan... Well, Khan didn't.

He should be the one out there taking on Martian soldiers, not Bulls-Eye. He was a genetic clone of the Conqueror Ape, himself. And yet he quivered behind his books and learning like a shield, coming out to fight only when he could hold back his inner beast no more.

Khan winced as the sounds of gunfire reached their ears. Damn that man. He wouldn't let him get killed just to protect Khan.

Khan bolted out from behind cover, his wide, heavy feet propelling him through the soft sand at an ungodly rate. He burst past an outcropping of stone twenty feet tall onto a pitched battle.

Already three soldiers were down and the fourth was struggling with Bulls-Eye in hand to hand combat. They wrestled while behind them the hovercraft tracked the pair with an enormous gun affixed to a turret on its top. The gun couldn't fire on Bulls-Eye without hitting the other soldier.

Khan didn't think that particular stalemate would last very long.

Khan circled around the vehicle. It had the same brass and copper construction as the spheres that had erupted from the soil to capture them, but that's where the similarities ended. Where those were massive and designed for tearing underground, the hovercraft was sleek and designed to slice through the air.

Khan leapt to a high boulder, his enormous hands pushing off the rough rock. He spun through the air, the lower gravity giving him a speed and agility he would have never had on Earth. He landed behind the turret. The hovercraft rocked, tipped from the impact.

The turret spun toward him, trying to track him. The raygun let out a blast of crackling energy, but he sidestepped it easily. A hatch behind the turret appeared to have the same magnetic seal their prison cell had and he quickly realized he wasn't going to get in that way.

But there was a large glass viewport in the front.

Khan grasped the ledge of the hovercraft with his feet and swung over until he was dead center in the window's view. The three crewmen inside startled and exchanged glances, began bickering over what to do about the upside-down ape in front of them.

Khan didn't give them a chance to decide. The jungle drums in the back of his mind flared to life. He pulled back his fist and threw every bit of strength into the punch, shattering the inch thick glass. His fingers caught a surprised soldier by the face. He hauled the man out through the hole and threw him to the ground.

Khan reached back into the cockpit and grabbed for another soldier. They backed away from his grasping hand, leaving the controls unmanned. The hovercraft pitched forward, tilted to its left, slammed into the dirt. Its engines whined as it wedged itself into the ground.

"I got this one, Perfesser," Bulls-Eye said behind him. The cowboy jumped onto the edge of the hovercraft next to Khan, shoved his raygun rifle through the shattered glass and let off a series of blasts.

"That got 'em," he said. He pulled the rifle back and slipped in through the hole. A moment later the engines died with a shudder and a heavy thud. The hatch behind the turret hissed and popped open like a cork. A moment later Bulls-Eye pitched the two unconscious soldiers out and to the ground.

By this time the Priestess had joined them. She stood staring with wide eyes at the unconscious men, the commandeered hovercraft. She looked at the two Centurions covered in dust. Khan his bow-tie askew, Bulls-Eye sporting a fat lip and black eye.

"Are you all right?" she asked.

"As rain, darlin'," Bulls-Eye said with a wide grin. He spit blood onto the ground. Leandra gave Khan a questioning look.

"He means yes," Khan said. Khan dusted red dirt from his kilt. "And more so, we now appear to have transportation."

The hovercraft sped across the desert. Bulls-Eye was a quick study and between him and Leandra they had gotten the vehicle operational in no time.

They had been traveling for several hours. The sun was beginning to peek over the horizon, dim and emaciated. The Martian winds had kicked up and the cockpit had filled with a fine layer of grit and sand before Bulls-Eye learned how to lower a blast shield across the shattered windscreen and discovered a viewer that lowered from the ceiling for him to look through.

The cockpit was unlike any Khan had seen before. Instead of a steering wheel or even a yoke, the controls were a set of large dials clustered on a pedestal. Bulls-Eye steered the craft by spinning them in different directions. If he went too far one way or too far another, large orange lights on either side of the pedestal would flash dangerously. It was a ridiculous way to pilot a craft, but Bulls-Eye seemed to manage just fine.

"You sure we're goin' the right way?" Bulls-Eye said.

"I told you already that we are." Leandra tapped a series of gauges that rolled up and down. From what he could gather the gauges were a sort of map but they operated in no pattern that Khan could understand.

"We're almost at the kingdom of the Monatu. They're the closest. They can get us transportation to the Inkidu lands."

"Provided that they don't have a teleportation technology that can assist us," Khan reminded her.

She tensed, then relaxed. "Yes. As you say."

"What can you tell us about them?" Khan asked.

"They were nomads a millennia ago. Instead of having a kingdom of their own they traveled wherever they liked. Some warred with their neighbors, some conquered, some lived in peace. Slowly, they began to pull together into cities, but it wasn't until the Weather Witches came to power that they put aside their more tribal tendencies."

"Can we trust 'em?" Bulls-Eye said.

"They have no love for Princess Cyclone," she said.

"I gather that's a common sentiment," Khan said. "But statescraft doesn't necessarily care whether there is love lost between nations. Pragmatism has a tendency to win out at the most inopportune times. We will have to tread carefully. Do you have any ideas on who we need to talk to? Anyone we can approach?"

Khan felt a shift in the engines, the hovercraft slowing. "What's wrong?" he asked.

Bulls-Eye pulled his eyes from the viewfinder, beckoned Khan forward. "Take a look, Perfesser."

Khan leaned forward, squinted through the eye-piece. "Oh, dear."

"What?" Leandra said. "What is it?" Footsteps sounded on the hull outside. She turned to Bulls-Eye. "Why don't we speed away? Or fight?"

"Because, Priestess," Khan said. "We are out-numbered, out-gunned and surrounded."

Bulls-Eye said. "Ain't nowhere for us to go, ma'am."

Khan tapped his chin in thought. "We can't stay in here all day," Khan said with a grimace. His face brightened with optimism. "And who knows, perhaps this is an honor guard come to greet us."

He pressed his hand against a control panel. The outer hatch popped open with a hiss and early morning light streamed into the vehicle. He slowly climbed the ladder, Bulls-Eye close behind him.

When he reached the roof of the hovercraft, he stepped aside to make room for Bulls-Eye and the Priestess and slowly raised his hands in the air. If the sight through the viewfinder hadn't been enough to convince him that a fight would be a lost cause, the army of centaurs in front of him certainly did.

These centaur soldiers surrounding them were nothing like the ones he had seen in the court of Princess Cyclone. Those were thin, spindly specimens compared to these massive brutes.

In the front they were very similar to men, but with ruddier skin, more angular faces and small tusks jutting past their lips. Their shoulders were not quite as broad as Khan's, and their musculature was more wiry than burly, but there was not an ounce of fat on any of them. They wore leather armor and carried wicked looking spears and raygun rifles.

But any similarity to humanity faded at the waist. From that point on even calling them centaurs was a stretch. Instead of horse bodies they had the heavy build and scaled skins of Komodo dragons covered in heavy, metallic barding. Long, dangerous looking claws grew from each paw and their thick tails waved lazily from side to side.

Khan had no doubts that, should they choose to, those tails could be used as weapons just as deadly as any other.

Bulls-Eye and the Priestess came up to stand beside him. The warriors stared at them, unblinking, unmoving. As Khan was about to break the silence, the group of centaurs directly ahead of them parted to clear a path for an enormous massive specimen of their kind, dressed in gleaming armor.

His skin was a lighter shade of red than the others, and his deep, black hair was swept back in a pony tail that fell halfway down his back. He was easily Khan's equal in height and breadth and his tail was armored with a series of sharpened plates that ended in a spiked club. His spear was almost twice as tall as he was and arcs of electricity danced among a set of nasty looking spikes at either end.

The centaur looked them up and down, eyes narrowed in disgust. He turned to the side and spit a thick wad of phlegm into the desert sand.

"Trespassers. Trespassers in our lands. As is my right, I, King Parsimal of the Monatu, demand blood honor from these unwelcome scourges." He slammed one end of the spear into the sand and sparks flew from the impact.

He pointed an armored hand at Khan. "You, barbarian, will fight me," he said, "or die where you stand."

Khan stared at the king in shock. Fight? This was ludicrous. That couldn't be right. He looked to Bulls-Eye for confirmation.

The cowboy shrugged. "So much for this bein' the welcome wagon."

CHAPTER SIX
PUGILISM IN THE DESERT!

"Face me, barbarian!" the king cried, slamming the butt of his spear into the ground with each word. "Face me and know your doom."

The soldiers spread out, creating an impromptu arena. There was nothing to do about it, Khan realized, except fight him.

"I could shoot him," Bulls-Eye said. "Right through that ugly kisser of his."

"I don't think that will actually solve our problem," Khan said, as he jumped off of the hovercraft into the red sand.

"You are weak, barbarian!" the king said. "Weak as your brethren. The Chosen? You?" He laughed. It was a loud, braying sound between a donkey's cry and a small earthquake. "You cannot defeat the Mighty Parsimal! I will feast on your flesh, make ornaments from your bones."

Khan flexed his muscles, readying himself for whatever might come. He didn't know the etiquette here. Should he strike first? Should he wait for his opponent to begin?

Clearly this was ritualized combat, but was it a form of counting coup where there was no actual bloodshed, like that practiced by some of the Plains Indians of North America? Or was this more akin to the one-on-one battles of the ancient Moche civilization of Peru?

Khan hoped it wasn't the latter. Those rituals only ended when someone's heart was torn from their chest as blood sacrifice.

The king stepped forward until he was inches from Khan. He towered over him, cheeks flaring, eyes aflame. He leaned in until he was nose to nose to the great ape.

"Make it look good," he whispered, and swung his spear at Khan's head.

Khan was taken off guard by the words and only barely ducked in time. His fur lifted as the electrified spear buzzed over his head. If he hadn't moved just then it might have taken his skull clean off.

Fine. If the king wanted it to look good, then Khan would make it look good.

He swung his fist in an uppercut that caught underneath the king's chin. And in the lower Martian gravity it was devastating. The blow snapped the king's head back, taking his body along for the ride. His forelegs left the ground and if not for the stabilizing tail it very well could have thrown him across the length of the impromptu arena.

The spear flew from the king's hand as his body came back down with a crash. His eyes weren't tracking very well. He stepped back, shaking his head.

"You don't have to make it look *that* good," the king hissed. "Look, I'm trying to help you here."

"Help me?" Khan said, indignant. "You're trying to kill—"

He was cut off as Parsimal's fists and forelegs slammed into his chest, knocking the wind out of him. It was like getting hit with tree trunks. Khan staggered back, wheezing. He saw spots.

Khan came to his senses as the king brought his hooves down. He rolled out of the way just in time. Khan leapt to his feet, his breath easing. He backed up, only to be prodded by the soldiers' spears as he got too close to the perimeter.

The king charged down upon him. Khan was too close to the edge. There was nowhere for him to go.

So he jumped.

Like all apes, Khan was a powerful climber, but he wasn't designed for jumping. He could leap to high branches when the mood struck him, of course, but he wasn't a monkey.

So when he leapt over the king's head and cleared the long, sinuous tail, he was as surprised as anyone.

His feet came down into the soft sand with a loud crash. He spun on his heels, as the king tried to do the same. But as Khan was victim of his own anatomy, so was Parsimal. He could flex the front half of his body, but the rear half took quite a while to catch up.

And before he could turn all the way around to face Khan and continue the fight, Khan grabbed his tail and heaved.

Khan spun and launched him like a hammerthrow. The king flew across the clearing, knocking over a group of soldiers on the other side like nine-pins.

Khan staggered, dizzy, unsteady on his feet. He didn't understand what was going on. Make it look good? What did that even mean? He hobbled toward the hovercraft. Maybe, if everyone was distracted, they could somehow escape? He shook his head again to clear it. No, that was insane. Surely someone would see them.

He was so caught up in his addled thoughts that he didn't notice the king's recovery behind him until the centaur grabbed him by the shoulders, spun him around and butted him in the head with a skull like an iron pot.

"Just trust me, you damn fool," Parsimal hissed. "Fall down and stay down. If you're going to survive this I need to show mercy. I can't do that unless I've beaten you."

"What?"

"If I don't beat you my men will kill you. That's how we do things. I can't offer you mercy unless you're on the ground."

Leandra had told him about their history as a nomadic people. Raiders, warriors. Of course some of their ancient customs would survive. Parsimal was their king. He had to constantly prove his right to rule.

"I see," Khan said. He brushed dirt off his lapels, crossed his eyes and pitched backward into the sand.

"You could have made it a little more showy," Parsimal said.

"Apologies," Khan said, cocking open one eye. "It's been a long day."

Parsimal pressed a foreleg onto Khan's chest, lifted his arms high and yelled, "I, King Parsimal of the Monatu have defeated the trespassers' champion! And as he was a worthy—" he leaned down, glaring at Khan, "—if stubborn opponent, I grant him and his companions mercy!"

He stepped off of Khan's chest, reached down and hauled him up by his wrist. "Welcome, our guest—," he paused. "What's your name?"

"Professor Khan."

"Professor Khan! And his companions to our lands!"

A cheer rose up among the soldiers. They rushed in, grabbing Khan and lifting him over their heads. Khan looked around and spied Bulls-Eye and Leandra getting the same treatment. Bulls-Eye had taken to it like a fish in water and was whooping like a madman, a wide grin on his face.

The Priestess wasn't taking it quite so well. He caught her eye, tried to convey that everything was all right. She seemed to understand and tried to ride out the ceremony with as much dignity as she could muster.

Perhaps things were looking up.

King Parsimal's city was a Spartan affair. Though clear evidence of technological advancement showed throughout, such as raygun batteries on the city's walls and an airfield loaded with sleek craft with stubby wings that Khan could only guess were rockets, the city kept a strong grasp on its nomadic roots.

The city's walls were rough-hewn stone, the buildings rustic and simple. The roads were paved in some soft, spongy material, presumably because the Monatu did not wear shoes. Stalls were lined up along the sides of the main thoroughfare selling all manner of goods, from technological devices whose purpose Khan could not grasp, to fruits and vegetables that Khan had never seen before.

As the king's procession went by, residents crossed their forelegs and bowed, and only openly gawked at Khan and his companions once the king had passed.

"I feel like I am on display," Khan said.

"Likely we are," Bulls-Eye said. The soldiers divested him of his raygun rifle and the cowboy looked almost naked without it.

"This is customary for them," Leandra said. "We are defeated prisoners given the status of guests. Before we can be allowed audience with the king we must be paraded before his people. This is a custom Cyclone has allowed them to keep."

"And the king, is that a hereditary title?" Khan asked.

She shook her head. "Every few years there is a coup to depose the reigning monarch. Parsimal has been king here for almost twenty years and has defeated all comers. Thus far Cyclone has not publicly interfered, but there are rumors that she has been behind the most recent coup attempts. He is popular with the citizens."

"That could make him quite a threat, yes," Khan said.

"So you think she's just tossin' enemies in his way to try and trip him up?" Bulls-Eye asked.

"Yes," she said. "And I think he knows it, too."

"That might explain his behavior," Khan said. If Parsimal was looking for allies against Cyclone, the Chosen One from Leandra's prophecy could be an advantage. Clearly Cyclone saw him as a threat.

The procession stopped at the palace gates, massive stone doors that opened smoothly through some hidden mechanism. King Parsimal turned to his three guests.

"I will give audience to my three guests in the throne room shortly. Burattus!"

A Monatu, thinner and more wiry than the others and dressed not in battle gear, but in a wide sweeping robe of red and gold brocade that stopped just short of his tail, stepped up behind the king. His face was long and thin and his tusks were needle thin parodies of the king's enormous fangs.

"Yes, my liege?"

"Ensure that they are given ample refreshment. No doubt they are tired and hungry from their travel through the desert. I will summon for them when I am ready."

"Your Highness," Burattus said, "surely this is a job for one of the servants."

Parsimal caught Khan's eye. "I wish you to see and give me your thoughts on them afterward, Burattus," Parsimal said. "Though they are honored in the palace one cannot be too careful."

"As you command, your Highness," Burattus said, distaste showing clearly on his face.

As Burattus led them away to another part of the palace, Khan couldn't shake the distinct feeling that the king had been talking to him and not to his aide.

The aide was every bit the huffy bureaucrat Khan had expected. He walked stiffly, his back straight, and every time he caught sight of Khan or Bulls-Eye his eyes narrowed and he gave a loud sniff.

The only one of the three who didn't seem to raise the aide's ire was Leandra. She moved with the grace of one who understood court and etiquette and, Khan began to realize, had an air of royalty about her. She wasn't merely acting regal, she was regal.

"Have you been with King Parsimal long?" Khan asked.

Burattus gave a non-committal grunt. A low growl began to grow in Khan's chest at the man's rudeness. Leandra's hand on his shoulder calmed him.

"I understand you've been Palace Administrator since before Parsimal took power," she said.

"Took," Burattus said. "Excellent word for it. Yes. I was with King Herakon before him. He was a king who understood that people had their place. Herakon would not have let—" he eyed Khan, "—barbarians into the palace."

Khan could feel his anger rise, but Leandra's touch warned him. He tamped it down.

"Herakon was well respected by Princess Cyclone, was he not?"

"Very. And his legacy will live again." He stopped before a set of rooms. "I don't know why you're with these two ruffians, Priestess, or why the king feels the need to entertain them, though I'm sure you both have your reasons. Each room has a valet. They will get you what you require and perhaps," he gave Khan and Bulls-Eye a look as though he had just bitten into a lemon, "some more appropriate attire."

"Thank you, aide Burattus. I appreciate your assistance," Leandra said.

The aide bowed his head low to her, turned and walked away, his tail barely missing Khan as he strode down the hall.

"Why, I never," Khan said.

"I think we just found ourselves a fox in the henhouse," Bulls-Eye said.

"That would explain Parsimal's coming to our aid," Leandra said. "If Cyclone makes a move against him, it is the old guard like Burattus she will work through."

Khan frowned in thought. "Then we don't have much time. No doubt she has spies in her various kingdoms. If word hasn't gotten back to her by now that we've survived, and that Parsimal has taken us in, it will soon."

"No doubt she already knows," Leandra said, "and I'm sure he is aware of it. As she has spies in Parsimal's court, he has spies in hers. He called you the Chosen when he confronted us in the desert."

"He was waiting for us?" Bulls-Eye said.

"I doubt it. I think he knew of your existence, saw a damaged Thavasian hovercraft far from its home and pieced it together. He's very shrewd."

"Then we best focus on the priorities," Khan said. He pushed one of the doors open onto an enormous apartment decked out in dark woods and marble floors. Tapestries and rugs of Martian landscapes adorned the walls and floor. An enormous, circular mattress lay in one corner, big enough for at least two centaurs to sleep in.

A very surprised valet stood to one side listening at a device jutting from the wall. A telephone of some sort, Khan guessed, though it had no mouthpiece. The valet recovered quickly, setting the device back in its cradle before hurrying toward the trio.

"Lords, m'lady," he said. "I received word moments ago of your presence. Food and beverages are being sent up now. Is there anything I can do for you?" He looked over their clothing with a critical eye. There was no judgment in that gaze, not like with Burattus, just the cool assessment of a professional. "I will get you new garments and if you like I will have yours cleaned and repaired."

Bulls-Eye looked down at his grime-covered, sweat-stained clothing and made a face. "I don't see what's wrong with my duds," he said.

Leandra patted his arm. "Then trust my judgment," she said. "You need to change."

"I'm keepin' my hat," he said.

She gave him a smile that lit up the room. Khan watched the cowboy melt in its gaze. "I wouldn't expect anything else."

"Yes," Khan said to the valet. "I believe all of those things would be perfect."

A sudden wave of exhaustion washed over him and he teetered a bit. There had been water and some rations in the hovercraft they had stolen, but it hadn't been enough to sustain his considerable bulk.

It had been at least a full day since he had slept and in that time he had fought a Mega-Mantis, been blown through space, stunned by rayguns twice, thrown down a pit and fought a centaur king.

He was, as Bulls-Eye might say, bushed.

The valet bowed. "Of course, sir. If you'll excuse me, I'll show the others to their rooms." Leandra and Bulls-Eye followed the valet out of the room, the cowboy casting a worried glance over his shoulder.

Khan waved him off. The man could do with some downtime himself. He never seemed to tire, but he was human, after all. The look on Bulls-Eye's face said he wasn't happy, but he went along, anyway.

Khan waited for the door to click shut then sat down on the bed. Five minutes, he told himself. Five minutes to close his eyes and then he would turn his mind toward what to do next. He knew they didn't have much time. Cyclone's troops could be on the move this very moment.

But surely, he could spare five minutes, couldn't he?

He lay back and was asleep before his head touched the blankets.

"Too late! Too late!" The cry came behind him as Khan struggled to run. He was clothed in rags, bound in chains. His feet sunk in the soft Martian sand as he tried desperately to escape. Tall cliffs towered toward the sky on either side of him.

Behind him he heard the cry again, "Too late! Too late!" Howls and hoots accompanied it, a low, wild dirge that echoed off the canyon walls and sent ice into his spine.

He pushed himself harder. He could feel the beasts that made that low keening cry approaching closer and closer. The canyon walls dropped away and soon he found himself running on an ancient plain. The chains were thick and hot around his waist, weighed down his arms and legs.

He was exhausted and afraid.

"Too late!" The screaming was right behind him. He risked a glance over his shoulder and saw a dozen faceless monsters with insect legs, lizard arms, snakes for hair. They were on him in an instant.

They beat at him with barbed scourges that tore into his side. He fell as the whips wrapped around him, slashing huge gouges of flesh from his bones. The beasts heaved and dragged him through the rocky sand.

"Too late! Too late!" they screamed over and over again, a mad keening that filled his senses. They pulled him along to a cliff, kicking and prodding him ever closer to the edge.

And pushed him over.

Khan bolted awake from the nightmare. He shook, sweating. He looked at the shadows stretched long and thin across the floor. The voices had been at least partially right. It was late.

But was it too late?

CHAPTER SEVEN
ASSASSINS IN THE PALACE!

He pulled himself off the bed. Someone had left a change of clothing draped over a high table next to a platter full of strange looking fruit, a large pitcher of water and a thick cup.

He eyed the fruit and water carefully for a moment before deciding that he was being paranoid and poured himself a glass of water. If the Monatu had wanted to do him harm there had been ample opportunity. And really, if you were going to murder someone, letting them take a nap first seemed counter-intuitive.

He selected a large mango-looking fruit and peeled off some of its thick rind before taking a bite. He ate three of them before realizing what he'd done. He forced himself to slow down, but still managed to devour four more.

The clothing they had left him consisted of a roomy blue and gold tunic with a large sigil of a pair of crossed hammers on the front, a thick leather belt and a skirt made of some silk-like material. The tunic was welcome as his houndstooth coat and shirt were a tattered mess, but the skirt was right out. His kilt was still in decent repair and he saw no reason to replace its thick material with the lacy affair they had left him.

He found a basin of water in the corner of the room and cleaned off some of the dust that had matted into his fur. Soon, clothed, fed and watered, he felt like a new ape.

A few moments after he cinched the tunic around his waist with the thick leather belt, someone knocked on the door. A new surge of paranoia ran through him, which he immediately discarded. He assumed he was still shaken from the dream he had woken out of, though no doubt his present circumstances helped.

It was odd, this feeling of being hunted.

He pulled open the door to see Bulls-Eye looking decidedly less like a ragamuffin, though he still wore his dusty Stetson. His new clothing was not unlike his old, but it had a more ornamental appearance. He wore leather pants with pronounced stitching along the seams, a dusty red tunic and a leather vest. A series of belts and buckles crossed his chest securing it awkwardly. Even his boots were new, and like the vest they had all manner of buckles and straps. Over all of this was a thin, rust colored duster that could easily blend into the Martian landscape.

But what really caught Khan's attention was the low slung gun belt with two holstered raygun pistols at Bulls-Eye's hips.

Bulls-Eye caught Khan's expression. "Sorry, Perfesser. I'da been here sooner, but it took me ten minutes to figure how to get these boots on," he said.

"I was more wondering about the guns," Khan said. "Where on earth did you get them?"

"The Priestess done give 'em to me. Don't know where she got hold of 'em, but I ain't about to look a gift horse in the mouth." He drew the pistols from their holsters, spun them around his trigger fingers and re-holstered them in one smooth motion.

"I'm a little rusty on the draw with 'em," he said, "but they'll do."

"Indeed," Khan said. That was rusty? "And where is Leandra?"

"She'll be along presently. Not sure what she's doin' in there. Primpin', maybe? Though heck if she needs it. She's a sight all on her own."

Khan chuckled. "Smitten, Mr. Gutierrez?"

Bulls-Eye jerked as though Khan had just dumped water on him. "What? No. No, sir. I'm just— I just appreciate the finer things is all."

"Speaking of which," Khan said, gesturing with a nod past Bulls-Eye.

Bulls-Eye turned and Khan watched him carefully. He still didn't really understand human courtship rituals, but it was obvious to him that the cowboy was quite taken with the Priestess.

And now, Khan suspected, he would be even more.

The Priestess was clothed in an outfit similar to Bulls-Eye's. Utilitarian and just as ornamental, but where it hung off Bulls-Eye's frame like a sack, it hugged hers as though tailored. Even her duster seemed to conform to her curves.

Her silver hair was swept back in a pony-tail and tied with a leather strap and instead of the guns hanging from Bulls-Eye's belt, she carried a long, curved sword in a red and silver scabbard.

"Professor Khan," she said. "Mr. Gutierrez."

"Hello, Priestess," Khan said. "I trust you got some rest."

"Some, yes," she said. She looked Bulls-Eye up and down, frowning. "You have those vest straps completely wrong, Mr. Gutierrez."

"I think," Khan said looking at his slack-jawed friend, "that he might prefer to be called Bulls-Eye."

She stepped forward, grabbed beneath his vest and began rearranging the belts. "Of course," she said. "Bulls-Eye. These are designed as armor as much as they are ornamental. And in this case they are also a statement."

Khan found himself distracted by the horrified look on Bulls-Eye's face. The man was at a complete loss as the Priestess cinched straps and pulled on buckles.

"A statement?" Khan said, finally registering her words. "How do you mean?"

"This is an archaic uniform from before Cyclone took power. The Desert Scouts were the first arm of the military to defy her. They led a populist uprising against her and they could have won, but she turned her powers of the weather on them during a crucial battle and they were all killed."

"I see," Khan said. "Were these clothes already in your rooms?"

"They were delivered by a valet who said they were from King Parsimal with his compliments. Once I saw what they were I asked the valet if he could get me the sword and Bulls-Eye a pair of guns." She eyed the cowboy carefully. "I assumed you knew how to use them."

He tipped his hat. "Thank ye, ma'am. I do."

"You're welcome. I fear you may have use of them soon. I think the king's choice in our attire is to tell his people that he is finally willing to openly defy Cyclone."

"And you as well?" Khan said. "You have the sword, got Bulls-Eye his guns. Do you support this plan?"

"I see no other options, Professor," she said. "I am already a traitor to my people. You are being hunted by them as well. Like it or not we need allies. And we need them now. Before it's too late."

Khan was shaken by her choice of words, but pushed the feeling away. Much as he was loathe to admit it, she was right. "Agreed," he said. "We do need allies. And if the only way to secure them is to play this game then so be it."

"Ain't it a dangerous game, though?" Bulls-Eye said. "I mean, if he's tellin' his folks who's side he's on, he's bound to have folks who won't be none too keen about it."

"True," Khan said, thinking back to the aide, Burattus. "If the two of you appear before the king's court dressed like that it will send a clear signal."

"It's worse than that," Leandra said, tapping the sigil of the crossed hammers adorning Khan's tunic. "This is the standard of the Inkidu. The barbarians marched into battle wearing this symbol before Cyclone loosed a powerful tornado that wiped out a thousand of their troops."

Khan frowned. Not only was Parsimal making his play against Cyclone, but it would appear that he was using the Inkidu prophecy as well. He disliked being played as a pawn.

"Then he will stand with the barbarians?" Khan said.

"If they can be found," Leandra said. "He may already be in contact with them."

Footsteps caught their attention and they turned to see Burattus at the end of the hall openly gawking at them. Aha, Khan thought. He knows what these uniforms mean.

"Burattus," Khan said. "I take it the king would like to see us now?"

"He— he would," Burattus said, something between shock, horror and disgust clear on his face.

Khan walked to the stunned aide, smiling. He didn't like him. It was childish, Khan knew, but he wanted to make him as uncomfortable as possible.

"Then let us talk to your king. I'm sure he has many important things to say to his people."

By the time they reached Parsimal's throne room Burattus had turned three deeper shades of red and was rapidly heading toward a fourth. He fidgeted with the staff of his office, tapping it loudly on the floor as he walked. Two guards opened the double doors and the aide marched inside, Khan, Bulls-Eye and Leandra close at his heels.

The throne room was full of Monatu men and woman dressed in their court finery. They milled about near the doors while a few at a time went to the king at the end of the hall to pay their respects.

Parsimal sat on a raised platform, his legs tucked beneath him like a sphinx. His armor was replaced with thin robes of red silk. A thin crown of finely worked gold lay across his brow. He held his staff across his forelegs, electric arcs dancing quietly at either end.

Burattus struck his staff on the marble floor three times. "Leandra, Priestess to The Weather Witches, and her two—" he faltered, "—companions, have arrived."

All conversation in the throne room stopped as everyone's eyes snapped toward Khan and his companions. The king let the tension sit for a moment and then leapt off his throne.

"Welcome, honored guests!" he said. "Welcome." He strode down the aisle toward them, pushing past Burattus and embracing Khan.

"We're part of your plan to attack Cyclone, aren't we?" Khan whispered as the centaur pulled him close.

"Figured it out, have you? I thought you might. And apologies. You won't like this next part. Be on your guard." Parsimal draped an arm over Khan's shoulder and turned to his assembled court.

"Citizens of the Monatu! My friends and advisors. Long have we suffered beneath the thumb of the Weather Witch, Princess Cyclone. We have seen her crush the Inkidu with her terrible powers."

The crowd could see where this was going. It looked to Khan as though the group was split fifty-fifty. Half of them were beginning to smile, nodding as the king spoke, while the rest wore looks of dawning horror.

But there were a few who wore neither. They looked impassively calculating, or outright angry. Khan could see Burattus and a few others slowly begin to congregate on his position.

"But now the Inkidu prophecy has come true. The Mighty Khan! Whose presence shows us that Princess Cyclone's rule is coming to an end. He, along with the Prophetess Leandra, High Priestess of Cyclone City, will lead his people, and all people, away from the tyranny of Cyclone."

Khan watched Burattus become increasingly apoplectic. He began to shake.

"We all know that the Inkidu are still with us," Parsimal continued, "raiding Cyclone's supply lines and harrying her troops. They have shown that they can strike from the shadows. But now it is time for us to band together with them and fight. Come the morrow I shall mount an expedition to find the leaders of the Inkidu and prepare for war."

"This is an outrage!" Burattus yelled. "How dare you!" The aide reached into his robes and pulled out a raygun. He began to level it at the king but Bulls-Eye was faster.

The cowboy drew a pistol in the blink of an eye and shot the gun from the surprised centaur's grasp. Immediately, his confederates drew their own weapons from beneath their robes and began blindly firing.

"Assassins!" the King cried. Guards swarmed in from the sides to protect their leader. A shot winged Parsimal and he roared in rage. Khan reached for Leandra to try to get her out of the way, but whether it was the uniform or the sword she had just drawn, she clearly wasn't looking for help.

She leapt into the fray, running toward the conspirators with the blade held high. Behind her Bulls-Eye drew his second gun and popped off shot after shot. Some of the conspirators dropped, others had their guns blasted out of their hands.

Leandra screamed and brought her sword down toward Burattus, but he blocked it with his staff. He swung it around to sweep her legs out from under her, but she hopped out of the way at the last moment and struck the pommel of her sword against his skull. The aide's eyes rolled up into his head and he dropped like a stone.

Smoke filled the throne room, thick as the chatter among the attendees. Soon all of the conspirators were unconscious, arrested or dead.

Parsimal rushed to Burrattus, grabbed the centaur by his lapels and hoisted him to his face. He slapped him a few times until he came to.

"I will beat the names of your cohorts out of you," Parsimal said. "I will see them exiled into the crater of the highest volcano, sent out into the desert wastes with nothing. You dare you call yourself one of the Monatu?"

He dropped Burattus to the floor and turned to Khan.

"Thank you. I knew this would force his hand, but I didn't know who was with him. I apologize for having to use you." He turned to Bulls-Eye and Leandra. The cowboy had calmly holstered his weapons, but Leandra was breathing heavy and hard. She looked a little wild-eyed.

"And thank you, Prophetess, and you... strange alien man for saving my life and the lives of many of my people. Now, if you'll excuse me, I have to attend to this mad business." He stepped away, barking orders to his guards.

When the king turned his back to them, Leandra's legs gave out and she sagged against Bulls-Eye. The cowboy hurriedly propped her up, concern writ large on his face.

"I don't know what came over me," she said. "I'm a priestess, not a warrior. I could have been killed."

"I dunno," Bulls-Eye said. "You looked like you knew what you were doin' out there. I was mighty impressed."

"Oh," she said. "Thank you."

"I must admit, it is odd," Khan said. "Have you never been formally trained?"

"No," she said. A dark thought seemed to pass across her face.

"What is it?" Khan asked.

"It's— It's nothing. Must have just been the heat of the moment."

Khan frowned. She had been about to say something else, but had stopped at the last moment. Why?

An ear-splitting klaxon sounded through the room. Khan wasn't sure, but echoes of the noise seemed to be coming from outside the palace, as well.

"Blast!" Parsimal yelled. He moved to the trio and ushered them toward his throne at the back of the room. "I had hoped to have another day before this happened."

"What is it?" Khan asked.

"Cyclone. I knew word would travel fast but I had thought it would take a little longer to muster her troops to attack the city. We need to get you out of here. I have a private rocket-ship in an underground launch site."

He pulled aside a tapestry behind his throne and rapped three times on a portion of the wall. The wall split open to reveal a passage.

"You can get to it through here. It's pre-programmed with the coordinates of one of the last known Inkidu cities. Once you're there, find their leader. You should have no trouble convincing them that it is time to strike back at Cyclone."

"Come with us," Leandra said.

Parsimal shook his head. "I must lead my people." He grinned. "Besides, I've been planning for this moment for a long time."

Khan put out his hand and the king shook it. "May we meet again under better circumstances, Your Highness," Khan said.

"May we meet again on the field of battle. Now go."

The trio hurried down the corridor to the bunker. Behind them the sounds of fighting grew. Explosions, raygun blasts, buildings crumbling beneath the onslaught.

The corridor opened into an enormous launch bay with a sleek, silvery rocket on the pad. It had stubby wings on either side and a tail fin that swept out far behind it. A couple of centaur technicians disconnected hoses and ushered them up a gangplank.

"The controls for the rocketships are much like the hovercraft we got from Cyclone's soldiers," Leandra said.

"Well, heck, that's simple then," Bulls-Eye said. "I'll get us outta here right quick."

"Are you sure?" Khan asked.

"Sure, Perfesser. Ain't nothin' that can be ridden I ain't figured out how to ride."

"Make it quick," one of the technicians said. "There's an auto launch and pilot. Red button on the panel. Can't miss it." Above them the roof of the launch bay began to iris open. Khan could see Cyclone's rockets filling the sky, raining electric death down upon the city.

Khan watched the destruction for a moment, marveling at the devastation being wrought upon the city.

And in the back of his mind a dozen faceless monsters screamed, "Too late! Too late!"

CHAPTER EIGHT
THE GOLEM OF STONE!

"I refuse to believe it is too late to retrieve them, Doctor," Amelia Stone said. She leaned against an overturned table in Edison Thomas' lab, her arms crossed and lips pursed in obvious anger.

"I didn't say it was too late." He waved a sheaf of papers in her face. "These readings say they're fine. Or should be fine." He looked at them and frowned. "I'm not sure what they mean, actually. Point is if these readings are correct they should be able to survive... wherever they have ended up just fine. For a while. But if we don't find something to replace that Atlantean crystal soon I may lose all possibility of getting them back." Thomas was scurrying around his lab, picking up pieces of shattered equipment, screws and bolts that had shaken off when his device had exploded.

"And unless you have that replacement," he said, peering up through his thick glasses, a single crack bisecting the left lens, "I'll kindly ask you to get out of my laboratory so that I can finish my work, and figure out where they've gone."

Amelia began to say something but stopped as Benjamin Hu stepped into the wrecked lab. He carried a large, leather-bound tome with a thick metal clasp to hold shut the flaking pages.

"We don't have it, yet, doctor," he said. He gave Amelia a questioning look.

"I haven't had a chance to tell him," she said.

"No, she hasn't said a blessed thing," Thomas said, "other than to berate me for my apparent lack of alacrity."

Amelia shrugged, but said nothing.

"I see," Benjamin said. "We may be in luck. From what we were able to find in the library there are potentially five other sites that might contain Atlantean artifacts. Two of them are on the continent, one is in Sri Lanka, one in Peru and the fifth is a barrow in Wales."

"Well, what are you standing around here for? Go get it!" Thomas said.

"We are about to," Benjamin said. "We have some of the staff packing gear and will be leaving within the hour." He set the tome on top of a ruined table and opened it up to an illuminated page showing a green glowing crystal that looked like a clawed hand.

Thomas leaned in, studying the picture carefully. "Hmm," he said. "Are you sure it has the same properties?" His eyes scanned the text. "Oh. Oh my, yes. Yes, that should do. Obviously we won't know the power it can generate until we get it back and I can run some tests, but this should do quite nicely."

"Excellent," Benjamin said, closing the book. "You were saying something when I walked in about not knowing where they are? I thought you said they were on Mars."

Thomas frowned. "Oh, that. Yes. Mars. Or something. I'm having trouble understanding some of my readings. All the location data points to Mars, but—"

"But?"

He sighed. "All of the rest of my data is... troubling. The important thing is that they should be fine. Air is breathable, pressure is normal. Look, let's just drop it, all right?"

Amelia gave Benjamin a questioning look that he answered with a shrug. "How long do you think it will take to make your repairs?"

"A day at most. If you're going to Wales to dig around in an old barrow it will take you at least that long to get there and back with it." A mischievous glint came into the doctor's eye. "I'll race you for it."

"I beg your pardon?" Amelia said, her voice tinged with shock.

"Yes, doctor," Benjamin said, "I hardly think that's appropriate."

"Not without some money on the table," Amelia said, cutting him off.

Thomas dug into a pocket of his lab coat. He pulled out a variety of pens, a slide rule, a half-eaten chocolate bar and a yo-yo. "Blast," he said. He thrust his hand in the other pocket, rummaged around a bit and pulled out a wad of pound notes.

He put the crumpled-up notes onto the table, smoothing them out as he counted them. "Five hundred pounds," he said.

Amelia and Benjamin stared at the bills.

"I can't believe the two of you are betting on this," Benjamin said, finally. "We have friends to rescue."

"I can't believe he's carrying five hundred pounds in his coat pocket," Amelia said. "It's a wager. We'll be back with your crystal before you have your contraption fixed."

"I'm a very fast worker."

"And I'm a very fast finder of ancient antiquities."

"If the two of you are quite finished?" Benjamin said. Neither answered. "All right, then. Good luck with your repairs, doctor. We'll be back as soon as we can."

"That money's mine, Doctor Thomas," Amelia said over her shoulder as she followed Benjamin out the door.

"Don't count on it, Miss Stone," Thomas said and went back to recovering pieces of his destroyed device.

The red and black Austin 10 was a dependable car, the most dependable brand in Britain if the adverts were to be believed, and Amelia Stone hated it.

It was a boxy machine, built for durability and utilitarian use, not speed, certainly not style. She would have preferred her motorcycle, and even offered the use of its sidecar to Benjamin.

But he would have none of it. Too much equipment, he said and showed her the ropes and crowbars, electric torches and winches that he insisted on loading into the boot. She knew he was right, of course, but the drive was long and slow.

And she wanted that five hundred pounds.

She didn't really want the money, of course. She simply wanted to win. She'd always had a competitive streak and she didn't see how a friendly wager between colleagues was a point of concern.

She looked over at Benjamin as he took turns far more slowly than she would have liked.

"How much further is it?" she asked.

"At least another two hours," he said. The road they were on was a winding affair that went past the occasional small village, and quite a number of sheep.

"Can't this thing go any faster?" she said. They were in a hurry after all, and the sooner they got the crystal the sooner they would get Khan and Bulls-Eye back. As Thomas had said, if they didn't get that crystal soon it might be too late to retrieve them.

"Yes, but I would rather get to our destination intact than not get there at all. *Festina lente.*"

Make haste slowly. Amelia hated that phrase. Patience was not one of her many virtues. She drummed her fingers on the edge of the door. He was right, of course. Retrieving Professor Khan and Bulls-Eye was too important not to proceed with care.

Provided they were still alive.

That was the unspoken thought that gnawed at her just as she knew it gnawed at Benjamin and Doctor Thomas. The Professor and Bulls-Eye could have been eaten by another one of those giant insects that had come through the portal, or been crushed in a rock slide, or died of dehydration, or any of a thousand other horrible fates.

Oddly enough, the presence of the Mega-Mantis was a positive sign. It meant that wherever they ended up there was air. It was a small thing, but Amelia would take whatever she could get.

They passed the rest of the drive in relative quiet, stopping the car every so often to get their bearings. Their map was imprecise. They had a rough idea of where the barrow was, but not its exact location. It was one of several mentioned in the Century Club's archives, but an exact mapping had never been done.

No doubt the locals knew of its existence, but driving around and asking every shepherd and public house patron could take weeks and get them nowhere. But Benjamin seemed to have another idea.

He pulled the car to the side of the winding road next to a wall of loose stones. Thick forest sat just a few feet away. "I think this is about as close as any map will get us," he said.

"What, you've got a special compass?"

"Something like that," Benjamin said, exiting the car. He opened the boot, pulling out a small wooden box inlaid with mother of pearl in a complicated design that made Amelia's eyes hurt to look at. He cracked it open, exposing two pairs of eyeglasses with multiple, colored lenses.

"These glasses were discovered in Paris in 1847 in the laboratory of Dr. Frédéric Goulot-Rouge." He handed one pair of the eyeglasses to Amelia. "What was left of the laboratory, at least. It was mostly rubble. No one's quite sure what he was working on."

He donned the remaining pair, flipping various lenses in front of each eye and turning them like some mad, nightmare optometrist. Amelia watched, fascinated, until he eventually settled on a complicated combination of lenses and settings.

"There we go," he said, taking her glasses and making the same adjustments. Amelia placed the lenses carefully across her nose.

And everything changed.

It was as though someone had turned the entire world into an Easter egg. Where there had just been brown woods, green leaves, gray stone and grayer skies, now there were vibrant purples and pinks, glowing blues and greens. The forest was a shimmering blast of color and focus that marked each tree so distinctly that she could make out individual striations in the bark, the veins of each leaf.

She looked down at her own hands and gasped. She could see her veins, bones and muscles. When she focused she could see individual cells of skin pulling her deeper and deeper into herself. She became dizzy.

"I wouldn't do that," Benjamin said, steadying her. She started to look at him, but he stopped her. "And you definitely don't want to do that."

"What are these things?"

"Hard to say," he said. "But with the proper adjustments you can see just about anything. Through walls, around corners. I find them very useful when I've misplaced my keys."

The images that swarmed her were overwhelming and her head began to throb. She pulled the glasses off her face and the ache immediately subsided. "I can see why you don't wear them all the time," she said.

"It takes some getting used to. And even with practice I can't wear them for more than a few minutes at a time. If you don't focus on anything in particular it doesn't hurt as much."

She tried it again, letting her focus fade out a little. He was right. It was much more tolerable.

"And these will let us see the barrow?"

"More, these will let us get in. The barrow itself exists in two places. Most sites housing Atlantean artifacts usually do. Without the glasses we might find the capstone, dig around for weeks and never find anything. But with these we'll see the folds in space that are hiding the real entrance."

Amelia let her eyes wander through the insane colors that danced in front of her. "What am I looking for?"

"Paisley," he said. "Or a feeling of paisley, at least. It's hard to explain. You'll know it when you... well, see might be the wrong word. Experience it, I suppose."

Something caught Amelia's eye and, inexplicably, her mind as well. It was as though her senses were suddenly cross-wired. As her eyes passed the trees she could swear she could feel their bark underneath her fingers, even though she was nowhere near them.

She focused a bit, willing away the pain as best she could. It took a few minutes to subside but when it did she could feel it. There, exactly as Benjamin said. A sense of paisley.

"Is that it?" she said, pointing awkwardly in the direction of the sense.

Benjamin squinted, a slow smile creeping across his face. "Yes," he said. "I do believe it is."

As Benjamin said, the glasses had gotten them through the real opening of the barrow. When she looked at the entrance without the glasses it simply wasn't there. All she could see was the barrow's capstone, a large slab of dolerite balanced atop three standing stones. But with the glasses, a vortex of paisley energy whirled at the center.

It was a strange sensation, stepping through, as though she had somehow been squeezed into a mouse hole and blown up to regular size a moment later. Then they were in a chamber that was far too large to be where it was.

She took off the glasses and rubbed her eyes. She was already getting a migraine. She clicked on her torch, adding its light to Benjamin's. Steep cavern walls with stalagmites and stalactites covered in some glowing green moss.

"Amazing," she said. "Are all barrows like this?"

"No," Benjamin said slowly. "Most are just burial mounds. Look for anything that looks out of the ordinary. These places sometimes have defenses to keep out interlopers."

Amelia stared at the beauty of the cavern. Out of the ordinary? This whole place was out of the ordinary. How was she going to find something that stood out in a place like this? A loud scraping of rock on rock sounded behind her. She turned and stopped.

"Does a giant man made of stone with an enormous club stepping out of the wall count?" she said.

"Yes," Benjamin said, turning to see the creature slowly pull itself out of the rock.

The thing sounded a monstrous shriek and slammed its club on the floor, shaking the cavern and sending motes of rock scattering to the floor.

"Run?" Amelia said.

"Run," Benjamin agreed.

They ran.

CHAPTER NINE
INTO THE DEPTHS!

Khan held tight to a handle on the wall as the ship bucked and dodged among the rays blasting around it. Bulls-Eye sat at the controls, knuckles white, eyes grim, as he turned dials this way and that, sending the ship careening in all directions.

Though the ship's controls were almost identical to the hovercraft they had stolen from Cyclone, the seats were designed for the centaurs. Instead of chairs they were wide benches to rest their mid-sections on with looped straps to hold them in place.

The benches were fine, but the lack of any safety harnesses that Khan and his companions could use meant hanging on for dear life every time Bulls-Eye banked the ship.

"How are you doing up there?" Khan asked.

"Like a long-tailed cat in a room full of mouse-traps, Perfesser. A little further and I think we'll be out of the worst of it, but I ain't makin' any promises."

Leandra pulled her eyes from a viewfinder at the navigation station. "If you can head north we might be able to make it to the borders of the Inkidu lands. Cyclone patrols it, but with the fighting here we might have time to hide the rocket and make contact with the Inkidu leaders."

"Sounds like a right good plan," Bulls-Eye said. The ship lurched as something hard hit the hull. "Only I don't think we're gonna get a chance to try it. Grab onto somethin' and hold on tight."

"I am holding on tight," Khan said.

"Well, hold on tighter."

Khan's stomach flipped as they lost altitude. Out a porthole he could see smoke and flames bubbling forth from one of the rocket's stubby wings. More fire hit the wing as they descended, buffeting the ship back and forth.

It was clear to Khan that Bulls-Eye had lost all control. The best he could do now was crash the ship as safely as possible. Through the forward windscreen Khan could see the ground loom toward them.

"What is that?" he said as he spied a dark blob in the upper right corner of the glass.

"Yes," Leandra said. "Can you aim for that?"

Bulls-Eye, shaking from his exertions on the controls, nodded. "I can sure as heck try." He cranked the dials to the right, the ship fighting him the whole way. The hull strained with loud shrieks and pops. Out the porthole, Khan watched in horror as one wing sheared away.

Soon the ship yielded and began to veer toward the dark shape. From this distance Khan still couldn't tell what it was. "Is it a field?"

"It's a cavern," Leandra said. "If we're where I think we are that might be one of the openings to the Underground Ocean, Regent Volus' domain."

"Ocean?" Khan said.

"What's the matter, Perfesser, can't swim?" Bulls-Eye asked.

"Uh... not as such, no."

"You're pullin' my leg."

"I'm too dense."

"Why you're one of the smartest folks I know," Bulls-Eye said.

"No, it means I'll sink like a stone. Gorillas have too much muscle mass. We don't float."

"We may not have much choice," Leandra said. "We're going to crash and better to do it in water than into solid rock. If we're lucky the water should be deep enough to cushion the landing. We can deal with your lack of buoyancy later."

The shape took on craggy outlines and Khan could see that she was right. It was an enormous cavern in the plains of Mars. It must be miles wide and who knew how deep. An ocean inside that murky dark? Khan wasn't sure if the thought gave him hope or terrified him utterly.

"And if it isn't?" Khan asked as the ship dipped below the edge and plunged into darkness.

"Then ain't nobody gonna need to bury us, Perfesser," Bulls-Eye said.

The cavern loomed in the windscreen. From so high up Khan had not realized just how huge it was. But now, as they cleared the lip and descended into the inky blackness, he was stunned at its enormity.

Bulls-Eye cranked the controls hard and the rocket's descent began to level out. He punched a button and braking thrusters kicked in to slow their speed. It seemed to be working and then a split second later the ship lost all power, the deafening roar of the engines replaced with an ominous silence.

The effect was immediate. Gravity reached up and yanked the rocket down. Khan was bounced off the ceiling. Bulls-Eye barely kept hold of his station and Leandra kept her place only by hooking both legs and her arm around a support beam.

The ship slammed into the water of the Underground Ocean with a crash. The remaining wing shattered as though it were made of glass. Rivets popped out and ricocheted around the cabin like bullets. Water shot through newly formed cracks. The cabin began to fill with water.

Khan picked himself up off the floor. He was dizzy and his head hurt, but mostly he thought he was all right. But he wouldn't be for long. Already the water was over his feet.

"We've got to get out of here before we sink," Khan said. No one answered him. Bulls-Eye and Leandra lay unconscious where they had secured themselves.

Khan's hopes sank along with the rocket. There was no way he could get them to the surface. The moment he went out into that water he would plummet to the depths.

No. He would not let that happen. His eyes scanned the battered interior of the rocket. Surely there had to be some sort of survival equipment for such an emergency?

He opened a promising looking box that had come loose from its place beneath the pilot's chair, but all it had in it was a ration of water, some stale looking biscuits that smelled of moldy cheese and a pamphlet entitled "Surviving To Serve Again In Cyclone's Army" with chapters like "How Not To Be Eaten By A Gritellian Sand Worm". Useless.

There had to be something that could save them. Then he had it. The rocketship was pressurized. It had its own air supply. Which meant there had to be some sort of oxygen tanks on board. He tore through the back of the ship and quickly found a row of massive oxygen tanks. He disconnected one from its moorings and hoses and dragged it to the front of the rocket. It was almost as large as a motorcycle.

Khan tore cables from the shattered cockpit and used them to lash his companions over his shoulders. It wasn't perfect, but as long as it kept them together that's all that mattered. He was going to need both hands and his feet if they were going to get out of this alive.

The ship's hatch was buckling inward and there was no way it was going to open by turning the wheel. There was too much pressure. But Khan thought, that might work to their advantage.

Khan tucked the oxygen tank beneath his arm, flipped toward the ceiling, grasping a support beam with his toes. There were advantages to having prehensile feet. With his free hand he grasped the edge of the hatch, dug in his fingers and pulled.

The water pressure did the rest. He yanked his hand back and pulled away as the door tore from its hinges from the torrential blast. Khan took in a great gulp of air, hoped he knew which direction the surface was and that they hadn't descended too rapidly, and heaved himself through the opening and into the unlit ocean.

He plummeted as he knew he would, though perhaps not as rapidly as he had expected. Was there more salt in this sea than in the oceans of Earth? That might work to their advantage.

He wasn't sure which way was up, but in the dim light he could see the directions the bubbles floated. He quickly oriented himself so that the oxygen tank pointed toward what he hoped was down and tore off the valve.

The blast of escaping oxygen shot him toward the surface. Moments later his head cleared. He held on to the tank as it sputtered the last of its air, propelling the three of them in increasingly smaller and slower circles until it finally came to a stop.

Khan held onto the tank for dear life. Between the increased salinity and the lower density of the spent tank he could stay afloat for a while. But for how long he didn't know.

Khan pulled Bulls-Eye and Leandra up and slung them over the top of the tank, hoping that they hadn't taken in too much water. Light streamed down from the cavern's entrance, and he could see the dim Martian sky far above.

Dark shapes flitted past, filling the sky. It took him a moment to realize that they were rocket-ships. Cyclone's presumably. And here in the freezing water, Khan and his friends were sitting ducks.

Confirming his suspicions one of the rocketships fired its raygun. It was a ridiculous shot and came nowhere near them, but Khan knew that that was just to find the range. More shots would come until they zeroed in on them and blew them out of the water.

Beneath him Khan felt something brush his leg. He startled. Of course. This was a planet that bred Mega-Mantises. Of course there would be something equally heinous in its waters. It seemed he had a choice.

Death from above or death from below.

Bubbles began to form in a ring around him. Small at first and then a seething, roiling mass of them, as though the water had begun to boil. Above him another shot came from a hovering rocket, closer this time.

Khan figured it was even money as to which would get him first, the rockets or the beast beneath the waters.

The bubbles increased in ferocity and he knew that it was over. What an ignominious death. To go out devoured by some feral ocean beast on another planet. He wouldn't take his death without some sort of fight, though. This thing wasn't going to have him that easily. He flexed his muscles, searching the water for any sign of something he could grab.

Whatever this foul beast was, it wasn't going to take him without a fight.

CHAPTER TEN
INTO THE LAIR OF THE FROG PEOPLE!

The bubbles surrounding Khan grew in intensity. Was this one gigantic beast, Khan wondered, or a swarm of Martian piranha? On Earth they could reduce a man to bones in mere seconds. He made a fist, ready to strike whatever horrific creature showed itself.

But instead of a giant shark, monstrous tentacle, or even a swarm of piranha, it was blasts from rayguns that burst out of the water. The beams sped toward the rockets, blowing them out of the sky. Deafened and blinded by the artillery barrage surrounding him, Khan didn't notice the divers surrounding him until they had grabbed him.

He started to flail, almost punching one of them, until he noticed that these were not Cyclone's troops, but the amphibious frog-like creatures that he had seen in Cyclone's throne room. They had wide faces, and enormous eyes. They had slits in their skin where their noses should have been.

"We need to get your friends medical attention," one of them said. His voice was a thick, croaking rattle. "The cannons will keep those rockets off us until we can get you to safety." He reached up to a metallic band wrapped around his forehead and clicked a button. "We have them. Bring up the submersible."

A low, disc-shaped vehicle broke the surface not far from Khan and the divers. They swam toward it and clambered atop the hull where the divers helped untie Bulls-Eye and Leandra from Khan's back.

"Are they breathing?" Khan yelled over the sounds of raygun fire.

One of the divers gave him a webbed thumbs-up as others put Leandra and Bulls-Eye onto stretchers. "They'll be fine, sir. We just need to get them below. We'll be safe once we're under the surface."

The frog-men were wearing suits similar to the ones divers wore back on Earth. They were designed to be worn in and out of the water. An amphibious uniform for an amphibious race.

"Incoming!" one of the divers yelled. An enormous chunk of debris from one of the damaged rockets landed in the water mere feet from the sub. A hatch opened and the divers carried Bulls-Eye and Leandra inside, Khan close at their heels.

The hatch closed behind them with a loud hiss and Kahn found himself inside a utilitarian room dimly lit with red lights. His ears popped as the room pressurized. He could hear rushing water outside and felt the fast descent as the sub slipped below the surface.

A door at the far end of the room opened and all of the divers stood at attention. A frog-man in a uniform similar to the divers', but with patches of insignia on his breast and shoulders, stepped into the room.

"Welcome aboard the *Whirlpool*, Professor Khan. I'm Captain Perrin. We received word from the Monatu that you might be headed this way." His voice held the same ragged croak that the divers' had. "The Lieutenant here will get you and your friends to the infirmary. I'll meet you there momentarily. We have much to discuss."

"If you'll follow me, sir," one of the divers said.

Khan could hear muffled explosions outside. "Are we safe?" he asked as he trailed behind the Lieutenant. At first he couldn't tell the frog men apart, but as his eyes adjusted to the dim, red light inside the sub he could tell that this one had jagged stripes running diagonally across each cheek. He noticed markings on the other frog-men that he passed. Diamond shapes on a forehead, tiger stripes around bulbous eyes.

"Absolutely, sir," the Lieutenant said. He waved his men through a hatch as they carried Leandra and Bulls-Eye on stretchers. "That's just the engines of those fallen rockets cooking off. We're well away from any potential harm. Cyclone can't touch us down here."

"That's good to know."

The Lieutenant led him into a large medical bay with beds that were all far too small for Khan, but easily accommodated his companions. Doctors hovered over their two patients and busily checked pulses and heartbeats, administering oxygen.

After the ordeal Khan just wanted to sit down. He found a low stool that seemed sturdy enough for his bulk. It sagged beneath him, but held.

One doctor broke off from the others and came to Khan. "How are you feeling?" he said.

Hounded, Khan thought. Hunted and used as a pawn in someone else's political game. Manipulated, played, set upon.

He settled on, "Wet."

The doctor laughed, handing him a towel. "I dare say you could be worse. You saved your friends there. If you hadn't broken out like you did we never would have gotten to you in time."

"Will they be all right?"

The doctor nodded. "Yes. They almost drowned, but your quick thinking saved them. They'll be unconscious for a while, yet. I suspect they'll come around by the time we reach port."

"Where are we going?" Khan asked. He rubbed the thick towel over his face. Between his sopping clothes and his fur it was going to take a lot to dry him off.

"To see the Regent," the doctor said.

Kings again, Khan thought. Khan wondered if this Regent was going to try to use him the way that King Parsimal had. He grimaced at the thought and masked it as a wince of pain.

"I expect you're a bit banged up after that. We'll see to your wounds and get you cleaned up. We have a cabin for you when we're done. We'll see to your clothes. You're very lucky, you know."

Khan looked at Bulls-Eye and Leandra lying unconscious on gurneys being attended by doctors and nurses. Telling someone they were lucky was the same as saying, "At least you have your health." Good or bad, you still had it.

The cabin Khan had been assigned was not designed for someone of his bulk. It was cramped and tight and he had to perform gymnastics just to get cleaned and change his clothes.

They had dried his kilt as best they could, though it was still slightly damp. The Inkidu tunic was too far gone. It was ceremonial, not functional, and it was little more than tatters. He felt naked, but going shirtless seemed the better option.

He made his way to the infirmary. Even the hallways on the sub were narrow. Frog-men stood aside or stepped into open doorways to get out of his way. Though it was hard to read their alien expressions, Khan felt that they were looking at him with something like awe. Or possibly fear.

And why not? Everyone knew of the prophecy. Even if it was just a fairy tale, it had power. He was a symbol and his presence meant something potentially more frightening than Cyclone's continued rule.

It meant change.

Bulls-Eye was awake and dressed. He sat on the edge of his gurney. A bandage was affixed to a cut on his forehead and poked out from beneath his Stetson. He stood stiffly from the gurney to greet Khan.

"How are you feeling?" Khan said.

Bulls-Eye looked back at the frog-men in the infirmary and dipped his head. "Damp," he said, his voice barely audible. "But at least my guns are dry. You?"

"The same," Khan said, lowering his voice to match Bulls-Eye's. "With the added indignity of being half naked."

"It suits you, Professor," Leandra said, stepping out from behind a partition. She cinched up her swordbelt. "Why are we whispering?"

Khan looked at Bulls-Eye. Bulls-Eye looked at the floor. "No reason," the cowboy said.

"I tend to disagree on the nakedness, Priestess, but thank you. And how are you?"

Unlike Bulls-Eye, Leandra had no bandages. Though Khan could swear she had taken just as much damage in the crash as he had. And her clothes were bone dry. Even Bulls-Eye's duster still showed signs of water in its hem. Curious.

"I'll live, thanks to you."

"Yeah, Perfesser," Bulls-Eye said. "Thanks for savin' our bacon back there."

"If it wasn't for your miraculous bit of flying we wouldn't have made it that far."

"Aw, heck, Perfesser. T'weren't nothin'. Those things is so automatic I just gotta press the button says GO."

Khan doubted it was nearly that simple. The cowboy seemed to have a knack for mastering anything that could be used to wreak insane amounts of havoc.

"Be that as it may, you saved us from certain doom at the hands of Cyclone's troops."

"Yes, Enrique," Leandra said, placing a hand gently on his shoulder. "It was remarkable."

The cowboy's olive complexion reddened. He stammered a bit and Khan decided to step in to save him any embarrassment. "The Captain wanted to see us," Khan said. "I understand we're going to see the Regent."

"Regent Volus," Leandra said. "I know little of him or his people, the K'kir. There are few of the K'kir at Cyclone's court and I've never had an opportunity to speak with them."

"We would be happy to educate you on our culture, Priestess," Captain Perrin said, stepping into the infirmary. "I heard you were up and wanted to let you know we'll be docking soon. And to discuss a little of what brought you to our kingdom."

"How much do you know?" Khan asked.

"The basics, I suspect. Appearing at Cyclone's court, being thrown to her Demon Dragon."

"We killed that varmint right good," Bulls-Eye said.

Though the Captain had no eyebrows, Khan could swear one eye cocked up a little higher than the other. "That alone might make her send troops after you. Do you have plans?"

"We're gonna—"

"Figure that out as time goes on," Khan said, cutting him off. "We really are just trying to get our bearings at the moment. Will we be seeing the Regent soon?"

"As soon as we dock."

"Excellent. We'll speak with him about our plans." Khan fell silent, hoping he had made his dismissal clear. The Captain, unused to being shut down quite so abruptly, said nothing. The awkward silence stretched.

"Very well," the Captain said. "We should be in dock in the next hour. The galley is nearby if you would like refreshment." He stood there, waiting for some sort of response. Khan didn't give him one.

"Well, then," he said, finally. "I wish you the best of luck in your travels, Professor Khan, Priestess and... strange man with a hat. Good day." He turned on his heel rather stiffly and marched out of the room.

"I don't look strange, do I, Perfesser?"

"He's an anthropomorphic frog, Bulls-Eye. To him I suspect we all look strange."

"Are you worried that he might be an agent of Cyclone?" Leandra said.

"Not particularly," Khan said. "But I am tired of being played as a chess piece. It's time this pawn learned to move on his own." He looked at Leandra. She wouldn't meet his gaze.

"I understand," she said.

"I don't," Bulls-Eye said. "Perfesser, this is one of them sub-text things, ain't it?"

"He's concerned that I too am trying to play him for a political end," Leandra said.

"Aw, heck, Perfesser, of course she is. We known that from the start. Either she wants Cyclone kicked out or she's settin' us up to find the Inkidu so Cyclone can wipe 'em out once and for all, includin' you on account of you bein' that prophecy ape. But it don't matter none. This fight's a comin' whether you like it or not. And if she can help us get there, all the better."

Bulls-Eye leaned over toward Leandra. "I don't think you're a-tryin' to sell us out none," he said. "'Sides, I think you're purty."

Khan considered this. The cowboy had a point, even if he was suddenly turning three shades of pink now that he seemed to realize what he had just said to the Priestess. Khan wasn't sure, but it looked as though she were turning a deeper shade of green.

Khan turned away to let them have their moment. Bulls-Eye was right, of course. Even if she was an enemy, keeping her close was the best strategy.

"Yes," Khan said, turning back to the two of them. "You are, as usual, correct. We've known from the start what your stated goal is. But I too have been clear on my goal, which is to find a way home. And to that end I will not be prodded, poked, or pushed in any direction not of my choosing. Do I make myself clear?"

"Yes, Professor," Leandra said. "I will not try to influence you in your choices. I will trust in the prophecy and I will trust in you."

Khan was expecting more resistance and he found himself slightly taken aback. "Yes. Well. All right, then."

A low, deep chime sounded throughout the submarine, saving Khan from having to figure out what to say next.

"I think we're here," Bulls-Eye said.

"Then let us go see the Regent," Khan said.

Khan and his companions were ushered off the submersible by a cadre of armed guards. When the hatch was opened and Khan stepped onto the dock, he paused to take in the marvel of engineering surrounding him.

The K'kir's city was hewn out of miles of solid rock. The cavern ceiling far above him twinkled with lights that illuminated the entire city in a muted approximation of twilight.

Buildings of impossible height reached toward the ceiling. Bridges of delicately carved stone connected the buildings in an intricate weave. Instead of streets at their bases there were canals with boat traffic to rival the cars of any city on Earth.

The sailors led the trio to an electric boat that zipped along the busy waterways until it emptied into a lake in the middle of the city. The palace at its center took Khan's breath away. If the city was an intricate web of interconnected buildings and engineering marvels, the palace was downright magic. It sprawled in all directions, its waterways and bridges decorated in complex and beautiful patterns. Spires of white, elaborately carved stone loomed up until they brushed the cavern ceiling.

The Captain led them through winding hallways, finally stopping at a non-descript door. The Captain knocked and opened it. Khan was expecting an ostentatious throne room, something to impress them.

Instead he stepped into a library. Shelves that reached to the ceiling two stories up lined the walls. Map tables and desks were spaced haphazardly throughout the room. Every surface was covered in books and scrolls.

And in the middle of it all, standing atop a rolling librarian's ladder, stood the Regent. He plucked a tome from a shelf and slid down to the floor with one hand along the ladder's rail. He was thinner than the other K'kir Khan had met, with wide spaced eyes and a streak of red running down from his forehead, stopping just before his nose. He was dressed in a loose, white suit made of the same material the sailors from the *Whirlpool* wore.

It occurred to Khan that perhaps the Regent actually had been trying to impress them. And if so, he had certainly done a good job of it.

"Welcome!" the Regent said as he hit the floor. "I have heard so much about you, Professor Khan! Welcome!"

Khan and Leandra bowed and, after a moment, Bulls-Eye followed suit. "Your Majesty," Khan said.

"Oh, none of that, Professor. Please." He turned to the Captain. "We'll be fine here, Perrin."

"Your majesty?" The Captain looked confused.

"I said we'll be fine. Go on, shoo."

"Yes, your majesty." The Captain and his sailors bowed deeply and left the room. The door shut behind them with a loud click.

The Regent let loose a sigh. "The military can be tedious," he said, "but like any tool they serve an important function. Now, Professor, Mister Gutierrez, I understand you're looking for a way to get home to the Chapter House in London."

Khan cocked an eyebrow. "You're remarkably well informed Your Majesty," Khan said. "I didn't know anyone here knew of London. Or the Chapter House."

"Yeah," Bulls-Eye said. "We ain't been here more'n a day or two and most of that time spent runnin'. I don't recall tellin' too many folks my last name, neither."

The Regent's wide, frog-like face split into a grin. "I am well informed, indeed, Professor. And more, I may have a way to grant you what you're looking for." He placed the book onto a nearby desk and clapped his hands twice, loudly.

A large, circular mirror, easily ten feet wide, descended from the ceiling. Its surface clouded momentarily and then, clear as though he were standing there himself, Khan watched a London street appear in the glass.

"Remarkable," Khan said. He reached for the surface of the glass and paused.

"By all means, please," the Regent said. "It's not fragile."

Khan touched the surface of the glass and it rippled against his fingers like the surface of a pond.

"Would you like to see another view?" He turned to Bulls-Eye. "Your home state of Texas, perhaps?" The glass clouded again and the scene shifted to a view of scrub brush on a desert plain.

Bulls-Eye frowned. "That's all well and good, Your Highness, but that don't much explain things."

"Enrique!" Khan said, appalled at the cowboy's lack of respect.

"Oh no, Professor," the Regent said. "He's absolutely right. Perhaps this will." The glass clouded once again and the scene shifted to the exterior of the London Chapter House of the Century Club. Several of the windows were boarded up and workers were cleaning up the recent wreckage to the walls that Dr. Thomas' lab accident had wrought.

"The glass can show several scenes from many different places on Earth and here on our own planet." He chuckled. "Mars. A fitting name you've given our home. We've been torn by war for centuries. Of course, we are not quite so poetic. My people have been studying your planet for decades. And, of course, the Centurions."

Khan frowned. The comment about war troubled him. "Invasion," he said darkly.

The Regent laughed. "Oh, my word, no! Science! Well, science and trade eventually, but I daresay we're still quite a ways from that."

The Regent hopped onto a table and crossed his legs. He was quite unlike any ruler Khan had ever imagined. More like an excited schoolboy than the leader of such an advanced civilization.

"This device," the Regent said, "allows us to tune into the natural frequencies of aether that surround all things. Once the frequencies are known it's a simple matter of tuning them in. There are limitations, of course. Some locales are easier to see than others and we don't have much control over our point of view. Stone and metal reduces the signal such that though we can see the building here we can't see inside it. On occasion we can even get sound, though for some reason that's trickier."

"Has everyone on this planet been studying us?" Khan turned to the Priestess.

"Doubtful," the Regent said before she could answer. "Princess Cyclone has a less advanced technology than what you see here that she stole many years ago. No offense, Priestess, but your people are more copiers and thieves than innovators."

"It's true," she said. "I've seen a similar device inside Cyclone's Viewing Room. She doesn't use it often because it is notoriously difficult to control."

"Pretty pictures are all fine and dandy," Bulls-Eye said, "but how does this get us back home?"

"My scientists have been working on this technology for decades," the Regent said. "And recently it's helped us crack the secrets of teleportation. We're nearly complete. We've managed to open small portals to other parts of the planet and even smaller ones to Earth. Nothing big enough to transport the both of you, but we think we have a solution. We're only a few days from perfecting it. And if it works..."

"And in return?" Khan asked. If there was one thing that he had learned in his time working with the Centurions it was that there was always a catch.

"Put in a good word for us with the other Centurions," the Regent said. "As I said, we're interested in trade with your planet and at some point we'll be ready for it. This is a first step. If we were to have the endorsement of the Centurions that would go a long way to help us."

"Aren't you concerned about what Cyclone might do to you for assisting us?"

The Regent laughed. "Cyclone's abilities are nearly useless down here. She has control of the weather. What weather is there under the sea? We have a trade agreement with her because it serves us, but her threats are weak at best. There will be repercussions, of course, but I've already recalled my ambassador and gotten my people out of her city. We can counter anything she throws at us. It's a necessary risk. I need to look to the future."

"And the future is Earth?" Khan said.

"The future is Earth," the Regent agreed. "And if you would be kind enough to accept my hospitality I can get you there."

Khan turned to Bulls-Eye who appeared deep in thought. "What do you think?" he asked.

"I think it's our best bet," the cowboy said. "Leastways we get ourselves a breather, not be jumpin' around like a coyote with his tail on fire. I say we go for it."

"We accept your offer, Your Majesty, and pledge that we will talk about your proposals for trade with the other Centurions."

"Excellent!" the Regent said.

For the first time since arriving on Mars, Khan dared to hope. He caught a glimpse of the Priestess, out of the corner of his eye, her face downcast, and that hope faded away.

What about the Inkidu? The other races of Mars? Would they have hope? He didn't believe he was a messiah, but clearly he was enough of a symbol that people were willing to hunt him down.

His thoughts grew dark even as the Regent's enthusiasm bubbled over. What would happen when he left? He put it out of his mind. Getting him and Bulls-Eye back to Earth was his highest priority. He was clear about that.

But was it the right thing to do?

CHAPTER ELEVEN
THE CAVERN OF CATASTROPHE!

Amelia ducked under the ponderous swing of the stone giant's club. Too close that time. She could hear the air as it whistled past her head. She tucked into a roll, drawing her pistol from its holster and popped off a round. It ricocheted harmlessly off the giant's skin.

"That's not going to work," Benjamin said. He danced away as the giant slammed a massive foot where the detective had been standing only a moment before.

"I had to try," she said.

They had run through the cavern, a space much larger than it had any right to be, to escape the stone giant. But there was nowhere to hide and they were running out of room. Soon they would be completely backed into the end of the cavern. With that enormous club there was no way they were getting past the stone giant.

"Shouldn't we have run into some treasure chamber or something by now?" Amelia asked. The giant swept a hand at her and she flipped over it easily. The monster was huge and immensely dangerous, but slow as a slug. The problem of getting past it was that it simply took up too much space. It was like trying to sneak past a wall.

"Yes," he said. The club crashed against a nearby stalagmite, cracking it in two. The pieces fell, barely missing him. "Can you keep it occupied a moment? I have an idea."

Amelia nodded, holstered her gun. She leapt to the giant's arm as it swung the club, pulling herself up. It swatted at her with its other arm, but by the time it got to her, she was already at the thing's shoulder.

She scurried to the side of the giant's head, ducking to keep from grazing the roof of the cavern. She could see the coarse cuts made from ancient tools, the chunks chiseled out to make an approximation of humanity. She wondered momentarily how it could see with eyes that were nothing more than dents in the stone. She began to discard that question as irrelevant and paused.

Maybe it wasn't. She grasped the giant's rough-hewn ears and swung herself to block its face with her body. Immediately the giant stopped. The arms froze in mid-swing, one leg stretched out, half-cocked at the knee.

"Hey," she said, "I think I stopped—"

Before she could finish her sentence the giant burst into motion, arms and legs flailing wildly in a mad dance. It spun in place, slammed its stone club against the ceiling. It rocked back and forth as if panicked by its sudden blindness.

Amelia clung to the giant as tightly as she could. It jerked its head from side to side, almost dislodging her. She tucked in tightly as the head slammed against the side of the cavern.

"Got it," Benjamin yelled. "Quickly now, before the passage closes."

She couldn't see what Benjamin had done but trusted that when he said she needed to move he meant it. She waited for the giant to spin until it faced him then launched herself backward off of its face.

She arced backward in a graceful curve, dodging the stone club by mere inches, spun herself end over end and landed firmly by Benjamin's side. He pulled her toward an opening in the stone that hadn't been there a moment before.

She leapt after him just as the stone giant re-oriented itself and brought its club down where she had stood just a moment before. The giant slammed its bulk against the rock, sending dust raining down on them but the passage was too small for it to follow. They were, for the moment at least, safe.

"A little distance from that thing might be in order," Benjamin said. He was wearing his multi-lensed goggles, which presumably allowed him to see how to open the passage. He pulled them off and rubbed the bridge of his nose.

"What, worried about a little rock?" Amelia said, grinning.

"Only when it's trying to kill me," he said, returning a smile of his own. He trained his electric torch on the passage before them. Amelia had lost hers playing leapfrog with the stone giant. This passage was less cavern-like than the one they had just exited; it had been carved out of the rock.

Whoever had done this had done a better job than on the stone giant outside. The walls were smooth with thin, almost imperceptible arches buttressing the passage. Though dim, the walls glowed with a pale blue light. Amelia squinted into the distance, blocking the light from Benjamin's torch.

"Noticed the walls?" she said. "It gets brighter further down."

"Then I don't think we need this." He clicked the torch off. It took a moment, but Amelia's eyes adjusted quickly to the gloom. They picked their way carefully down the passage. It was slow going but there was no telling what sorts of traps they might run into down here.

Twice they stopped to edge past obvious pressure plates, and a rockfall almost crushed them when Benjamin accidentally triggered one as he walked past. A spike-lined pit inexplicably appeared beneath them as if it had suddenly popped into being rather than being revealed by a trapdoor. If not for Amelia's quick reflexes, they both might have died.

"How long have we been down here?" Amelia said. There didn't appear to be any end to the passage.

"Minutes, days, hours. Hard to say. These chambers often exist outside regular time. What would be a minute to us could be a day outside. Or more. Or less, even. Once I left a chamber like this in Mongolia three days before I went inside."

Amelia laughed. "And did you meet yourself?" she said.

"Yes," he said, face deadpan. "He was very confused." He continued down the passage, testing the floor for more traps.

Amelia was never quite sure if Benjamin was telling the truth. Considering some of the odd things she'd encountered with him, he probably was.

She followed, taking the other side of the passage to explore. A few moments went by and she stopped. She reached into her coat pocket and removed her glasses. Even looking at them made her head feel tight. She took a deep breath and put them on. Immediately the passage flooded with light emanating from glowing symbols written along the walls. She couldn't read them but they were clearly a language of some sort. Soon it grew too bright; she took the glasses off and slipped them back into her coat, blinking rapidly.

"Benjamin," she said. "Put on your glasses." He looked over his shoulder at her, catching on immediately.

"Aha," he said. He adjusted a lens or two on the glasses perched upon his nose. "Ancient Alantean. Yes. I see." He studied the words for a moment and then purposefully strode off down the passage.

"Benjamin, the traps!"

He waved a hand over his head. "Just a moment," he said. When he came to a depression in one of the arches, he reached in and pushed. There was a loud click and the room rearranged itself to show all of the traps it had been hiding. Walls slid aside, pit traps appeared, their spikes receding into the floor.

Benjamin pushed his hand further into the depression. "And if I twist this that way and push." There was another click and a low earthy rumble began to echo through the chamber. A moment later a section of wall shifted to the side revealing a room from which spilled a soft, green glow.

"Is that it?" Amelia asked, stepping carefully toward the opening.

"The resting place of The Spear of Brân Fendigaidd the legendary Welsh king Brân, The Blessed."

"He's not going to come to life and try to kill us, is he?"

"He's not here. This is just his spear." Benjamin placed the spectacles on his nose and peered into the room. "I think it's safe. Come take a look."

Amelia leaned into the opening. It wasn't a large room, maybe fifteen feet on a side and twenty high. In the center, propped up atop a large dolerite slab, was a broad spearhead made of a jade-like material. It glowed a fierce green and bathed the room in its unearthly radiance.

"I don't trust it," Amelia said.

"Nor do I. But needs must when the devil drives, yes?"

Benjamin put the glasses back on, stepped gingerly into the room. His eyes scanned back and forth for potential traps. "I see no triggers," he said. Amelia followed closely at his heels.

"Nothing at all?"

"Nothing," he said.

"I still don't trust it."

Within a few moments they were at the pedestal. Amelia could hear a low hum coming from the spearhead. They both knelt to look at it more closely.

"Pressure plate," she said. "Has to be."

"I see no seams, or other breaks in the surface." Benjamin traced his finger near the bottom edge of the slab where it lay on the floor, almost, but not quite touching. "If there is one it's well hidden. A counterbalance of some sort? But would it detect increased weight or decreased weight?"

Amelia stood, walked around the slab, looked at the spearhead from multiple angles. "Aw, to hell with it," she said, finally, and snatched the spearhead from its resting place.

Immediately a large stone dropped across the entrance, sealing them inside.

"I knew there was a pressure plate," she said.

The room began to shake, sending motes of dust cascading to the floor. A low rumble came up from the floor. Cracks began to appear in the walls.

"I think this could be very bad," Benjamin said. "Why did you do that?"

"Because—" Why had she done that? She'd been accused of being impulsive in the past but never suicidal. And it wasn't like this was the first treasure hunt she'd been on. She knew the risks.

The spearhead in her hands pulsed, its unearthly light rising and falling. She had the sudden urge to sit down and wait for the inevitable. It was such an alien thought that she could tell that it wasn't her own. She shook off the feeling as best she could, but it lingered.

"It's the spear," she said. "I think— I think it's trying to control me."

"Interesting," Benjamin said. He opened his satchel to her. "Here, this should help."

Now that Amelia had the spearhead she didn't want to let it go. Again, she realized the thought for its alien nature and reluctantly dropped the artifact into the satchel. The room was plunged in darkness as soon as he closed the flap. And with the light so went the feeling of wanting to surrender.

"The bag is lined with arcane symbols and a copper mesh, like a Faraday cage."

"Whatever works," she said, taking Benjamin's torch and flicking it on. "Now let's find a way out of this place before it—" A chunk of rock dropped from the ceiling, cutting her off.

She sidestepped it easily, but Benjamin, still fastening the clasps of his bag, wasn't so lucky. It bounced off his head and drove him to the floor.

"Benjamin, are you all right?"

"Yes," he said. "Mostly." He sat up, blinking in the light from her torch. "But I've lost the spectacles." He grasped blindly along the floor, looking for them. Amelia bent to help him.

"Here," she said as her hand came upon them. They had skittered across the floor to rest against the stone slab. Forgetting her own pocketed pair, she pulled Benjamin's on and immediately saw why he had wanted them.

The cracks in the walls were widening, and behind them she could see a pale outline of a passage, a set of crude stone steps heading skyward. She could also see the stress fractures in the ceiling and the floor. If they didn't get out soon they weren't going to get out at all.

She grabbed Benjamin, hauling him to his feet. She shoved him toward a large tear in the far wall. "This way," she said. "There are stairs or a ramp or something."

Benjamin didn't argue, and just wedged himself through the tight opening. Once he was through he reached for her to guide her through the crack after him, but loose stone fell and he jerked his hand away before it could be crushed.

"Go," she said. "Get that thing back to Thomas. And get that five hundred quid!"

"Amelia!" Benjamin cried, but more stone fell, filling the gap even as it widened. If she responded he couldn't hear it. A crash of stone sounded behind the wall as more of the room collapsed in on itself.

All around him the passage was crumbling. He closed his eyes for a brief moment, a silent prayer for his fallen friend, then turned and rushed to the safety of the exit.

CHAPTER TWELVE
BETRAYED IN THE FROG KING'S PALACE!

"I don't know if I trust 'em, Perfesser," Bulls-Eye said. He leaned against the wall of the Regent's laboratory, arms crossed and glaring at the crowd of scientists tinkering with a device not ten feet away. One of them glanced up, caught sight of him and quickly dropped his gaze back down to his work.

The room was abuzz with K'kir scientists puttering about, taking readings, adjusting dials. He could only follow a little of what was actually being worked on. One of the K'kir scientists tried to explain the more technical aspects of the devices around the room, but it was like listening to Edison Thomas going on about his quantum devices and such. Still, it was fascinating to watch.

"So far they're the only people we've encountered who haven't tried to kill us, beat us or imprison us," Khan said. "I think that warrants some consideration."

Bulls-Eye sighed. "I know that," he said. "But they just look so... so..."

"Alien?" Khan said.

"I was gonna say peculiar, but yeah. Alien. They're nice enough folk, but they got them frog eyes that give me the willies."

Khan gave him a sideways glance. "You have a problem with frogs?"

"It ain't a problem so much as it's an agreement. I don't go frog giggin' and they don't look at me with them big ol' eyes of theirs." He shuddered.

Khan had a memory of Bulls-Eye sweating in Cyclone's throne room, remarking on the K'kir diplomats and how nervous he seemed, his drawn-in behavior in the submarine infirmary. His vague, not quite hostile behavior around most of the K'kir.

"My word," Khan said. "You're ranidaphobic."

Bulls-Eye stood straight, puffed up his chest. "I ain't no such thing," he said. "Why I'm as hygienic as the next guy."

Khan tried to parse out what the cowboy thought he had said but quickly gave it up as a lost cause. "It means fear of frogs," Khan said.

"Oh. Well. Yeah, I suppose that's right." He looked at the floor, a sheepish look on his face. "You won't go tellin' the Priestess, will ya?"

"Tell me what?" Leandra said, coming into the room. She still wore her Desert Scouts uniform and sword belt, though the duster was nowhere to be found.

"I— Uh, that is—" Bulls-Eye stammered, glancing at Khan for assistance.

Khan felt sorry for the poor man. His feelings for the Priestess were obvious and he couldn't imagine that she wasn't aware of them by now. Clearly, it was time to help him, even if his manner suggested this wasn't the sort of help he was looking for.

"Bulls-Eye was concerned that you might not like to accompany him on a walk through the palace. I understand there are some beautiful subterranean gardens that he would like to show you." He nudged the cowboy out of his stammering stupor. "Wouldn't you?"

"Uh. Yes. Yes, I surely would. Ma'am. If you'd care to I would very much like to show you the sights."

The Priestess cocked her head to one side, a slight smile on her lips. "If I'm not to call you Mr. Gutierrez, I think you can stop calling me ma'am. I would be happy to join you."

"Oh, yes, ma— I mean, sure. I gotta finish something up here right quick and I'll catch you in the hall?"

"All right," she said. It was clear to Khan that she was trying very hard not to laugh. She turned and sauntered out of the room.

Bulls-Eye turned on Khan, betrayal in his face. "Why'd you go and do that, Perfesser? I thought we was friends."

"We are. That's why I did it. Go. Enjoy yourself. Besides, it will get your mind off of frogs."

"I don't know how to sweet talk a lady. I'm no good at it. And where's these subternian gardens you're talkin' about?"

"Subterranean. Ask one of the palace guards. He'll show you the way."

"I ain't gonna forget this, Perfesser," Bulls-Eye said. He tried for a steely gaze, but it just came across as a squint.

"Then let us hope for both our sakes that it goes well. Seize the opportunity, Bulls-Eye. *Carpe diem.*"

Bulls-Eye gave him a final glare. "Don't know what carpets got to do with all this," he muttered as he walked away.

Bulls-Eye was nervous. He told the truth. He didn't know how to talk to a lady. There wasn't an interesting bone in his body.

What was he going to talk about? Roping steers? Riding through the desert after cattle rustlers? His time in Old Ironfeather's Wild West Show where he learned trick riding and shooting? How he rescued Calvin Coolidge when the outlaw Black Brannigan and his gang of cutthroats kidnapped him while the President was visiting Texas?

He'd never done anything impressive. He was dull as ditchwater and that was all there was to it. Especially next to a lady like Leandra.

"You're quiet," she said as they walked across one of the palace's many ornamented bridges. The water below them reflected the pinpoints of glowing stone far above their heads like stars bathing the palace in a twilight glow.

The whole place reminded Bulls-Eye of some kind of fairytale. Palaces, kings… even a frog prince. He suppressed a shudder. It wasn't true what Khan had said. He wasn't afraid of frogs. He was just… nervous around them.

That was it. Nervous.

"I'm just a little worried is all," he said. He plucked at the Desert Scouts uniform he wore. "I know you mean well and I'm on board and all, but the Perfesser, well, he don't much care for bein' used."

Leandra frowned. "I know. And I don't mean to, but the people need a symbol and like it or not, he's the only one we have."

"I get that. And I figure the Perfesser knows it, too. He's a smart cookie. But it don't mean he likes it."

Leandra stopped, leaned against the bridge railing, worry creasing her face. Her green skin was pale in the twilight. "Do you think if the K'kir find you a way home that he'll leave?"

Bulls-Eye paused, letting the statement wash over him. She hadn't asked if he would leave. There hadn't been any concern in her voice over his going away.

"I don't rightly know," he said. "With somebody like Cyclone runnin' around though, I can't see him thinkin' it'd be good for anybody. Here or back on Earth."

"And you?" she said. "How did you put it? You're on board? If he leaves will you help us fight?"

His heart swelled, and he was about to pledge an oath right then and there, but a moment of caution stopped him.

"I think I would," he said. "I think I'd have to. But I need to know more. I got questions and I ain't had a chance to sit down, take a breather and ask 'em. Like what's with this prophecy? And what's Cyclone's problem? I get that she's just meaner'n a dyspeptic rattlesnake, but how come? And what's a Weather Witch, anyhow?"

Leandra laughed, but then her face grew somber. "I have no idea what a rattlesnake is, but yes, I suspect that she is. Weather Witch is a title. For as long as we have history there have always been Weather Witches. But they were a force for peace. Powerful and terrible if crossed. But they only intervened when order broke down and always looked for a peaceful solution before they would resort to using their powers."

"Right," Bulls-Eye said. "I remember this. And then Cyclone came around and— Wait. If there were always Weather Witches and Cyclone was just the latest one, that means there were others when she showed up. What happened to them?"

"Cyclone murdered them. In the space of one evening she killed almost everyone in the temple of the Weather Witches. Some in their sleep, some in open combat. Only those she deemed worthy and who pledged their oath to her survived. Over a hundred died that night in a fierce battle that tore the temple to shreds and laid low much of the city."

"But why?" Bulls-Eye asked.

Leandra shrugged. "Pride? Spite? She believed that our world was corrupt and needed the Weather Witches to rule with an iron fist. Our people had fallen into hard times and lawlessness. Political in-fighting, open conflict with the other races. She lay the blame for our decline squarely on the Inkidu and their conquering ways. Believed they should be eradicated."

"Can't imagine the Weather Witches liked that idea much."

"They didn't. She was publicly censured for her radical ideas."

"And she killed 'em for it."

Leandra nodded. "She didn't stop there. She had her supporters, many from the military, and they rampaged through the city. There were purges. Almost everyone in government was killed. When the smoke cleared people cheered. But they had no idea what they had unleashed."

"Folk often don't. They get all swept up in the hullabaloo. So she didn't just stop once she was in charge, huh?"

"No. It just got worse. All who defied her were put to death." She smoothed out a wrinkle in her uniform. "There was resistance, but when she killed the Desert Scouts that all but disappeared."

Bulls-Eye could guess what happened next. "And then she needed to keep the rabble under control, didn't she? So she sent her troops after the Inkidu. Called 'em barbarians and such like. Gave the people something to hate more than they hated her."

Leandra looked up at him, surprised. "Yes. She sent troops after the Inkidu. She all but destroyed them. Only scattered tribes remain living in the bombed out shells of their former cities. There are rumors that they fled underground to rebuild, to survive." She considered Bulls-Eye more carefully. "That was... surprisingly astute," she said.

Bulls-Eye laughed. "I ain't been educated, but I ain't stupid. And I know how people see me. Just some desert rat cowboy who's quick with a gun. And that suits me just fine."

A smile tugged at the corner of Leandra's mouth. "I can see that being useful," she said. "I sometimes wish I could do the same."

"Nah, you don't need that. You're smart and educated and awful purty. Folk'd line up just to pay attention to you."

She blushed, the green of her cheeks deepening, her red eyes growing darker. "Thank you," she said. "But at home I'm more a pariah than anything else."

"Because of the prophecy?"

"Partly," she said. "No one likes to hear of their doom. But there are other things. I—" She chewed her lower lip, worry creasing her face. "There's something I should tell you. Cyclone is—"

A burst of gunfire erupted from the water beneath them, hitting the railing next to Bulls-Eye's hand. Another inch and it would have taken it clean off. Bulls-Eye drew his rayguns, popped off two blind shots into the water. There was a gurgling scream.

Loud bangs sounded from below and dozens of cabled grappling hooks flew over the railing to stick into the stone of the bridge.

"Thavasian soldiers," Leandra said as the first of the silver uniformed soldiers were pulled up to the bridge by the retracting cables. Their uniforms were more form fitting than the ones Bulls-Eye had seen in the palace and they sported airtanks on their backs. Instead of the rifles he had seen, these ones carried wicked looking knives and pistols.

Leandra drew her sword and Bulls-Eye gawked as arcs of electricity danced along its curved blade. She ducked under one of the guards' swinging fist, stepped up behind him and stabbed him ruthlessly through the heart. Electricity arced across his body and he fell twitching off the sword.

Bulls-Eye wondered momentarily why she hadn't used the sword's power in their fights at the centaur king's palace, but put the thought away as he dealt with more pressing concerns. A dozen soldiers were advancing on him, firing their pistols.

Bulls-Eye rolled to the side, feeling the heat of the rays brush over him. He'd never be able to take them all out with his pistols without getting drilled himself. Instead he fell backward and fired into the air above them.

They laughed, clearly unimpressed. Until Bulls-Eye's fire dislodged a chunk of stone from the bridge above them to land on their heads, taking ten out in one blow.

The other two dodged out of the way in the nick of time, but their distraction gave Bulls-Eye ample time to shoot one and knock the other over the side of the bridge.

He turned to see Leandra fighting three soldiers, her electrified blade slicing through the air, crackling with each sweep. She dodged, feinted, parried. Her swordwork was artistry; every time it looked as though her attackers had an upper hand, she revealed it as a trap and drove her blade home.

Bulls-Eye stared at her. She danced like a ballerina of death. He'd never seen anything so beautiful. The last of her opponents dispatched, the electricity disappeared from the sword. She wiped green blood off its blade onto the uniforms of her fallen foes.

"We gotta tell the guards what's goin' on," Bulls-Eye said as he rushed over to Leandra. In the short time he had dealt with his bunch, she had taken down three with her electrified sword.

"I think they know," she said. Above him, Bulls-Eye heard the eruption of gunfire, the sounds of pitched battle. Grapple lines shot up from the water, pulling soldier after soldier up to the higher bridges.

"This won't do at all," Bulls-Eye said. He waited until the soldiers were high above him, almost at the top of their ascent, before he let loose a fusillade of fire from his twin pistols and mowed down a good twenty of the grappling hooks.

"Serves ya right," he yelled after the soldiers as they plummeted back into the water.

"We need to find the Professor," Leandra said. "That's who Cyclone will be going after. Come on." The electricity around her sword crackled back to life, illuminating her face like an avenging angel. She rushed across the bridge back toward the laboratory.

"Beautiful," Bulls-Eye said and raced after her.

CHAPTER THIRTEEN
CYCLONE ATTACKS!

Khan felt a vibration in the laboratory floor. An intermittent thud that traveled up his legs. One of the scientists working nearby glanced up, a frown creasing his face.

"You felt that, too?" Khan said. The scientist nodded. He looked around at the others who were slowly becoming aware of something not quite right.

In the distance Khan could hear something. Yelling? Was that gunfire? "Quickly," he said. "Barricade the door." The scientists stood dumbfounded as he dragged a heavy piece of machinery toward the door. "There's a fight, you fools. And it's coming this way."

Outside the unmistakable sounds of battle increased, snapping the scientists out of their reverie. Two rushed to Khan's side, helping him bar the door. Others began shutting down equipment, gathering notes.

"Hopefully this is just a drill," one of the scientists said, though he looked doubtful. He slid a lab bench against the doors. "Protocol demands that we destroy much of our research if we ever come under attack, so they don't do drills often. Too many setbacks."

Someone screamed outside. "I don't think it's a drill," Khan said. "Is there another way out of the room?" He couldn't see any other doors, and none of the vents in the walls appeared to be big enough to admit the K'kir scientists, much less his larger bulk.

The scientist shook his head. "That's the only way in or out," he said.

The door shook in its frame as something heavy hit it. A body, Khan thought. The door shook again, this time as gunfire punched a burning hole into it.

"Everyone get back," Khan said. He ushered the scientists, some of them picking up pieces of equipment to use as clubs, behind him. It was only a matter of time before the door broke down and with only a handful of panicked scientists, Khan knew that it was going to be up to him to keep them all alive.

More gunfire, more screams. The door shook with a powerful blast that pushed it inward only to be stopped by the mound of tables and heavy equipment piled against it. Blows hammered the door again and again, but each time, it held.

For a brief moment Khan let himself hope that the attackers would stop before they breached the door. But with one final, monumental blow the door blew off its hinges in a shower of sparks and splinters. Smoke filled the room as half a dozen of Cyclone's troopers barreled through the open doorway, stepping over blasted equipment and chunks of wall.

The jungle drums clamored on the inside of Khan's skull and he was there to meet the first soldier with his fist. He connected with the soldier's skull, cracking the helmet under the blow. The soldier crumpled like a marionette with cut strings and Khan moved to the next one.

"We don't want to kill anyone," the soldier said, leveling his raygun at Khan.

"Then perhaps you shouldn't be pointing that thing at them," Khan said as he swiped the gun from the soldier's hands. He threw the weapon aside and gave the soldier an uppercut that sent him flying across the room.

The other four soldiers, realizing that Khan was the only threat in the room all raised their weapons to bear, but before they could shoot, a flurry of blasts from the doorway shot the weapons from their hands.

"On the ground afore I take your fool heads off, too," Bulls-Eye said, stepping into the room. The panicked soldiers fell to their knees.

Leandra rushed in behind Bulls-Eye. "Are you all right, Professor?"

"I'm fine, but we need to get everyone to safety."

"I don't think there's a safe place around right now," Bulls-Eye said. "Cyclone's goin' full out."

"How did they get in?"

"No one seems to know for sure," Leandra said. "Near as anyone can tell she sent swimmers in through the city canals to surround and assault the palace. It's a little chaotic."

"They're here for us," Khan said. "We should surrender."

"We don't know that for sure," Leandra said. "They could just as easily be here because the Regent has openly defied Cyclone."

"No, we're here for the Chosen One," a soldier said. Another elbowed him violently in the ribs.

"Shut up, fool," the second soldier said. "Do you know what Cyclone will do to you if she finds out?"

"She can't do anything to us," the first said. "She's not here. Maybe this way they won't kill us."

"By becoming traitors?"

"By becoming pragmatists," Khan said, leaning in and glaring at the soldiers. "Tell us what's going on and we might let you live."

Khan had never been comfortable with intimidation. Even when confronting wayward students who refused to pay attention in class he always felt somewhat comical, not believing that he could actually be seen as threatening.

"I dunno, Perfesser," Bulls-Eye said. "I was kinda looking forward to skinnin' em alive and hangin' their innards from the ceilin'. Make it all festive-like."

Khan's stomach turned at the image. "Indeed," he said. He laid a hand heavily on each soldier's shoulder. "Gentlemen," he squeezed with enough force to show that he could apply much more, "unless you would like me to turn you over to my associate here, you will tell us everything you know of this attack. As has been pointed out, your ruler is not here whereas I and my bloodthirsty friend are." He squeezed harder, feeling the joints shift beneath his hands.

"He makes a compelling argument," the first soldier said, his voice strained.

"Fine," said the second one. "Yes, we're here for you. We're to take you back and destroy the palace."

"Destroy the palace?" Khan said. "How?"

"The force-field generators," the soldier said. "The cave system we're in is sealed from the ocean outside by a force-field. If the field goes, the ocean comes rushing in and destroys everything."

"Surely there are backups," Khan said.

"There are," one of the scientists said from the back of the room. "Six of them."

"We have strike teams to take out each one in a coordinated attack. They've already taken the control rooms. Once we give the signal that we've gotten you they'll complete their tasks and set charges to destroy the controls."

"Well, they won't be getting the signal that you've gotten me," Khan said. "That should buy us some time."

The soldier shook his head. "Not much. If they don't receive the signal from us within half an hour they're to assume that our mission was a failure and destroy the controls anyway."

"That sounds like my—" Leandra said and stopped. "That sounds like Cyclone all right."

Khan looked back at her and wondered at what she had almost said. No time to deal with it now, though. He looked over at the scientists.

"Can any one of these backups keep the force-field from collapsing?"

"Easily. They're kept in steady rotation so we can always be sure that they're functioning."

"Least we don't have to save 'em all," Bulls-Eye said.

"Small blessings," Khan said. "Even if we could get word out to the troops in time they may be too occupied trying to hold off the main invasion force."

"So we do it ourselves," Bulls-Eye said.

"And if we fail?"

"We need to warn the citizens," Leandra said. "There has to be some plan to evacuate the city."

"We'll do it," one of the K'kir scientists said. "We can raise the flood alarm. It will sound a general evacuation alert." He picked up one of the fallen ray-guns. "And we won't let anyone get in our way."

"We need to know where the closest control room is," Khan said.

"They're scattered throughout the palace so that if something catastrophic happens to one it doesn't destroy the others. The closest one is by the Regent's study."

"The big library with that vision thingamabobber?" Bulls-Eye said.

"That's the one. Go two doors past it and you'll find one of the auxiliary controls."

"Then let's not waste more time," Khan said. He looked at Cyclone's troopers, and back at Bulls-Eye. "We can't have these ones warning their fellows."

"On it, Perfesser." The cowboy leveled his pistols at the soldiers, who scrambled to get out of the way. They were too slow and Bulls-Eye dropped them with a stun blast before they could blink.

"That should keep 'em out a good, long while."

"All right, then," Khan said. "Let's do this."

As the elevator ascended to the control room floor, Khan wondered how best to approach their task. Stealth? A ruse of some kind? A full-on fight? His companions seemed bent on the latter, each gripping their respective weapons with grim purpose.

Perhaps he could convince them that subterfuge was the best approach. Caution was always the smarter approach.

Then the elevator door opened and the decision was made for him.

The hallway was filled with the carnage of pitched battle. K'kir and Cyclone troopers lay on the floor, unconscious or dead. Further down the hall the fight waged on, filling the air with the sounds of gunfire and the clang of swords.

Before Khan could stop him, Bulls-Eye rushed headlong into the fray, Leandra close at his heels. Khan watched in amazement as every shot the cowboy made hit its mark. The man was a devil of whirling energy, spinning and weaving to make shots that didn't seem physically possible.

But it was when he saw arcs of electricity burst around Leandra's sword that he was truly struck dumb. The lightning seemed to be an extension of her as it danced along the blade, occasionally shooting out to strike an opponent. It acted as both sword and shield and seemed to have a mind of its own.

He watched the battle, mesmerized. It ebbed and flowed like the tides. The flashes of fire, the screams of the wounded, the sounds of steel upon steel. Blood and smoke, fear and anger flowed together into a stink of war. It snaked its way into his mind calling forth the jungle drums that beat in his heart, filling him with their savage rhythm.

A stray raygun blast sizzled over his shoulder and burned a hole into the elevator wall.

And Khan snapped.

He filled his lungs, let loose a mighty jungle roar and charged into battle. He was blind with rage, felling all who came within range of his swinging fists. He knocked over Cyclone troopers and K'kir soldiers like bowling pins.

He could distantly feel the burn of gunfire, the bite of steel into flesh, the pummeling blows of fists and rifle butts, but not a one could slow him down. He loped through the combatants knocking them aside like a tidal wave, a hurricane, some heathen god of vengeance.

He was Khan, Conqueror Ape, and nothing could stop him.

Instinct propelled him toward the heaviest fighting. A group of Cyclone troopers were clustered at a doorway holding off the K'kir soldiers. To Khan's hypnotized mind they were all enemies to grind beneath his feet. He tore through the ranks of friend and foe alike and within seconds he was through the door.

A keening wail burst through hidden speakers in the walls, its alien sounds snapping him out of his delirium. He started at the Thavasian trooper limp in his hands. He dropped the soldier and looked around at the carnage.

Behind him, Bulls-Eye and Leandra stood staring at him as though seeing him for the first time. Thavasian troopers and K'kir soldiers alike lay in crumpled heaps. He could only dimly recall what he had done. Shame swept over him like a wave.

A handful of K'kir soldiers still stood in the control room before him and, stepping from behind them, the Regent.

"Thank you for the assistance," the Regent said, sheathing a sword green with the blood of his enemies. His face was haggard and stained with blood. "But I fear you're too late. They did their damage before we could get here and I have heard reports of the other control rooms equally sabotaged."

"I'm sorry, your Highness," Khan said. "We only just learned of their plot. We sent some of your scientists to sound the alarm."

"Thank you. That may very well have saved my people."

"Your highness," one of the soldiers said, pushing a panel on the wall in a complicated sequence, "we have to get you to your transport. We don't have much time." A section of wall slid silently out of the way revealing an elevator.

"Yes, Captain, of course. Professor, I am sorry that our attempts to get you home have been cut short. But if you and your companions will join me I can at least get you to safety."

"Much obliged, Your Kingship," Bulls-Eye said, tipping his hat.

A nearby explosion rocked the room. Smoke billowed in from the hallway. Khan could hear footsteps and the sizzling sounds of electricity. A bright blue arc crawled crazily along the ceiling.

"Oh, no," Leandra said, her face growing pale. "We've got to get out of here. Now."

"What is it?" Khan said.

"I know what it is," Bulls-Eye said. He gripped his pistols and strode toward the door. "And I aim to fix it once and for all."

The remaining K'kir troopers surrounded the Regent while their captain shoved him into the elevator. Soldiers grabbed at Khan and Leandra, pushing them after him into the elevator.

"No," Leandra said. "Professor, you can't let him go."

"I don't understand," Khan said. "What is it?"

"Cyclone. She's here."

Arcs of electricity danced through the open doorway like mad heralds announcing the Princess' arrival. She strode into the room with purpose, struck a pose in the doorway, her chin held high and lightning radiating from her fingertips.

Bulls-Eye let loose a flurry of gunfire. But as his shots reached the corona of lightning blanketing Cyclone's body they evaporated like rain in the desert.

Cyclone glared at the cowboy who stood his ground and kept firing. She lifted a hand and a bolt of lightning shot out. Bulls-Eye ducked out of the way, but the lightning snaked its way around to his left and hit him in his side. He fell unconscious to the floor.

The K'kir soldiers unloaded their weapons at her, giving Khan the moment he needed to grab the unconscious cowboy and drag him to safety.

"Inside," the Regent cried. "Quickly. My men will hold her off long enough."

Khan didn't argue. He clutched Bulls-Eye to his chest and squeezed into the small elevator. He watched in horror as Cyclone unleashed the fury of her powers on the K'kir soldiers.

The doors closed on the grisly sight. Khan's last view of her was her standing atop a pile of dead soldiers. Laughing.

CHAPTER FOURTEEN
ESCAPE UNDER THE SEA!

The elevator shot like a bullet into the depths of the palace. Soon the stone shaft gave way to glass and Khan could see that they were headed to a submarine moored in a chamber deep beneath the palace.

"It's not much but it will get us away from the assault and the destruction of the city," the Regent said. He rubbed his temple with a webbed hand. "I can only hope that the evacuation orders went out in time. Cyclone is not going to get away with this."

"If the force-fields fail the way you're expecting won't she be caught in the tidal wave, too?" Khan asked.

"No," Leandra said. "She's mastered teleportation. She always has an escape plan. Many of her soldiers might die, but she'll survive."

"Then I'll make her pay," the Regent said. He looked down at Bulls-Eye unconscious in Khan's arms. "How is he?"

"I don't know," Khan said. "His breathing is shallow, but he's still alive. Do you have medical facilities on board?"

"Yes," the Regent said, "but it's completely automated. I don't know what it will do with his physiology."

"It's not that different from mine," Khan said. "Would it would work on one of the Inkidu?"

The Regent frowned. "Aside from bandaging wounds and helping with any bleeding, no. And I fear your friend has more severe issues than that."

"We need to get him to the Inkidu," Leandra said. Khan shot her a glance. Was this another part of her plan to fulfill that damnable prophecy?

No. The earnestness in her voice, the way she looked at Bulls-Eye lying limp in Khan's arms told him the truth. This was all about him.

"Agreed," Khan said. "If we can get him stable enough to travel, can you get us to the Inkidu's lands?"

"Easily. But I can't take too long. The attack has already set things in motion and I must get back to my people. My generals are waiting for my commands."

The elevator entered the submarine through a hatch in its roof, which sealed behind it. The room was sparse with a grilled floor and vents along the curved walls. Immediately the water was pumped away. A moment later, the elevator opened.

The Regent stepped out and quickly hurried to a hatch that opened at his touch. "I'll get the systems started. Down this hall is the sickbay. Get him onto a bed and the machines will do the rest. Don't worry, if they don't know what to do, they won't do anything. They won't make matters worse."

"Don't you have a crew?" Khan asked, hurrying through the door after him.

"Normally, yes, but there was no time to get them here. Fortunately, I don't need them." He pointed to a side corridor. "Sickbay's down there. We'll be off in a moment."

The sickbay had half a dozen beds over which hung a large hemisphere with mechanical arms and camera lenses sticking out of it at odd angles. As Khan got Bulls-Eye into one of the beds he felt the submarine begin to move.

Once he had Bulls-Eye in place the contraption over the bed came to life. Cameras whirred as they focused on the new patient, arms gently prodded. A moment later it stopped and a red light began blinking on its shell.

Before Khan could investigate what it meant he felt a sudden lurch beneath his feet. A moment later it tilted violently, almost throwing him and Leandra to the floor and Bulls-Eye out of his bed. Khan found straps on the bed and cinched the cowboy in tight. Another lurch of the submarine almost threw him into the wall.

"What's happening?" Leandra said.

"I don't know," he said, but he suspected. There was no way Cyclone was going to just let them get away. "I don't think there's anything more we can do for Bulls-Eye at the moment."

The Priestess looked down at the unconscious cowboy, worry creasing her face. She touched his brow, then turned and strode to the door. "The Regent might need help," she said.

Khan followed her on unsteady legs. The submarine shuddered again, its metal shell straining with a loud groan. The submarine was designed for a small crew, none of whom were of Khan's size, and he found himself having to shimmy sideways through a couple of doors. The bridge was larger with enough room to maneuver in, but still cramped. Half a dozen stations were spaced throughout the room, their functions Khan could only guess at. There were no windows, but a large, split screen in the front of the room showed an image of the darkened sea ahead on one half and an outline of the submarine and three glowing green blobs behind it on the other.

The blobs were gaining.

The Regent sat alone at a station in the middle of the room, staring intently at the screen, turning dials, pulling levers. The sub banked suddenly. Khan steadied himself against a bulkhead.

"Is your friend secure?" the Regent asked.

"As possible as it is to be under the circumstances," Khan said.

"Good. We're under attack."

"I suspected," Khan said.

"Cyclone's been busier than I expected. She's managed to move troops and submersibles into the area without being detected." The sub shuddered as something hit the hull. "And we have three of her subs on our tail right now."

"How much danger are we in?" Leandra said.

"Oh, quite a lot," the Regent said. "But I know these waters and the terrain. There's a hidden tunnel nearby. Once we get there we should be fine."

"Won't they follow us in?" Leandra said.

"Oh, I certainly hope so. You might want to hold onto something."

Leandra fell into a seat and strapped herself in. Khan grasped a nearby rail with hands and feet.

A moment later the submarine plummeted into a steep dive. Khan held tight to the railing. The screen showed the looming sea bed, a massive boulder directly in their path.

"Shouldn't we turn?" Khan said. He tried to keep the anxiety from his voice, failed.

"Where would the fun be in that, Professor?" On the screen the boulder shifted, sliding away to show a deep pit beneath it.

And the three large batteries of torpedo launchers.

The Regent slid the submarine through the gap between the launchers as they disgorged their torpedoes into Cyclone's oncoming subs. The green blobs on the screen winked out in a vaporous cloud of phosphors.

"The tunnel will seal behind us," the Regent said. He turned a series of wheels, sat back and let out a deep breath. "We're safe for now. The autopilot will take us to an exit some distance away. From there I can get you to the surface."

"How far to the Inkidu's lands?" Khan asked.

"We'll surface on the border," the Regent said. "As to how long before you encounter them, though, I couldn't say. Their cities are husks, their villages few and far between. There are rumors that they've gone underground but my spies never got confirmation."

"We'll find them," Leandra said. "They'll help us. They have to."

Khan was not so hopeful. Find them they might, but would they help? Could they? A civilization in ruins, if it existed at all? What if all they found were nomads and broken villagers? It didn't sound promising. But the look on the Priestess' face was so earnest that he kept those thoughts to himself.

"If this underground city exists the likeliest entrance would be in the ruins of their capital," the Regent said. "The Inkidu have conducted raids on Cyclone's troops from time to time and they appear to originate from that location."

"And Cyclone knows this, too, I imagine," Khan said.

"Of course," the Regent said. "The area is constantly bombarded. Yet the raids continue. I can get you a map that shows routes that might be safer than others, as well as supplies. The area is a wasteland and it will be at least a day before you reach the city."

"I don't see any other choice," Khan said.

The Regent stood. "Then let's see to those supplies."

Khan stood atop the hill, red dust swirling at his feet, Bulls-Eye unconscious and strapped to his back in a makeshift litter. The miles of Martian desert stretched before him, an empty wasteland of rock, sand and the ruins of an entire civilization.

The bones of the Inkidu's once grand cities thrust up from the dirt, grasping and clawing their way from the dust. Twisted girders, scattered brick, paving stones encrusted with a generation's worth of sand littered the desert. The devastation was total.

The Regent had dropped them off not five hours earlier at an underground beach with a path that led to the surface. He had given them a map, supplies and a makeshift litter so that Khan could carry the unconscious Bulls-Eye on his back. They emerged into the dim Martian afternoon, the sun low in the sky. The destruction he saw left him stunned.

"This is all Cyclone's work?" Khan said.

"Yes," Leandra said. "Some of these craters are decades old and some," she pointed to a series of fresh holes pockmarking the surface, "are much newer. She occasionally bombs the area and sweeps it with storms so that nothing new can grow here. She murders the few scattered tribes that scrape by. And when she isn't obliterating them she takes them as slaves."

"And you honestly believe that the Inkidu have survived this well enough to be a threat to her?"

"If it's not them, someone is harassing her troops in disguise."

"Raiders, perhaps? Rovings hordes of bandits?"

Leandra stopped, her eyes scanning the horizon. "This way," she said. "I want to show you something."

Curious, Khan followed her as she wound her way past the rubble. It was impossible to tell what the buildings had been, but the remaining stone had been quarried with great care. Decorative carvings could still be seen even under years of weathering. Whatever these structures had been, they had been grand.

"Here," Leandra said, as they topped a hill looking down on a twisted hulk of metal and glass. It was enormous. Hundreds of feet long, dozens high, dug into the ground at strange angles and bristling with ledges, towers and turrets. Doors were spaced along its rusted surface too high for him to reach. At first Khan thought that it was a wall, some defensive bulwark in the city that had been destroyed. But then he realized that it was a vehicle.

Massive holes rent its sides from artillery fire. Pieces of it had been melted into slag. "An Inkidu vehicle?" he asked as they made their way down to it.

"One of Cyclone's," Leandra said. "This is one of her flying dreadnoughts. The pride of the fleet. Nothing could stop it. It was destroyed less than a year ago when it came out here."

Khan could see the lines of a battleship now that he knew what he was looking at. Impressive engineering. Even more impressive was the sort of ordinance that could bring it down.

Khan scraped at the surface and it was so mottled and brittle that when he touched it, huge piles of rust came off in his hands. Something occurred to him. "A year? That's not possible. This is decades of wear."

"Yes. That is why Cyclone is so afraid of the Inkidu. It's not just rayguns, not just cannons. They have technologies we've never seen before that do more than punch holes and melt metal. And then they vanish. How do you hide the kind of weaponry that can bring down a ship like this?"

"Underground," Khan said. But where? The Regent said his people had an idea of its location but could never find them, and this was a race that knew the subterranean passages of Mars.

"That's their primary advantage. If they came out into the open for very long they'd have more than just Cyclone's dreadnoughts to contend with."

Khan gazed out across the wasteland of ruined buildings. "Her weather powers did all this?"

"Mostly, yes. She—" Leandra looked up in alarm. "Do you feel that?"

"Feel what?" Khan said. Besides an increase in air pressure that had him swallowing to clear his ears, he felt nothing. He stuck a finger in his ear and wiggled it around.

"That's what I was afraid of," Leandra said. She grabbed his hand and pulled. "We need to find cover and fast."

"Dear Heavens, why?" Khan said, and then his eyes caught the horizon. "Oh, no."

Clouds were gathering in the distance, thick and ominous. Pouring in as if pulled forth from a magician's hat. From a single point they coalesced and expanded into a tremendous wave.

Khan ran after Leandra as she ran across the desert. "What is it?" he asked, afraid that he already knew the answer.

"Cyclone. Either this is one of her regular storms that she sweeps the lands with or—"

"Or?"

"Or she knows we're here. Either way we have to run."

CHAPTER FIFTEEN
THE DEADLY DESERT!

Khan glanced at the storm behind them. It darkened the sky, blotting out the sun. It had ceased its swell and instead was visibly moving toward them. Lightning shot through the clouds, illuminating the landscape like flashbulbs.

Slowly, menacingly, a face appeared in the clouds and sheets of blown desert sand. Princess Cyclone. Her eyes searched the lands, lightning bursting forth from them to char the ground. Could she see out of those storm-filled eyes? Could she sense the world around her?

Could she find them?

Those terrible eyes of smoke and lightning searched back and forth and then stopped, locked on Khan. He froze as they loomed in his vision, filled his mind with terror. And then, so loud he could hear nothing else, he heard Cyclone's voice.

"Barbarian! Assassin! This is pointless. You don't belong on this world. You are on a fool's errand. I can see into your mind, Professor. You hope to defeat me? My lightning will cook you like a fatted calf, my winds will scour you until you are nothing but bleached and pitted bones. I will devour your soul and—"

Khan felt a stinging slap on his cheek and the words died in his mind. "Professor!" Leandra yelled, her voice drowning in the sound of the wind. She pulled him along and he followed, dazed.

Leandra stopped at a devastated building, an emaciated shell of cracked concrete and skeletal girders, rusted and crumbling. "Quickly!" she said, "In here." She pulled Khan inside the building.

Khan ran inside after her, the winds pushing him along. At four-hundred pounds he was hard to move, but the winds did an impressive job of shoving him aside. He kept one hand on Leandra's and the other on the straps securing Bulls-Eye to his back.

"How will this protect us?" Khan yelled over the noise. Besides the winds he could hear thunder close behind, could feel the rumble in his feet as the lightning struck the ground. Tremendous explosions sounded outside.

Leandra drew her sword and arcs of electricity burst around it giving them enough light to pick their way through the ruin. She pointed to a corner of the building. A set of stairs led down.

"If we can get some cover on top of us we might survive," she said.

"Or we might be buried alive."

"I saw one of those lightning strikes take out an entire platoon of armored Monatu warriors in one hit. What do you think it will do to us?"

"Agreed," Khan said and followed her down into the darkness. The stairs were covered in dirt and debris and they stepped as carefully as they could, the only light the crackle of electricity surrounding Leandra's sword. As they descended into the bowels of the shattered building the noise of the storm grew distant, but not distant enough.

After two floors of stairs Leandra stopped, looking up. "Quickly, grab hold of something," she said and wrapped herself around a rusted girder. Khan reached for a pipe jutting out of the wall but he wasn't fast enough.

An explosion sounded outside and the ground bucked violently beneath him, throwing him to the floor. He twisted himself so that he wouldn't land on Bulls-Eye and worked to pull the cowboy off of his back so he could shield him with his body.

The shaking went on for almost a minute. Chips of concrete and mortar rained down from the ceiling. Soon the three of them were covered in dust and sand, rust and powdered concrete. Outside the storm raged on, but it lessened and grew quieter as it passed them over.

"Is it safe?" Khan said when the quiet had returned.

"Not yet," Leandra said. "That was the worst of it, though. A few more minutes and we should be fine. There's usually some residual damage as some remaining structures fall."

Sure enough Khan could hear distant crashing above them as some structures, already pummeled and frail, disintegrated even further.

"I saw—" Khan started, but the possibility was too astonishing. He let the sentence linger.

"Her face," Leandra said. "In the storm."

"So I wasn't hallucinating?"

"No. That was her. That's one of her powers. She can control the storms, see through them. She frequently uses that in battle or when she's searching something out."

"I hear her voice."

"Yes. She can project her voice into your thoughts through the storms. Did she say she could read your mind?"

"Yes."

"She can't."

"She knows we're here."

Leandra nodded. "It's a logical choice. We need to get to the Inkidu. I'm not surprised she appeared."

"Interesting," Khan said. He wondered how many of the storms that had raged over the desert had been to purge the land and how many had been to search for the insurgents.

Bulls-Eye gave a muffled groan. Khan looked him over. He was breathing, and had shown signs of waking earlier, but had fallen back into unconsciousness. Aside from some dust and dirt, he appeared none the worse for wear. This was the most sound he'd made since the palace attack.

The machines on board the Regent's submarine had finally figured out how to treat the burns from Cyclone's lightning bolts, but those wounds were superficial. There was no telling what other damage might have been done.

Leandra was on Bulls-Eye in a flash, checking his pulse, worry creasing her face. She raised the sword to give more light. "Does he need water, do you think?" she asked.

"Tarnation, woman!" Bulls-Eye croaked, his hands feebly batting at her. "Enough with the pokin' and proddin'. I ain't some side of beef." His voice was dry and cracked, a whisper of its former strength. "And where the heck are we?"

"Underground," Khan said. "A storm struck. We had to find shelter." He gave Bulls-Eye a quick rundown of what had happened.

"And she does this all regular-like?" Bulls-Eye said.

"Yes," Leandra said, "though this storm was specifically for us."

"Perhaps we should see how bad the damage was," Khan said.

The three of them made their way up the stairs and out into the ruins. Khan couldn't see how the devastation that had been visited upon this place could be made worse. And then he saw it.

The storm had been fierce. A swath of chewed up ground, furrows dug several feet deep, stretched to the horizon. Many of the nearby buildings, already damaged by countless similar storms and bombardments, had finally given up and disintegrated into ash.

Even the buildings still standing showed the effects of the storm. Floors had been sheared off, rusted metal scoured until it shone, stones rough hours before worn down to a polished sheen.

Anything alive that had stood in the storm's path would have been pulverized. Khan shuddered to think what would have happened to them had they not found shelter.

Bulls-Eye gave a low whistle. "And Cyclone done did this?" he said. "You think she'll go and do it again?"

"Not any time soon," Leandra said. "A storm of this magnitude takes time to come back from. She's powerful, but she only has so much strength. We should be safe from another one for a while."

"How long a while?" Khan said.

Leandra shrugged. "A day? Maybe two? Hard to say."

Khan eyed the horizon. The sun was beginning to dip down. It would be dark soon. "Perhaps now is a good time to set up camp," Khan said, "and get you up to speed."

"Back downstairs?" Leandra said.

The building behind them groaned as if in protest, metal straining and buckling. A tall girder twisted and fell, pulling tons of rubble down where they had found refuge just moments before.

"Or perhaps not," Khan said.

"Wish I'd been awake for that submarine ride," Bulls-Eye said. He lay propped against a rock in front of the camp fire. He was still weak and walking was a challenge. He had insisted on standing on his own and immediately fell over.

Khan had expected as much and was there to catch him. It was clear that the cowboy still needed rest. With luck Bulls-Eye would feel better in the morning, but if not Khan could easily carry him. The thought of being carried about didn't seem to sit well with Bulls-Eye, but he wasn't so stubborn that he couldn't recognize the need.

"It was harrowing," Khan said. "I honestly wasn't certain we were going to survive."

"I knew we would," Leandra said. She took a bite from a fruit Khan had found among the supplies the Regent had given them. It was something like a soft-skinned durian, with a thin, edible rind and bumps where the Earth equivalent would have had spikes. Khan had already eaten three of them.

"With all the chaos and turmoil surrounding us I have difficulty believing that," Khan said. "We came very close to dying several times."

"Close to, yes," the Priestess said. "But we didn't. That's the prophecy."

Khan rolled his eyes, but said nothing. If believing in this ridiculous prophecy kept her going then Khan wasn't about to disabuse her of the notion.

"I know you don't believe me," she said, taking another bite. "But it's true. You'll see."

Khan said nothing. An awkward silence descended upon them.

"There's somethin' I don't understand," Bulls-Eye said finally, sipping water from his canteen. His voice was cracked, barely grew above a whisper.

"About the prophecy?" Leandra said.

"Nah, that's simple. The Perfesser here's gonna lead all them other Martian gorillas out of the desert or some such. I got that fine. I been thinkin' and somethin's been eatin' at me." Bulls-Eye took another sip of water, coughed. Khan started toward him, but the cowboy waved him off.

The fit subsided and he took a long, ragged breath. "I don't mean no disrespect, Leandra, but I gotta know. What have you been doin' with Cyclone?"

"I don't understand," she said. Khan caught a strange look that passed across her face for a moment. Was that panic? He couldn't tell. It was gone so quickly he wasn't entirely sure that it had been there in the first place. "I'm not with Cyclone."

"Not now, no," Bulls-Eye said. "But you were for a long time, weren't ya? How come you ain't never tried something before?"

"The prophecy—"

"Prophecy or no, you never thought to do nothin' before?"

"He does raise an excellent point," Khan said. He poked at the fire with a piece of rebar they had found in the ruins. "You could have left sooner. Could have tried to contact the Inkidu before we appeared. Why now?"

Leandra frowned, her eyes staring into the distance. "I was the first to dream the prophecy. Or at least the first to publicly announce it. I had shown the gift when I was a child and was brought into the Temple of the Weather Witches to train. The Priestesses are... different from the Weather Witches. Their skills are in telling the future, not in controlling the weather. Some can do both, but that is rare and no one has shown that power in over a hundred years. It was there that I saw the visions and relayed the Prophecy."

"But you said everyone had been killed in the Temple," Bulls-Eye said. Khan looked at him sharply. "We talked a bit before Cyclone attacked us. Cyclone went crazy and killed all the other Weather Witches and everyone in their Temple."

"Most everyone in the Temple," she said. "By the time she found me I was the only Priestess left. And I was the one who had given the Prophecy. She felt it was in her best interest to keep me alive. I've been a virtual prisoner since."

She rolled a pebble between her fingers, tossed it into the fire. "Yes. I could have defied her sooner. But what would it have gained me? Too many pretenders to the Prophecy have appeared. And they have all died. I would have died with the rest of them. Think less of me if you will, but I made a choice and I stand by it."

"And this time is different?" Khan said.

"Yes," she said. "This time is different."

"I am not your puppet," Khan said. "I am not a pawn. My friend needs help and I intend to find it for him and then I intend to get us home."

"Oh, shut yer trap, Perfesser," Bulls-Eye said. Khan closed his mouth with a snap, surprise writ large on his face. "I'm sorry, Leandra," the cowboy continued. "That's been eatin' at me and I just needed to know. I meant no disrespect. I know you had your reasons, I just needed to know what they were."

He turned to Khan and glared at him. "And as fer you, ya overgrown monkey, we're past all that. Prophecy or no, we're here. Look around ya. Cyclone's crazier than a grizzly with a beehive up its butt. She ain't gonna stop 'til what's left of these folks is ground into dust. If you don't wanna help, then that's fine. But I aim to put a stop to her. So go ahead and find a way home, ya coward, but I ain't goin' with ya. Not 'til we're done here."

Anger bubbled up inside Khan. He stood, loomed over Bulls-Eye, who stared him down without blinking. "Did you just call me a coward?"

"I did. And I'll keep doin' it 'til you prove me otherwise."

Khan and Bulls-Eye glared at each other until Khan turned to Leandra and said, "Does the Prophecy say what I will do? How I will do it?"

"No," Leandra said. "Only that 'The barbarians will find their champion in one such as they clad in all black.'"

"And how can you be sure it's me? How do you know it isn't just an Inkidu in a black uniform? How can you pin all of your hopes on me? I can't lead battles or inspire troops. I'm a professor, not a champion. I'm no messiah. I'll get everyone killed."

It struck him as soon as the words were out of his mouth. That was it, wasn't it? His anger, his reticence. It wasn't that he was afraid that he would be used, that he would be some political game piece.

It was that he was afraid he wasn't up to the task.

"I get it, Perfesser," Bulls-Eye said, his voice soft. "I truly do. Ain't nobody envious of the position you're in. Not me, not the Priestess here. Maybe the Prophecy's wrong. Maybe we're all gonna snuff it. But that don't matter none."

"How can you say that? I could get you killed." He pointed at Leandra. "I could get her killed. Does that mean nothing to you?"

Bulls-Eye winced. "It does, but that don't change nothin'. We're not doin' this because we want to. We're doin' this because it's the right thing to do."

Khan opened his mouth to argue but nothing came. He had no argument. Like it or not, the cowboy was right.

"Hmmph." Khan went back to his place by the fire, crossed his arms. "We should get some sleep," he said. "If we're going to do this then we'll need rest."

A wide grin cracked Bulls-Eye's weathered face. "Knew you'd see it my way."

CHAPTER SIXTEEN
A NEW DILEMMA!

Benjamin Hu dragged himself up through the last few feet of tunnel, pushing the soft earth and soil out of his way. He pushed and pulled, tearing clumps of dirt. He raged against it, his anger and frustration fueling his escape.

He knew it was a fool's errand to stay behind. There was nothing he could have done. He would have died along with Amelia. The crumbling chamber had begun to bring down the passage he was in and he was forced to run. Like a coward.

Perhaps there was a way he could go backward in time. Not unheard of. He'd done it before, if only on accident. Perhaps there was something back at the Century Club that might help. Some piece of arcane lore hidden within its library. Or the Spear tucked securely in his satchel. Doctor Thomas was working with time travel. Maybe together they could turn back the clock and save Amelia.

The thoughts wormed their way through his mind as he continued to dig. Finally, with a great heave he broke the surface and pulled himself into the night air.

"About time you showed up," Amelia said, sitting against an oak a few feet away. "I've been here for hours."

Benjamin started. "Amelia! How did you escape?" She helped dig him out the rest of the way, hauled him to his feet.

"There was another passage," she said. She dusted clumps of dirt off of his coat. "The falling rock exposed a new passage and the glasses showed the way. What, you think I'd let you escape and not find a way out, myself? Please, Detective. I'm better than that."

"You've been out here for hours, you say?"

"About three. My journey to the surface was quite a bit smoother than yours, I must say. I was going to head back to London, but when I found the car I realized you hadn't gotten out, yet. Considering what you had said about how that place might affect time, I thought it best to wait."

"Thank you," he said. "I was certain you were dead."

"To be honest, I wasn't sure I was going to get out myself."

He held himself back. He wanted to jump. To grab her and hug her. But he didn't. It just wasn't something he did.

"Well, I'm glad to see you survived, Miss Stone," he said, instead.

She gave him a broad smile. "Likewise, Mister Hu. Shall we get back to London?"

"An excellent plan," he said and followed her to the car.

Amelia dropped Benjamin's satchel onto the workbench where Thomas had fallen asleep. It hit with a loud thud, rattling the tools scattered on the bench. Thomas startled awake, his glasses falling off his face and onto the floor.

"Five hundred pounds, Doctor Thomas," Amelia said. "Pay up."

"Hardly," he said, retrieving his glasses and settling them onto his long nose. "I finished yesterday. Where have you been? It's been two days."

"Dammit," she said.

"I told you we should have stopped for a newspaper to check the date," Benjamin said coming in behind her.

"It doesn't matter," Thomas said, opening the satchel and looking inside. The glow from the spear lit up his face like a spotlight. He blinked. "Why don't I want to touch it?"

"I think it might have some properties that can influence your mind," Benjamin said. "As protection. Whether in its defense or as protection from it, I'm not really sure." He pulled a vial of brown liquid from a coat pocket. "I stopped in my room to pick this up. I think it might help."

He unstoppered the vial and dumped its contents into the bag. Sparks erupted from the spearhead and it sizzled like a hot frying pan dropped into cold water. They all reared back from the light show, shielding their eyes.

A minute later the sparks died down and disappeared, and the sizzling quieted. The glow coming from the spearhead dulled.

Thomas peered into the bag again. "Yes, that's better. What is that?" He reached into the bag to retrieve the spearhead.

"Basilisk blood, mostly," Benjamin said, and Thomas froze. "Oh, it's perfectly safe."

"Basilisks exist?" Thomas said.

"On a small island in the South China Sea, yes," he said.

"I see." He reached back into the bag and pulled out the spearhead. It hummed when he touched it, a low, quiet pitch that shifted as he poked at it.

"Yes," he said. "I think this will do. I'll have to run some tests to make sure that it doesn't explode the minute I plug it in, but that shouldn't take long." His glasses slid down from the bridge of his nose and he pushed them back up onto his face. "We have a bigger problem, though."

"It will bring in another one of those giant insects?" Amelia said.

"Not quite, but it's related. My calculations indicate that the portal opened on," his face contorted into a grimace, "Mars, for lack of a better word, but I don't know exactly where. If I tune in the coordinates, adjusting for time, orbital rotation, all that, I'll get us a portal there, but—"

"It might be on the other side of the planet from where we want to be?" Benjamin finished.

"Exactly."

"So how do we fix it?" Amelia said. "You do know how to fix it, don't you?"

"Yes," he said. "But I can't do it."

"Why not? Do we need some other magical doohickey?" she asked. She turned to Benjamin. "We need another magical doohickey, don't we?"

"No, no," Thomas said hurriedly. "Nothing like that. I have the item here." He pulled a large device from under the workbench that looked something like a railroad spike with a dinner plate attached to the end.

"What is it?"

"I call it either a quantum resonance tracker or a folded space-time transducer. I'm not sure which, yet."

"I told you we needed a magical doohickey."

"It is not magical and it is not a doohickey!" Thomas said. "Sensors in the end here will analyze the chemicals of whatever substance it is immersed in and pick out the quantum frequencies which are then transmitted to my computers and help pinpoint their origin."

Benjamin and Amelia looked at him with blank faces.

"Stick it in the Mega-Mantis and it will tell us where it came from, which should be close to where Professor Khan and Bulls-Eye were sent."

"Magical doohickey," Amelia said.

"I think I see the problem," Benjamin said before another argument could erupt. "The beast would crush you before you got anywhere near it."

"Not to mention the difficulty of breaking the carapace to get a reading. I've been analyzing mantises to see where they have a weak spot. The joints are the weakest, but they're not exactly safe. The best bet seems to be a spot behind the head."

"Wait," Amelia said. "You're serious? This has to go into that monster?"

"It won't work otherwise. Just holding it won't give it enough data to analyze. And it's going to need to be there for a while. I thought about shooting it in with a harpoon or something, but I'm afraid it'll shake loose."

"All right, then," Amelia said. "Who wants to wrestle the giant man-eating insect?"

CHAPTER SEVENTEEN
SECRETS REVEALED!

Khan stood watch at the edge of the camp. After traveling a bit further from their storm shelter they settled on another bombed out building with a low overhang and a missing wall. Not quite a cave, but it allowed for some shelter from the elements and a more easily defensible position. There was nothing like a basement they could retreat to, but it was the best they could find. Khan hoped Leandra was right about Cyclone's need to recharge before sending out another storm.

Of course, that also meant that there was nowhere for him and his companions to go should things get dicey. But in this blasted wasteland it was the best they could do.

Khan had opted to take up Leandra's sword while he guarded their camp. The trigger guards on Bulls-Eye's pistols were too narrow and he couldn't get his meaty fingers into them. He inspected the blade, looking for the trigger mechanism that allowed it to flare into life with arcs of electricity, but couldn't find one. As far as he could tell it was just a sword.

Well made, and perfectly balanced, but just a sword. Odd.

He walked a few feet out from the opening of the building, the firelight behind him casting a dim glow across the sand. The ground was tightly packed, and he knelt to brush some sand away. As he suspected, there were paving stones beneath.

At one time this had been a vibrant city, the streets brimming with traffic. The remnants of buildings marked out the city blocks. They had first spotted the blasted out buildings hours before they made camp. If it was all one continuous city it may once have rivaled, or even exceeded, the size of New York.

Khan felt a flare of disgust and anger. The fears of a madwoman, the expediencies of politics. Whatever had forced this onto the Inkidu didn't matter. This was an outrage. Bulls-Eye was right. This could not stand.

A sound to his left pulled him out of his thoughts. A heavy thump, and something dragging through the sand. He hefted the sword in his hand, toyed with the idea of turning on the electric torch to see what had caught his attention. The stars and twin moons of Phobos and Deimos shining in the night sky were not nearly enough to see by.

He stopped just short of flicking the switch on his torch. If whatever was making that sound was dangerous it might call undue attention to himself and if it wasn't he didn't want to scare it away.

He caught a glimpse of a shape nearby that shifted a bit in the sand. Not a lot, just enough for him to catch sight of it. The Martian equivalent of a rabbit? He had seen few animals since he had been on Mars. The beast beneath Cyclone's palace, the Mega-Mantis who had come through, but that was all. Given the races he had encountered so far on the planet, it was conceivable that there would be some similarities to Earth animals.

Curiosity got the better of him and he creeped up to the wriggling shape. It sounded as though it was snuffling in the dirt the way a pig might go after truffles. Its silhouetted body seemed pressed against a large boulder and twitched with the motion. It was awfully loud. It must not have many predators if it were making that much racket.

Finally he could take it no longer. He had to see what this little creature looked like. He flicked on the torch, blinked as his eyes adjusted to the light.

The twitching animal turned out to not be an animal.

It was a nose. The boulder he thought it was pressed against, though, that was an animal. A very large animal.

It looked something like a bear. Only a bear the size of an elephant with enormous tusks curving up out of its mouth and forepaws tipped with claws the length of Khan's forearm. Deadly certainly, but Khan couldn't help but wonder if they were designed for digging more than fighting.

The thing reared up on four of its six legs twenty feet into the air and let loose a bellowing roar. The sound tore the air and Khan could feel his fur blown back from the strength of it. The creature fell back to the ground with a crash, its massive feet cracking the hard-packed Martian soil.

Khan leapt back to avoid the enormous tusks as the beast swung its head from side to side. They missed him by inches. Had they scored a hit, they'd have torn through Khan as though he were paper.

Khan weighed his options. Calling for help wasn't one of them. Bulls-Eye could barely walk and he'd certainly be no good in a fight. No, Khan had to lead the beast away from his friends and somehow escape to double back. By now he was sure Bulls-Eye and Leandra were awake after the beast roared. This way he might be able to give them some time to get into hiding.

He swung the sword in a wide sweep as the beast swung its tusks back toward him. Steel rang on bone and sparks scattered from the impact. Khan's entire arm went numb from the blow and he staggered back to regain his footing.

Khan took a moment to reorient, made a split second decision. He dropped the sword and leapt to the thing's face, using one of the tusks as a foothold. The thing was even more terrifying up close. It had eight eyes like a spider set above a tiny slitted nose and its face was split by a wide mouth that sported, along with the two enormous tusks, a series of thick, crushing teeth.

Plant eater, Khan thought in passing as he scrambled across the thing's eyes to get to its forehead. The tusks must be for self-defense, not that the knowledge did him any good. He had startled it in the dark and it reacted. If he'd just bolted it might have left him alone.

Too late to change things now. He'd gone on the offensive. Perhaps running away would have been a better choice, but Khan was weary of running. He'd been on the move ever since he'd gotten onto this planet. He'd barely had time to eat, sleep or even appreciate the fact that he was on Mars. A whole other world. Instead everyone was trying to make him something he wasn't, trying to play him against each other. Well, he was done with that. He was done with running.

Khan perched atop the beast's head. It was covered in thick fur with bony plates underneath. He grasped it behind the ears, flashing back to Bulls-Eye riding the Mega-Mantis back on Earth when this whole mess started. If he could pull hard enough, maybe he could steer it like a horse.

The beast grunted, shook its head like a wet dog. Khan flew, holding onto nothing but handfuls of hair. He slammed into the hard-packed dirt leaving a furrow a good ten feet long.

Khan groaned as he lifted his head, a wave of dizziness crashing in on him. He'd lost his torch; flung somewhere in the distance by the beast's wild shaking. Even in the dark, though, he could see the silhouette of the monster looming in front of him.

And then it started to charge.

"Professor?" Leandra said, running toward him. She froze when she saw the six-legged bear-thing charging toward him.

"Get out of here," Khan cried. Instead she ran in front of him. Khan yelled to her to get back, to save herself, but she wasn't listening. She raised her arms high.

Bolts of lightning burst from her hands.

They enveloped the charging beast, setting it ablaze. It screamed in agony and fear. Khan watched appalled as electricity and flames danced along its surface. The air filled with the stink of ozone, the stench of cooking meat. It convulsed, staggered, fell headlong into the dirt. It shuddered one final time and lay still.

"My god," Khan said. The implications of what just happened burst on him like a bomb. "This has all been a ruse. You're a Weather Witch like Cyclone."

"No," she said, running to where he lay in the dirt. Her skin glowed with electricity and Khan could see panic on her face. "Not like Cyclone. Nothing like her. You don't understand."

"Then start explaining," Khan said, pulling himself unsteadily to his feet. "Or are you going to kill me the way you felled that beast? Why have you been hiding this? Are you working for her or are you playing your own game?"

"Neither. She's—" Leandra faltered. "She's my sister. I've been a virtual slave since she took the throne. If it wasn't for my having given the Prophecy I would have died years ago."

"I thought the Priestesses only had the gift of Prophecy, not that." He waved at the still burning corpse of the beast.

"Some have both. It's rare. I didn't know I could do it until we were in the Monatu lands. And I didn't have any control over it until we were attacked in the K'kir palace. Please, Professor, you must believe me."

That would explain the lightning around the sword. It wasn't the sword that had could project electricity, it was her. She looked very distraught. She was either a very good actress, or she was telling the truth.

"How well can you control it?" Khan asked.

"Not well. I hadn't meant to kill the animal. Just frighten it. And in the K'kir palace I hadn't even tried to summon the power but it came anyway."

She sat heavily on the ground, her whole body deflating. She wasn't just afraid she'd been discovered, Khan saw, but that she had a new power that she didn't understand how to use.

"That must be terrifying," Khan said.

She nodded. "I'm afraid. Especially now. What if it doesn't come when I call it? Or worse, what if it does and I can't control it? What if you'd been in the way? What if Bulls-Eye had been in the way?"

"I believe you," Khan said. "I don't know how Bulls-Eye is going to feel about it, though."

"You can't tell him," she said quickly. "I don't— I don't think I could face him if he knew."

"He might be upset that you hadn't told him, but I doubt—"

"He'll hate me. I know he'll hate me. Please. Promise you won't tell him."

Khan was taken aback by her earnestness. "All right," he said. "If that's what you'd like. If you want to keep this secret, we should probably start moving before daybreak. If Bulls-Eye sees what happened he'll have questions."

"Thank you, Professor."

"At some point you know you're going to have to tell him."

"I know," she said, walking over to retrieve the sword that the beast had torn from Khan's hands. "But not right now."

Khan adjusted the straps on the litter that held Bulls-Eye to his back. He seemed improved yesterday, but as the sun rose and they trudged through the Martian desert he was visibly worsening.

He hadn't woken, but he was hot to the touch and he'd stopped sweating. Khan stopped every so often to let Leandra pour some water into him, but it didn't seem to be helping.

"The lightning that Cyclone used to hit him," Khan started.

"I don't know what it does," Leandra finished. "It isn't merely lightning. Sometimes she'll use that on prisoners to make them suffer. Sometimes she'll call electricity from the sky or create wind or rain. Her powers are over all the weather and some things beyond."

"Will he die?" Khan said.

Leandra looked away. "If we don't get him help soon, yes."

They traveled in silence as the dim sun rose behind them. It cast pale shadows across the sand. They had left the city behind an hour ago, but as they crested a high dune Khan could see the blasted ruins of another not far away.

Once again Khan was overcome by the devastation. How much hatred did it take for one person to do this to an entire civilization? Not much, Khan feared, thinking back to some of Earth's greatest villains. How many people had Alexander The Great slaughtered in his pursuit of empire? Napoleon? His own creator, Dr. Methuselah, or his genetic progenitor, Gorilla Khan?

"It's going to start getting hot soon," Leandra said. "I'd like to get Bulls-Eye into shelter. He'll be more comfortable when he—" She caught herself before she could finish the sentence.

When he dies, Khan thought, letting the words ring hollow through his mind. He couldn't conceive of it. Bulls-Eye had always seemed indestructible. It was as though the man were made of rubber. Whatever you threw at him, merely bounced off his stubborn hide.

"Yes," Khan said. "There's a building not far that looks suitable. We'll make camp there."

Khan caught a flash of movement in the distance. "Did you see that?"

Leandra peered into the distance. "No, I— Wait. Yes. Someone's down there."

"Cyclone's troops?" Khan asked.

"I don't think so," she said. "They would have announced themselves by now. With gunfire. It's possible, though. I'd say we should be careful, but there's not much cover out here." She felt Bulls-Eye's forehead with the back of her hand. "Or much time."

The slope was steeper than they expected and they half hiked, half slid down the rest of the way. At the outskirts of the city they could see that it wasn't Cyclone's army, but signs of life. Some small remnants of civilizations in this barren wasteland. Clotheslines for laundry, a windmill, pumps for wells.

"This doesn't look like an army," Khan said.

"No, it doesn't. But I know they're here. They have to be here. We just need to look hard enough and I know we'll find them."

"Find an army? In this?" He fingered a scrap of clothing hanging from a line. It was holed and falling apart.

Khan saw no one at first and then, as though melting out of the shadows, the Inkidu stepped forth. A dozen blue-furred gorillas, thin to the point of emaciation, shorter than Khan, each holding a crude spear made from a piece of a ruined building. This was no army.

One of the largest stepped forward brandishing his spear as though he had no idea what to do with it. "You," he said, eyes wide.

"I am Professor Khan. And these are my companions—"

"The Prophecy!" the leader cried, raising his spear into the air. "Our salvation!" The others joined their leader, shaking their spears to the skies like savages. They hollered and hooted. Khan was appalled to see a once powerful people reduced to being mere monkeys.

One of the Inkidu, a smaller female dressed in a rag shift, scurried through the dancing throng. "Professor Khan," she said. "Priestess. And your unconscious companion is named Bulls-Eye, yes?"

"Y-Yes," Khan said, surprised.

"I'm Agent Hillard. We need to get you into the city quickly. Cyclone's sky patrols are about to begin their sweep of the area and if you're not under cover they'll spot you. And we need to get your friend some medical attention."

Khan looked around him at the ruined buildings jutting up through the ground. "Isn't this the city?"

"Oh my word, no," Hillard said. "Come with me. The others will keep on for some time. We've established a number of 'rituals' we use to fool Cyclone's people. They're surprisingly effective. If all you're looking for are savages that's all you're going to find." She turned to the crowd. "Let's do Great Hunt Number 72. The Graal Beast that the Priestess took out last night to the east should make a good excuse."

"Yes, ma'am," the other Inkidu said in unison, snapping to attention. It occurred to Khan that these weren't savages at all, but highly trained soldiers playing a crucial role.

"Nice work on the Graal Beast, by the way," Hillard said. "I wasn't expecting that at all. Lightning, huh? Interesting. Now, come on." She turned and strode into one of the bombed out shells. Khan and Leandra stared after her in silence for a moment.

"I think we found the army," Khan said and followed Agent Hillard.

Hillard stood waiting for them at the back of a barren room with a dirt floor. Three posts were jammed into the ground at odd angles. Though they looked like normal pieces of debris Khan couldn't determine what they were for.

"Step in close," Hillard said. "And hang onto a post." Khan and Leandra followed her instructions as she flipped open a panel with a complicated sequence of pokes and prods on the wall revealing a series of glowing buttons.

"This is going to move pretty quickly, so hold tight." She punched a button and with a short, sharp jerk the floor dropped out from under them.

Hillard wasn't kidding. The elevator dropped at an ungodly speed until the opening above them was only a speck of light. Markers along the shaft indicated depth and Khan lost count after about a hundred as they sped past. Khan's ears popped several times as they descended.

Eventually the elevator began to slow and with a low rumble and squeal of brakes came to a stop in front of a steel door that wouldn't be out of place in front of an airplane hangar. The door slid open with a hiss of hydraulics, spilling light onto the elevator.

Inkidu troops in heavy plate armor, helmets and steel skirts marched in to surround them. Their breast plates sported the pair of golden crossed hammers that marked them as Inkidu. Each one carried rayguns in their hands and swords at their sides. Two of them held a stretcher between them.

Though larger than Hillard they were still smaller in stature than Khan. He was taller, more heavily muscled, but their eyes were filled with a grim purpose he could only guess at.

One soldier with a helmet plume like a Roman soldier greeted Hillard with a salute.

"Get them to medical," Hillard said. "The human needs immediate attention. He's been hit by one of Cyclone's wasting bolts." She glanced at Bulls-Eye. "I honestly don't know how he's still alive."

"Yes, ma'am," the soldier said. "Professor, Priestess, I'm Colonel Patrus. Follow me, please." Two soldiers helped unstrap Bulls-Eye from Khan's back and lay him gently onto the stretcher.

Khan paused momentarily as it dawned on him that he was trapped underground with an entire platoon of heavily armed soldiers. He had been stunned to see the troops appear and wasn't sure if they were prison guards or an honor escort.

But if they could cure Bulls-Eye he didn't care which they were.

The soldiers led them through corridors hewn out of solid rock to a medical facility. They were met partway there by a team of Inkidu doctors with a large contraption that looked something like an iron lung. They lifted Bulls-Eye from the stretcher and slid him inside. It closed with a loud clang that sounded far too final for Khan's liking.

"Those bolts that Cyclone used on him cause the body to create its own poison," the Colonel said. "That machine will pull the venom out of him and retrain his cells to stop producing the venom. It takes time. He'll be there for at least a day, possibly longer."

"Hillard said she was surprised he was still alive," Khan said.

The Colonel gave the Priestess a pointed glance. She looked away and said, "Most only last a few minutes."

"I see," Khan said. He had known the situation was grave, but not how grave. "Thank you for not telling me. I might have lost hope."

"I'll take you somewhere you can get some food and drink. And clean the dust off."

The Colonel led them to a series of rooms that reminded Khan of his short stay with the centaurs, but with furniture that suited his frame. It was nice to finally have somewhere to sit that fit him.

"Professor, this is your room. There are fresh clothes available for you. Priestess, you're next door."

"Do you have anything that might fit me?" she asked.

He looked over the Priestess' uniform. "The Desert Scouts," he said. "A noble band. I served with a platoon of them years ago. I've heard of the risks you've taken. You do the uniform proud, Priestess."

Surprise flashed across Leandra's face, and quickly disappeared. "Thank you," she said. "I hope to."

"There's a fresh uniform in the room for you. We knew you were in our lands the minute you stepped off of Volus' submersible. I'll have someone come by to collect you in a couple of hours. Queen Deena will want to see you as soon as possible."

"Thank you, Colonel," Khan said. Khan hadn't heard of an Inkidu queen. Another leader. Though he had already accepted that he would help these people in whatever way he could, he still wasn't comfortable with politics. No matter what anyone might call him, he was still a pawn.

"I look forward to meeting her highness," he said, plastering a smile across his face that he hoped looked sincere.

"And she looks forward to meeting the both of you. I'll be sure to let you know how your friend is faring as soon as I hear anything." He nodded briskly at them and turned to stride down the hall.

"An audience with the Queen," Khan said as soon as the Colonel was out of earshot. "What do you know about her?"

"Nothing," Leandra said. "I didn't know they had a queen. They've hidden themselves remarkably well. I'm not sure even Cyclone knows."

"Interesting. If what we've seen so far is any indication they seem well organized."

"Do you think they'll be ready to take on my sister's army?"

"I don't know," he said. "But I think we're about to find out."

CHAPTER EIGHTEEN
THE WARRIOR QUEEN!

Khan bit into a peach-like fruit that had been in a bowl by the door and examined himself in a broad mirror. He picked at a thread on his new Inkidu tunic. It was blue with the gold sigil of the crossed hammers on its front, identical to the one he had discarded. By now his kilt was a shredded mess, but they had left him a similar one almost as good. Better in some ways. It had pockets.

The room itself was exquisite. Though he was larger in frame than the Inkidu, he saw that everything was designed with his body type in mind. The bed, the chairs, the height of the tables. Back on Earth everything he had was either custom built or cobbled together to accommodate him. He hadn't realized just how much that rankled him until he had something to compare it to.

Someone knocked softly on the door. Not demanding his attention, but politely requesting it. He pulled it open expecting the Priestess, but instead found himself before a burly soldier.

"Professor, Queen Deena requests your presence in the throne room."

Khan was getting tired of throne rooms. What was wrong with conference rooms, or offices? Or a library like in the palace of the K'kir Regent? He'd never met so many rulers in his life.

"Of course," Khan said. "And the Priestess?"

"She's been asked to confer with the Inkidu seers. They have questions about the Prophecy."

Khan cursed himself for not paying closer attention. He had stupidly expected that they would be kept together. He would have to try to find her later. Right now, though, he didn't see any way to change that. He didn't even know where in the city to look.

"Please," he said, composing himself quickly, "lead the way."

He followed the soldier through a series of wide, arching corridors hewn from solid rock, stark and utilitarian. It must have taken an enormous effort to build this under the nose of Cyclone and her minions. How long had it taken? And what price was being paid by those still on the surface? Khan wondered if all the surface dwellers were in on the ruse, or if some of them were ignorant of the fact that an entire city, the remnants of their civilization, sat beneath the planet's surface.

Soon the soldier brought him to a set of imposing double doors. Heavily armored with wide rivets holding steel plates to its surface. Even given the city's utilitarian design, the doors were unusually Spartan. He hadn't expected ostentation—it wasn't as though the Queen was receiving visiting dignitaries. But he had expected something less dungeon-like.

"If you'll step inside, sir, you'll be announced to the Queen." The soldier threw back a large bolt and pulled one of the doors open with a loud groan.

Khan frowned. At the very least they should have oiled the hinges. He stepped through, an uncomfortable feeling in the pit of his stomach. Something was wrong.

He turned to ask the guard if they had gotten the wrong room only to have the door slam heavily in his face and the bolt thrown. A part of him hoped that this wasn't what it appeared, but even as he surveyed the empty room with only the one door he had come through, he knew there was no hope. He was trapped.

Khan pounded on the heavy door, the sound echoing through the chamber. This was just another prison cell. Khan wondered if this Queen Deena were any better than Cyclone.

A hiss of escaping air brought his attention to a floor vent. A moment later sickly, green gas bubbled out of the gap. It had a cloying, sweet stench. Khan didn't know what it would do to him, and he had no intention of finding out.

Panic and rage flooded into him. He had come so far, been through too much. He was not going to let this happen to him. Not while Bulls-Eye was alone and vulnerable in Inkidu hands. Reason left him, pure animal ferocity taking its place.

He pounded again on the door, throwing the force of his entire body behind the blows. A dent appeared, then another. The door bent, hinges buckled. A large rivet loosened from one of the steel bands reinforcing the doors. Khan grasped it and pulled, tearing it free. A space opened between the doors. Khan tore at the gap.

The doors ripped open with a shriek. Clear air filled the chamber, blowing away the thick gas.

Five soldiers rushed in only to meet the swinging mallet of Khan's fist as he swung it in a wide arc.

He felled three of the soldiers with that one blow. The remaining two flanked him, one jumping for his legs, the other for his head. Khan spun his body, kicking wildly. He felt a satisfying crunch as his foot connected with the face of one as the other knocked him to the floor.

Khan and the remaining soldier wrestled, the soldier trying to get a purchase on Khan and hold him down. But Khan's greater bulk worked for him. He managed to push the soldier far enough away that he was able to punch him.

The soldier fell back, stunned. Khan paused, looking for more attackers. Something wasn't right. Certainly if they'd meant to kill him they would have just shot him, not come running inside, not with poison gas...

"Enough!" A female Inkidu with dusky blue fur strode into the room. Something in her voice snapped Khan back to reality and he stood there, blinking at her.

She was Khan's height, equally muscled. She wore a battle-scarred breast-plate, and an armored skirt like the other soldiers. She slammed a spiked scepter that looked more deadly than any blade to the ground with a sound like thunder that reverberated through the room.

Imperial. The word popped into Khan's mind. Not imperious, not the sort of arrogant demands of a child, but Imperial with a capital I. Her very presence commanded respect. She was, Khan was certain of it, Queen Deena.

Khan shook the thought away. "You tried to kill me," Khan said.

With two quick steps she was nose to nose with him. "You're an idiot," she said.

Khan had been called plenty of things but never that. "I beg your pardon?"

"Do you have any idea how many pretenders to the Prophecy come waltzing in here? Some long lost subject who claims to have grown up in the desert far away from my rule? Painted fur, or coated in coal black. All ruses by Cyclone to fool us into bringing a brainwashed traitor into our midst. That gas would eat through any paints or dyes we've seen before. And it wouldn't have done a thing to you."

A light went off in Khan's head. "This was to see if my fur was actually black? To see if I actually fit the Prophecy?"

"Yes. Congratulations. You figured it out. Do you want a prize?"

"Considering how many people have tried to kill or capture me in the last few days I think it's understandable that I'd be a little resistant to being gassed."

"Are you resistant to a blow to the head to knock some sense into you? Because I can arrange that."

Khan pointed to the fallen soldiers slowly pulling themselves up from the floor. "You tried that," he said. "It didn't work."

The Queen glared at him, lips curling into a snarl, then, much to Khan surprise, burst out laughing.

"That was phenomenal!" she said, punching his shoulder with a fist like a mallet. His arm went numb momentarily, but Khan refused to flinch.

"Does that mean I passed your test?"

"It means I believe you're really that color. But beyond that, I don't know what to make of you. I know you're from Earth. And I know what my spies have told me about your exploits, but I don't know if you're working for Cyclone or not. You did show up with her sister, after all."

"What would it take to convince you that I'm here to help?"

"Help? Really? From what my spies have told me your goal so far has been to do nothing but get off our glorious rock of a planet. You want to help us? Or do you want us to help you?"

She knew far more than Khan had expected. He shouldn't have been surprised, she clearly understood espionage and subterfuge if she had managed to keep her people's location a secret from the rest of the Martian races for so long.

"As I was recently reminded, assisting your people in their fight against Cyclone is the right thing to do. Whether I get off your 'glorious rock of a planet' or not."

"I see. And you think you can do something? You think you can wander in here with your Prophecy and your pet human and put right decades of wrong? Just wave your magic hands and all will be right with the world?"

"It's not my Prophecy." Khan said. "I'm a stranger here. I want nothing to do with all this politicking and backstabbing. I want to get my friend and myself back home safely. And at every turn this ridiculous Prophecy sees fit to steer us into ever greater danger. I've been threatened, punched, shot at, dropped down bottomless pits, fed to cave-dwelling dragons, drowned, gassed and generally made to feel miserable. If you want my help I'll give it. Otherwise, I would prefer all of this to end."

The Queen studied him, her gaze level. "Anything else?"

"A decent cup of tea would be nice."

"I'll have someone get right on that."

"Does that mean you believe me?"

"That you're not working with Cyclone? Yes. That the Prophecy is more than just a bedtime tale for young pups? Hardly."

"Then we're agreed on something."

Surprise appeared on the Queen's face. "You don't believe the Prophecy? Just think of the power you could wield if it were true."

"Have you listened to nothing I've just said? True or not, all it's done is make me a target. And worse, a pawn."

"You're the first one who's come to us who hasn't claimed to be the Inkidu savior," she said. "Who hasn't demanded we follow them or demanded my head."

"I am a teacher of antiquities, not a messiah."

"We'll see about that," she said, a mischievous glint in her eye. "Come with me. We have much to discuss."

Khan followed the Queen down corridors of stone, the five soldiers he had defeated limping along behind. He wasn't sure if they had held back or not. He knew he was strong, particularly in Mars' lower gravity, and he had been in fights before where the red mist of battle had taken his rationality, so it was certainly possible that he had defeated them through skill.

But these were trained soldiers. Veteran warriors. They had battle scars and their armor was well used. He flexed his fingers. His knuckles were bruised and his arms were sore from the short fight. He looked back at them and they all glared at him. Perhaps he really had won that fight.

"Do you prefer to be called Khan or Professor?" the Queen asked.

"Professor," Khan said.

"Khan it is, then. I like that better, anyway. I understand it is the name of a great general in Earth history. A ruthless warrior."

"It's a title, actually," Khan said. "Mongolian originally, though it's a term that has spread throughout Central Asia. Roughly translates to king. You're probably thinking of Genghis Khan, leader of the Mongol Empire which he ruled with an iron hand from 1206 to 1227. He—"

"I stand corrected," the Queen said, cutting him off. "Professor it is. Here we are." They entered a long room with a polished stone conference table in the center at which sat several Inkidu warriors. Colonel Patrus was there and next to him, to Kahn's surprise, sat Leandra.

"Welcome to my War Council, Professor," Queen Deena said. "Now that you're here the Prophecy can really get started."

CHAPTER NINETEEN
CAGE MATCH!

"I don't see why I'm the one going into the cage." Amelia said, tightening a wide, leather belt around her stomach. A thick, metal cable attached to its back went through a series of pulleys on the ceiling and down to a motorized winch at the far side of the room.

She eyed the Mega-Mantis in its titanium and steel cage. It stared at her with alien eyes.

"Thomas certainly can't do this," Benjamin said, checking that the cable was secure. It was threaded through a series of thick, leather loops on the belt and held in place with a padlock. "Can you imagine him in there?"

"He'd try to quantum it to death, or something," Amelia said. She felt like a worm on the end of a hook. "But you could do it."

"I could," he said, "but you and I both know that you could do it better."

Her face went sour. "You're just trying to stay out of that bug cage."

"Yes," he said. "But it doesn't mean it's not true."

"I hate you."

"Noted."

"If you two are finished, we're on a schedule here," Thomas said.

"Just give me the magical doohickey and let's get going," Amelia said.

"I told you," Thomas said, "it's not magical. It's a quantum resonance tracker." He handed the device to her. "Once you crack the carapace and get it in place, hit this switch on the side. That will start the analysis. The softest spots are at the joints and the safest is—"

"Yes, yes, I know," Amelia said. "Behind the head. How long do I need to hold this thing in before I can get out of there?"

"Twenty minutes."

Silence filled the room.

"Twenty minutes?!" Amelia said. "I won't last ten with that thing."

A slow satisfied smile crept across Thomas' face. "Gotcha," he said. "You just need twenty seconds. Once the analysis is complete it will transmit the information to my computer here." He showed her a handheld device brimming with vacuum tubes and blinking lights.

"If anything starts to go wrong we'll pull you out of there," Benjamin said. "Just try not to get the cable tangled. Thomas and I will distract it as you get into place on the top of the cage. Good luck. Don't get killed."

"Thanks," she said. The Mega-Mantis watched her warily as she walked to the far side of the cage. It couldn't turn its body in the cage, but it craned its neck almost completely around to track her. A ladder was welded to the side of the cage. She stepped near it, but didn't climb. It was too close to the bug's spiked legs for her comfort.

"I'm not going up there with that thing staring at me," Amelia said.

"Hey, ugly... bug thing!" Thomas yelled. He picked up a stone from a pile that he had pulled from one of the decorative ponds in the Chapter House gardens and threw it at the beast. It bounced harmlessly off its chest.

The Mega-Mantis ignored him.

"Let me try," Benjamin said. He opened his satchel, rummaged for a bit. "I'm sure I have something. Oh. I forgot I had that in there. This should do the trick."

He pulled out a device that looked like a hand-mirror with a clouded glass and an ornate handle, but had a series of exposed gears and cogs on its back. He twisted a small dial at its base, setting the gears in motion. A low hum rose amid the clicking and whirring of cogs.

"Is that bag larger on the inside?" Thomas asked.

"Sometimes."

"Huh. What does the mirror do?" Thomas asked.

In answer Benjamin pointed the clouded glass toward the Mega-Mantis. The sound rose in pitch and a moment later a green beam of light shot out of the glass toward the cage, striking the Mantis in the chest.

The effect was immediate. The monster reared up on its hind legs as much as it could, slamming its head against the top of the cage. It leapt forward, crashing against the cage. It rattled, but the bars held.

Amelia took advantage of the distraction and scurried up the ladder. The top of the cage had an opening for dropping food down to whatever animal it held. Considering that the cage was designed to hold dinosaurs some of that food would likely be alive, kicking and the size of a moose. It was more than large enough to admit her.

She dropped down onto the Mega-Mantis' back, using the spiked end of Thomas' quantum resonance tracker to give her purchase. The giant bug flailed. It screeched a terrible noise. Even with its frantic thrashing, she was up behind the giant bug's head in no time.

The green beam faded from Benjamin's strange device and the Mega-Mantis finally registered Amelia's presence. The flailing began anew, but this time it reached up with its forelegs in an attempt to scrape her off its back.

The thick spikes dotting its legs came worryingly close, but it was the head that Amelia was most concerned about. The insect began to slam it against the bars, and Amelia had to slide down the neck to keep from being crushed.

Now or never, she thought, and slammed the spike into the closest crevice on the thing's neck that she could find. Thick green blood welled up around it.

If she had thought it had been a wild ride before, now it was even worse. It bucked like a bronco on fire. Amelia's boots lost their purchase on the slick carapace. She hung by the resonance tracker counting the seconds. Five, ten, fifteen...

"Don't let go, yet," Thomas yelled. "It's almost done."

Twenty, twenty-five, thirty, thirty-five...

"You said twenty seconds!" Amelia said. Her grip was loosening as the Mega-Mantis did its best to throw her and the offending spike off of its body.

"Almost there. Don't let go!"

"I don't think I'm going to have much choice."

"Got it. Get her out of there."

Amelia heard the winch kick in and the cable pull taut. She pulled the device out of the Mega-Mantis' hide and pushed off with her feet. She grabbed the lip of the hatch and shoved her way out as the Mega-Mantis threw its head back into the bars. It missed her by inches. Amelia kicked herself off the edge of the cage as the cable slackened, allowing herself to get clear.

"I have the coordinates," Thomas said. Benjamin and he ran to Amelia to get the cable belt unlatched. "I wonder, though, if only one dataset is sufficient. Maybe we should do it again."

"No," Benjamin and Amelia said in unison. The Mega-Mantis howled as if in agreement.

CHAPTER TWENTY
A CRUCIAL CHOICE!

"The Prophecy is a sham." The Inkidu warrior claiming this stood and pounded his fist on the table. "Are we to put our soldiers at risk for it? Are we to have them follow on faith?"

The arguing had started the moment Khan sat down at the table. Twenty Inkidu warriors all yelling to be heard, yelling to get their points across, yelling to suggest strategies, yelling to yell.

Khan was the outsider, so he said nothing. Many angry fingers pointed at him and Leandra. Comments were made about his alienness, about his authenticity. Was he really from Earth? How did they know? He just appeared out of the desert. Maybe he was a mutation with his black fur, an abomination that had been co-opted by Cyclone to be a spy and lead them astray. He had brought a Weather Witch into their midst, after all.

And Queen Deena let it rage on. She watched her war council argue with each other as though it were a tennis match with twenty players and half a dozen balls. After twenty minutes she cleared her throat. Everyone fell silent.

"What do you think?" she asked Khan.

"About? I've heard a dozen different topics."

"The Prophecy. Do you think it's true?"

"It's poppycock."

Another round of arguments and finger pointing threatened to erupt, but the Queen stared it down. "I happen to agree with you," she said. "Whether or not it's true is irrelevant. My troops are ready to move, and Cyclone is clearly afraid. That gives us an advantage. But I want an even bigger advantage. I need my people to believe the Prophecy, too."

Khan knew this was coming. Knew that he was going to have to be a pawn. He sighed. "Yes, I assumed as much. You need a figurehead. Someone to rally around. Fine. I can be that. Say the Prophecy is true and that I'm their messiah. Cart me out to wave to the troops."

"It's not that simple," the Queen said. She looked over her advisors. "I know you all have your own opinions on this matter, and I have listened to each of you these last few days. I have made my decision. We will, as Professor Khan suggests, 'cart him out to wave to the troops.'"

"That won't work," Colonel Patrus said.

"Why not?" Khan said.

"As I said, it's not that simple." The queen turned to face Khan full on. "We have lived with this Prophecy nonsense for decades. We have had so many false saviors that people are tired of hearing about it. Our doctors have even coined a phrase for it. Prophecy Fatigue."

Khan was beginning to see the problem. "Then how do we break that? How do we renew their faith in it?"

"If the people are going to rally behind you they need to believe you're serious. They need to believe that you might actually prevail. We need to make them believe in the Prophecy again. And that means that you need to prove yourself in battle."

Khan blinked at her. Had he heard that right? "Battle?" he said.

"Yes. Nothing too difficult," the Queen said. "We don't want to risk you losing."

"It has to be public," one of her advisors said.

"And big," said another.

"Vitrepian Land Worm," said a third.

"Ridiculous," said a fourth. "They only grow to twenty feet. A child could kill one by stomping on its head."

"Porculis Fire Ant," someone said. "Tall as a house. Skin gets to a thousand degrees and it farts flames."

"Out of season," said the first.

Soon the room was full of suggestions of terrible sounding beasts that Khan could fight. Ragnar Bore Beetles, The Double-Headed Ice Snakes of Hormise, Spike-Tailed Hurricane Snails, Insanity Sharks, Lorogran Acid Hedgehogs.

"You have hedgehogs?" Khan asked the Queen.

"Three hundred feet tall with poison tipped spines and teeth the size of your head," she said. "They make excellent guard animals."

Khan felt a little sick.

"I can't do this," he said. "You want me to prove myself by battling some hellish beast. You do know what happened in the desert, don't you? I had to be saved fighting a spider-eyed bear. And you want to set me against giant, poisonous hedgehogs? This is madness. I can't do it. I won't."

Everyone stopped their bickering to look at him. The Queen lay a hand on his shoulder. "I understand," she said. "I can't make you do it. That won't work. But I would like a chance to convince you."

"I don't see how you can."

"Everyone," she said, "this session of the council is adjourned." She stood and headed toward the door. "Professor, if you'd follow me?"

Khan caught Leandra's eye. She looked stunned. Somehow he doubted that Cyclone's court worked like this. She shrugged, too overwhelmed to be any help. Khan sighed and followed the Queen out of the conference room.

The two walked unescorted down the empty corridors in silence for some time. Khan wasn't certain of the etiquette here so he took a speak-when-spoken-to approach and said nothing.

"I was just becoming an adult when Cyclone took power," the Queen said. "I lived on the surface in the palace. War wasn't unknown to us, but there was a balance between us and the other kingdoms and the Weather Witches helped maintain that. They were expert diplomats, powerful allies and terrible foes. It wasn't easy, but my parents made it work for us. We prospered."

"I understand that Cyclone murdered the other Weather Witches," Khan said.

"She did, save her sister. That's an interesting development, by the way, her showing weather powers. We knew they were related, but not that she had power beyond her gift for prophecy."

"Neither did she. Some of your advisors seemed to think she's a threat."

"She's not," the Queen said. "If Cyclone had known about it she would have had her murdered years ago. She is what she says she is. Family won't hold Cyclone back for long. She murdered her mother and five of her other sisters, after all."

Khan stopped, aghast. "That's horrifying."

"Yes. That's Cyclone. When she sent her troops against us she was at the head of the charge. We weren't expecting it. We had a truce with all the other kingdoms and the Weather Witches didn't war. She laid waste to our cities. We were totally unprepared."

"Her own people rebelled."

"The Desert Scouts, yes. Our military was broken, but we still had some pieces of it. My parents were killed in the first assaults and I was left to take command. We are not a lead from behind sort of people. Once the Desert Scouts came to us we thought we could win. We were wrong."

She stopped at a door behind which Khan could hear the sounds of heavy machinery, placed a hand against it.

"My parents built this city as an overflow to save some of the population should an all-out war occur. It hadn't been finished when Cyclone struck. Even with the losses we had taken it couldn't hold everyone. We saved who we could. Continued the construction."

Aside from the troops Khan had encountered and the endless corridors with blank doors scattered throughout, he had seen nothing indicating any kind of city life. Everyone he had met was a soldier.

"Where are the citizens?" Khan asked. "Where are the children?"

"Struggling," the Queen said. "This door, one of many, leads out to our underground city. We keep them locked and barricaded. Not to keep our people in, mind. But to keep any invaders out. Where we are now is our front gates. More fortress than palace, certainly." She opened a panel next to the door, punched in a code on large buttons. The door hissed and slid aside.

The sounds of industry flooded into the corridor. Through the opening Khan could see a massive cavern, hundreds of feet high filled to the brim with machinery the size of skyscrapers. Lights glittered off every surface, casting the smoke-laden air a dull, devilish red. Gears and cogs moved gondolas across cables from one building to the next. Catwalks connected each structure and Khan could see thousands of people scurrying about, working, and traveling.

"Wait," Khan said. "Those machines. People are living in them?"

"They are. We don't have the space to separate our industry from our living quarters. We can only build out or up so far without being detected. These machines supply our air, our heat, our water. They grow our food. And they are failing."

"What do you mean?"

"Without trade we cannot keep them going indefinitely. And when they finally die we cannibalize them for parts to keep the rest going."

"How long?"

"My scientists tell me we have about two more years before we are unable to support the entire population."

"And after that?" Would the Queen sacrifice some of her people to save the rest? How would she decide? How could she decide?

"There won't be an 'after that,'" she said. "Because we will be on the surface, rebuilding our homes and Cyclone's head will be on a pike. My people are desperate, Professor. We are refugees of the surface. We have nowhere to go but up where we will be slaughtered."

"But your war machines," Khan said. "I've seen what they can do. Certainly you could fight."

"We don't have enough material for an extended war. We have to make a fast, brutal and decisive strike. If we just go to the surface we will hold out for a while, but Cyclone will eventually burn us down. To survive we have to take the fight to her."

"I see. You have to win. Cyclone has to merely not lose."

"Precisely. If we don't win right out of the gate it will become a war of attrition. We'll be slaughtered."

The Queen stepped through the door and down a winding flight of steps that led to a rusty catwalk. Khan followed, overwhelmed by the sights and sounds. Here were those citizens and shopkeepers and families he had been wondering about. Here among the machines, huddled around the technology that kept them alive.

As he approached the far building people stepped aside to let the Queen pass. They were soot stained, wearing clothing that had been patched and re-patched so many times that Khan couldn't tell what the original garments looked like. Many of them were battle-scarred; some of them were missing limbs.

The Queen acknowledged each of them with a quiet thank you. Some of them gave Khan surprised looks as he went by. He could hear whispers behind him. Surprised voices spreading who knew what rumors about him.

"A brilliant move," Khan said behind her as they continued their walk.

"And what is that?" she said. She sounded subdued and would not turn her head to look at him.

"Not only are you showing me the face of your war, the victims you want me to help, but you're showing your people the face of their 'savior.'"

"It was my plan, yes," she said. "Did it work? Have you changed your mind, or do I need to show you the orphanages? The children blinded by Cyclone's constant attacks are particularly heartbreaking."

"No," Khan said. "You don't need to show me the orphanages." He touched her shoulder and she turned to look at him. Tears filled her eyes threatening to spill over. This must be agony for her to see her subjects like this, and knowing that she can do so little to ease their suffering. It was a calculated move bringing him here, but it did not mean she felt her subjects' pain any less keenly.

A tear ran down the Queen's cheek and Khan surprised himself by gently wiping it away. Even more surprising was that she let him.

They stood a long moment looking at each other, saying nothing. Khan felt a flutter in his chest, a new sensation he couldn't identify.

"I don't need to see anymore," he said, his voice cracking. "I'll fight whatever monster you decide I must to win over the troops. If your people are to win this fight they will need hope. And if you think I am the one who can give it to them, who am I to deny that?"

The Queen reached up and took his hand in hers. She smiled slowly, wistfully. "Thank you. The fight to show off your skill will be rigged, of course, but it won't be that rigged. We can't have you losing, but we can't have you walking into the arena to fight the body of a dead Acid Slug. We'll find something suitable."

Khan looked out at the city stretching through the murky cavern, the tall spires of lights, the belching smoke. These people deserved much more than to hide beneath the rock away from the life-giving sun. Khan would not allow this to stand.

"I'll do it," Khan said. "For your people. For you."

CHAPTER TWENTY-ONE
INTRIGUES IN THE PALACE!

When Khan and the Queen returned to the conference room they found the Priestess alone. She paced the room, her face a mask of worry and thought. She didn't notice they had arrived until Khan cleared his throat and said, "I'm going to go through with it."

She blinked. "Oh. Good. That's very good. Thank you. I knew I could count on you."

"He's agreed to his role in this," the Queen said, "but what about your role, Priestess?"

Leandra looked at her, surprise on her face. "I don't understand."

Khan looked back at the Queen, possibilities ticking through his mind. He had a guess what she was about to say, but stayed quiet.

"We are about to depose your sister, end her rule in as violent manner as we can. If I can crush her skull myself I will. Does that bother you?"

"She murdered our parents," Leandra said. "Our other sisters. I want to see her dead as much as anyone."

"I thought as much," the Queen said. "But after that, then what? Vengeance has a shelf-life. You've survived this long because that fire kept you going. What happens when it goes out?"

"I— I don't know," Leandra said. "I hadn't really figured it out past getting the Professor to you."

"I have an idea, if you'll hear me out," the Queen said. "When Cyclone falls there will be a lot of angry people. Her citizens, the other kingdoms. What do you think the Centaurs will do? The K'kir? Me?"

Doubt slowly spread across Leandra's face as the full import of what she had set in motion finally registered to her. "You can't be serious," she said. "You'll go in and kill everyone, not just Cyclone?"

"Not beyond those who fight for her," the Queen said. "Everyone has suffered under her. But the other rulers? Who can say? Or even the people within the city? When they see a void in power, when they see no Weather Witch to maintain order, what will they do? It could be very, very ugly. But—"

"But?" Leandra said.

"But if that power vacuum was filled, if it closed before anyone else could move on it, that could be avoided. If it were one of the other kingdoms, everyone else would fight amongst themselves, and even the citizens would rebel. There would be no peace."

Leandra sat heavily in a chair and sighed. "But if a Weather Witch, one with power, one that the people knew, took charge..."

"Exactly," the Queen said. "You know there's only one choice."

The Priestess hesitated, her thoughts plain on her face. Khan knew this couldn't be an easy decision for her. But surely she had to have thought of it before.

"I do," she said after a long moment. "Yes, I'll do it. I'll take my sister's place. But if you want to avoid that prolonged battle, that ceaseless war, I will have your assurances that when Cyclone is deposed, that's it. No more fighting between my people and yours."

"And the other kingdoms?"

"I will have to work with each of them in turn, but if I can get word out to them before we attack I might be able to negotiate the same."

"That I can arrange," the Queen said with a slow smile. "I've already started making contact with them. And they might already be under the impression that you will be taking Cyclone's place."

Leandra stared hard at her for a long moment and then laughed. It was a humorless sound. "Nicely played, Your Highness," she said. "Have you spread the word that I've come into my powers as a Weather Witch?"

"And then some. I had the dead Graal beast you incinerated in the desert delivered outside Cyclone City as my spies spread the story about how it was killed. With a little embellishment, of course."

"You're very good at this," Leandra said. "How do I know I can trust you?"

"How do I know I can trust you?" the Queen said. "Trust is a fickle thing. Today we can have it; tomorrow it might evaporate like rain in the desert. Politics is an ugly thing, Priestess. Or should I call you Princess, now?"

"Until I sit on the throne Priestess will do."

"I'll have documents made up and we can haggle over the details of our truce. But in the meantime." The Queen extended her hand. Leandra stood and took it. "To our future."

"To our future."

"Something else you might want to know," the Queen said. "Both of you. Your friend is awake. We were able to stop the poison and reverse the effects. He's not fully recovered, but his body isn't trying to kill itself anymore. If you'd like to see him, he's still in the infirmary."

"Thank you," Khan said. "Leandra, go on ahead. I think he would like to see you more than me."

"Are you sure, Professor?"

"I'll be along. I have things to discuss with Her Highness."

Leandra bowed to the Queen, and quickly left.

"Nicely done," Khan said once the Priestess was out of earshot. "I was wondering how you were planning on keeping the peace once Cyclone was out of the picture."

"I'm still working on some angles with the K'kir and the Monatu, but I think they'll be fine. The Alivons, the bird people, might be a bit harder. They've been Cyclone's allies for a very long time. They won't be easy to convince. We may find ourselves in the middle of a protracted war anyway, once this is all over."

"Can you survive that?"

"With the other kingdoms' help, certainly, but—"

"But allies are fickle things," Khan finished.

"They are. But that's for later. For now, I suggest you see your friend and get some rest. You have a big day ahead of you tomorrow. I'm leaning toward the giant hedgehog."

Khan's stomach roiled. "With the poison spines?"

"And the razor sharp teeth the size of your head, yes. It'll be fun."

"For you, maybe," Khan muttered as he left the room.

Khan wrinkled his nose at the smell of bleach and antiseptic as he stepped into the palace infirmary. Like everything else in the palace it had the feel of a battlefield encampment more than any kind of permanent structure. Khan wondered if that was by design. Keep it mobile in case of attack.

The trip to the infirmary had been an odd one. He had no escort, but everyone was watching him with something between reverence, fear and excitement. Even during his early days at Oxford when he was seen more as curiosity than scholar he had been met with less enthusiasm. He was beginning to feel a little like a celebrity.

The infirmary's reception area was a large room carved out of the rock with hallways branching off in several directions. A single desk sat near the entrance with a burly Inkidu receptionist keeping track of who came and went in a large ledger.

"You're here to see the Earthling?" the receptionist asked, glancing up from his ledger.

"Well, technically, I'm an Earthling, too," Khan said. "You see—"

The receptionist grunted, jotting a note in his book. "Down hall number 3," he said. "Eighth recovery bay on the left." He pointed over his shoulder with his thumb to a hallway.

"Uh, thank you." Khan said. Any feelings of celebrity evaporated. Khan headed down the hall, counting the curtained off bays. He stopped as he heard raised voices.

"I don't care about none of that," Bulls-Eye said loud enough for Khan to hear it down the hall. His voice was strong and he clearly had his dander up.

"Well, you should," Leandra said. Her voice angry. "It's all based on a lie. And I don't know why you can't see that." Leandra pulled the curtain aside and stomped out of the recovery bay, scowling. She stopped when she saw Khan.

"Maybe you can talk some sense into him," she said and stalked down the hall.

Khan poked his head in to see Bulls-Eye wearing the same scowl. "Hello," he said, a little nervous.

"I don't understand her at all," Bulls-Eye said.

"What happened?"

"She told me she was Cyclone's sister and that she was a Weather Witch."

"Ah, that." Khan felt a great relief. Since the cat was, as they say, out of the bag, Khan didn't have to keep it a secret from his friend. "I discovered that in the desert. She saved my life."

Bulls-Eye threw up his hands. "Now this makes even less sense!"

"I don't understand."

"I told her I didn't care that she was Cyclone's sister. None of that matters. And that just made her mad. Like I'm supposed to be upset with her, or somethin'."

"She was very adamant that I not tell you about it. She was afraid you'd be upset."

"But that's just it, I ain't upset. She ain't her horrible princess sister goin' around killin' folk for lookin' cross-eyed at her. It ain't her fault she's related to a maniac. But now she's all mad at me for sayin' so. Aw, heck Perfesser, I just don't get her."

Khan had to admit that he didn't get it, either. He weighed his options. He wasn't quite sure how to react. Show encouragement? Sympathy? Outrage?

"I'm supposed to fight a giant beast to cement my position as the Inkidu champion and I may not survive it," Khan said, opting for changing the subject. He told him about Queen Deena's plan.

"Ah, you'll be fine," Bulls-Eye said when he'd finished.

"Did you hear the part about the giant beast?" Khan said. "They want me to fight it. And kill it."

"Well, of course they do. You wouldn't be much of a champion if you couldn't do that."

Khan sighed and sat heavily on the edge of the bed. "I know. And I understand why. I just don't like it."

"I know you don't like it, Perfesser, but ya gotta."

"Do you ever lose control?"

"Oh, sure, Perfesser. Why there was this time in Abilene when I got snockered and woke up the next day in San Antonio without my pants."

"That's not what I mean," Khan said. "I get... rages. All I can think of is the battle."

"Sometimes that's what's called for."

"But I become a mindless brute. I lose myself."

"I know. I seen it. But you always come back. That's the important thing. And for this one it sounds like you could use some mindless brute. Whatever she picks you to fight it ain't gonna be easy. She don't want you dead, but she can't make it look like she's thrown the fight. Folk'll see through that in a hot minute. So when you get in there you let that brute out and you go kick some butt."

"I'll have to kill it."

"You've done it before."

Khan sighed. "Of course I have."

"This is just like those times. So don't fret none. You'll do what needs doin'. That's who you are."

An orderly stuck his head through the curtain. "I'm sorry, but visiting hours are over. He needs to get some sleep."

"When will he be out?"

"Soon," the orderly said. "Possibly tomorrow. We'll know more once the doctors have another look at him."

"Oh, I'm fine. I feel like I could wrassle a steer."

"Be that as it may," Khan said, "he's right. You still need rest."

"Hey, Perfesser, could you do me a favor?"

"Of course."

"See if you can find out what's eatin' Leandra. I don't understand what's goin' on."

"I'll see what I can do," Khan said and left his friend to his recovery.

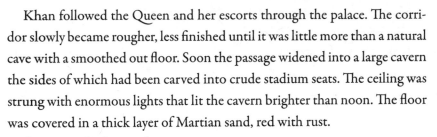

Khan followed the Queen and her escorts through the palace. The corridor slowly became rougher, less finished until it was little more than a natural cave with a smoothed out floor. Soon the passage widened into a large cavern the sides of which had been carved into crude stadium seats. The ceiling was strung with enormous lights that lit the cavern brighter than noon. The floor was covered in a thick layer of Martian sand, red with rust.

"An arena?" Khan said.

"This is where you'll fight as our champion," the Queen said. "All of our warriors complete their training here. Each squad fights a beast pulled from the wastes. You will fight a Desert Demon of Kroom."

"Desert Demon?"

"Of Kroom. It was one of our cities before Cyclone wiped it off the map. They're giant beasts with two heads, teeth dripping with poison and twelve legs ending with huge talons the size of your head." Khan's eyes went wide. "Don't worry. We've removed the poison sacs."

"That still leaves the claws."

"And the teeth in the two heads. At least we didn't get the hedgehogs."

"Yes, of course." He had forgotten about the hedgehogs. Khan felt queasy. He could think of several other ways a giant, two headed beast could kill him even without poison. "How will I defeat it?"

The Queen shrugged. "You're the champion, you'll figure it out. My men will escort you to the dressing chambers. You're on in two hours."

"Two hours? I can't be ready in two hours. I need training. I need to size up my opponent, learn how it moves."

The Queen gave him a level gaze. "And if I gave you a day or a month or a year, you would have no more insight. The only difference it would make is that my people would see you as weak. I cannot afford that to happen. The people need a champion. They need a symbol to bolster them, to give them strength. They need you, Khan."

"I'm useless to you if I die," he said.

"Then don't die."

Khan stood in a holding chamber, a large metal gate separating him from the arena. He could see the silhouette of his opponent pacing back and forth through a similar gate on the other side. In a few minutes both gates would open and the fight would begin.

Next to the terror that had set his knees to shaking, Khan felt ridiculous. He wore an Inkidu skirt of armor plates and a top that was nothing but buckles and straps. He carried his spear awkwardly in both hands, unsure of how to hold it. He wasn't sure which was more likely, him being torn limb from limb by the Desert Demon or impaling himself on the spear.

"You've never been in a fight like this, have you?" Khan turned to see Colonel Patrus. The soldier had snuck up quietly behind him. He had last seen him in the conference room where so many ghastly suggestions were thrown about of what Khan's opponent should be.

"I've been in battle before. I'm no stranger to it, but no, not like this. I've never been a gladiator."

"I know. There was no time for training. That was not the Queen's decision."

"I'm sorry? I thought her rule was law."

"It is, to an extent. But there is a parliament who can, and does, put pressure on her. Not everyone wants to see you succeed."

Khan felt suddenly very claustrophobic. "And you? Do you want to see me succeed?"

"Very much. I follow my queen not just out of duty. She is the best leader we have ever had in the most trying times we have ever faced. Whatever some politicians might think, my people need you to succeed."

"Thank you. I hope to live up to the expectations."

The Colonel smiled. "That's why I'm here. If you look at your spear you'll notice a button about half-way down. When pressed it will release a toxin into the tip. It's under pressure. Strike the beast with that, hit the button. It'll fall in a matter of seconds. It will be fast and painless."

Khan looked over the spear until he found the button. "I take it there's only one shot?"

"Yes. And it's not exactly a hair trigger, so you shouldn't have trouble with it going off accidentally. And you'll have to do more than deliver a scratch. Embed it firmly into the beast's hide, then hit the button. Also, the beast has been drugged and, well, it's pretty old. It's had a long life. So it shouldn't have too much fight in it."

Khan turned the spear over in his hands. "I see you don't have much faith in my abilities?"

"We have a saying that perhaps your human friend might appreciate. If you're not cheating, you're not trying."

"I imagine he would." Outside a steady chant of 'KHAN KHAN KHAN' was steadily growing. "More of your doing?"

"We're trying to make you a champion, Professor," the Colonel said. "With little time to do so." The gate shuddered, heavy chains pulling tight. Slowly, it rose. The Colonel slapped Khan on the back. "When the beast comes out, run in close before it can bring its heads or its forelegs in. Strike fast, hit the button."

"Any other advice?" Khan said.

"Don't die."

CHAPTER TWENTY-TWO
ASSASSINATION BY MONSTER!

Khan stepped out onto the red sand and froze. The stadium was packed with Inkidu all chanting 'KHAN KHAN KHAN' with an occasional cry of 'THE PROPHECY!' thrown in for good measure. There were thousands in the stadium all looking at him, all expecting him to fulfill their ridiculous prediction and lead them out of these caverns to victory.

A voice nagged at him. What if he couldn't? What if he failed them? What if he failed *her*? What if he succeeded here only for disaster to take them later? He shook the thought away. He wasn't the one who would be leading the troops. He was a symbol, a figure-head. He wasn't their leader. He was their hope.

He knew what he had to do. He needed to prove that he was worthy. That he was their Prophecy come to life. He gripped the spear in both hands, raised it above his head and let loose a mighty roar. The sound echoed off the cavern walls, fed back into itself and when it finally died away the cavern was silent.

All of the Inkidu looked at him expectantly. His eyes searched the stands until they fell upon the Queen. Khan needed to say something. Not just to the Inkidu, but to Deena.

"I am here to prove my worth," Khan cried, his voice reverberating through the cavern. "And when I do we will take to the surface. We will drive back Cyclone. We will take back what is rightfully yours. The Inkidu will walk under the sun once again. And we will do it together." He finished with another roar. This time it was met with wild cheers.

It was hard to see from this distance, but he thought he could see the Queen smiling.

Yes, Khan thought. This was right. This was as it should be. He was giving these people a second chance. All they needed was hope. And he would be that hope.

The gate holding his opponent slowly rose and the crowd fell silent. The beast leapt out of its enclosure and onto the arena floor.

What he had been told didn't do this monster justice. It looked as though someone had crossed a snake and a scorpion with a lion. Twenty feet long at least with a low slung back and spider-like legs that allowed it to telescope its body high into the air. The two heads sat at the end of long, sinuous necks and were crowned with thick manes of black fur. Its red eyes glowed and green ichor dripped from its teeth.

That was wrong. He had been told that the poison had been taken out. Had he been lied to? Had someone switched the defanged beast with this one? Khan cast his gaze up into the audience and quickly spied the royal box. The Queen was standing, looking furious. Had she seen the poison dripping from its jaws, too?

The beast let loose a deafening roar. If he had been lied to it didn't matter right now. He needed to survive. Remembering the Colonel's words, Khan leapt between the snapping heads. One of them shot to where he had been standing, slamming itself into the ground with a thunderous crash, while the other looped to track Khan's movement. It snapped at him, missing him by inches.

It was fast, but Khan was more nimble. If this monster had been drugged, then Khan was a monkey. He thrust the spear up into its chest, but before he could strike one of the forelegs shot out and knocked him away.

Khan flew a good ten feet and skidded in the dirt, raising a plume of red dust. The spear went flying and embedded itself into the floor. Khan rolled to a crouch. The Desert Demon charged. There was no way he would reach the spear before the beast was upon him, so he didn't even try.

Instead he jumped, letting his Earth strength in the lower Martian gravity propel him high into the air. The Desert Demon snapped its heads at the spot where he had stood, green spittle flying from its teeth, the ground smoking where the poison struck.

Khan came down on one of the Desert Demon's necks as it raised its head. He slung his arms tight around the neck and heard a snap as the neck bones cracked from the shock. The beast let out a high pitched scream and the head swung to the ground when the neck finally couldn't support it any longer. The other head looped around and snapped at Khan, but Khan was ready for it and simply let go.

Its teeth closed on its neck, severing the already wounded head from its body. Green blood burst from the wound and the remaining head jerked back, flailing wildly. Khan rolled clear as the legs danced madly around him, striking randomly at the ground. It was losing a lot of blood.

The creature staggered, let loose a thin cry and toppled. Its remaining head whipped about for a moment, but even that grew furtive and finally ceased. Khan stepped warily toward the creature. It was panting and its thick, black tongue lolled out of the side of its mouth. It gave a slow, low groan.

Khan was horrified. Not at what he had done but at what he had been forced to do. This could have been a quick death, painless. Whoever had swapped out the drugged beast for this one hadn't wanted Khan to survive and in so doing had only inflicted needless suffering.

Khan walked back to the spear embedded into the ground and pulled it free. He was only distantly aware of the murmurings of the crowd. He knelt down to the Desert Demon's head, looked it in the eyes. "I'm sorry," he said. He slammed the spear into the beast's head right between the eyes and pressed the button to release the poison. A loud hiss erupted from the spear and a thick, blue fluid bubbled up out of the wound. The beast jerked once and then finally fell still.

A mad cheer erupted from the crowd. Khan looked up at them all. He had done what he had set out to do. He had won them over. Or most of them, at least. Someone up there had tried to kill him. That was all right,

Khan thought. He'd gotten used to it. Khan tossed the spear aside and glared defiantly at the assembled Inkidu. Some, he knew, would take that as his acknowledging his victory. But whoever had set him up would know the challenge for what it was.

Bring it on, he thought. Khan would be ready.

"That was an assassination attempt," Leandra said after Khan had told her what had happened. She had been in the stadium by the Queen's side watching the whole thing. "The Queen was furious, and now I know why."

"I hate politics," Khan said. "Politics gets people killed." They sat in Khan's room. He had washed up and changed back into his kilt and tunic. He had met the Queen briefly, but she was distracted and Khan suspected this was the reason why.

Leandra paced back and forth, her hands behind her back. "We have guards posted outside," she said. "There's no way anyone will try to kill you."

"Really? Why not? They've certainly been trying ever since I got here," Khan said. "At some point there will be an opportunity and someone will take it."

"Not as many opportunities as you might think," Leandra said. "The arena was their best chance. Their job is much harder, now. You're the Champion of the Inkidu. Anything they do will have to look accidental. Otherwise you'll just be a martyr."

Khan thought about that. Given the propensity of the Inkidu to follow strange apes that prove themselves in single combat with giant, double-headed beasts, he wasn't sure the logic followed. But she was right. Any assassination attempt would have to look accidental. If they outright killed him it would backfire, showing them merely as traitors to the crown. And now, if the reactions in the arena had been any indication, the people were behind him.

Most of them, anyway.

Khan startled when someone knocked on the door. He was ready to spring into action, though whether that meant attacking a would-be assassin or leaping behind a chair he wasn't sure. His nervousness must have been showing because Leandra put her hand on his shoulder and said, "Come in."

The door slid open and a burly Inkidu guard ushered Bulls-Eye into the room. The cowboy looked healthy, though he walked with a slight limp. He was dressed back in his Desert Scout uniform, though it looked as though a tailor had finally fitted it to him properly. It no longer hung on his frame like a scarecrow.

Leandra was on him in a flash, taking him in her arms. "They let you out?" she said. "I thought you'd be in there for at least a few more days."

Bulls-Eye returned the hug. "Nah, I got me a bull's stamina. Ain't no hospital keeping me cooped up. Docs gave me a clean bill of health and sent me on my way."

"It's good to see you up and about," Khan said, putting out his hand to shake. Bulls-Eye ignore the proffered hand and pulled the surprised ape into an embrace.

"And good to see you, too, Perfesser," Bulls-Eye said. "Heard you was fightin' a wicked, poison-headed monster."

"It had two heads," Khan said.

"I always miss the fun."

"This one wasn't," Leandra said. Bulls-Eye's expression grew dark as she relayed what had happened in the arena.

"And you're sure it weren't just some mix-up?" he said.

Khan thought about that. It was an interesting thought. But no, that didn't follow. This was too important to mess up that badly. "I don't think so. We haven't heard anything from the Queen since we left the arena."

"Well, if it means anything there's an awful lot of hustle and bustle goin' on out there. I almost got run over by all them soldiers runnin' around."

"Soldiers? Are we under attack?"

Bulls-Eye shrugged. "No idea. They looked like they was gettin' ready for somethin'. The Queen sending her folks off to war, maybe?"

"So quickly?" Khan said. "I suppose that makes sense. They've been planning things for a long time now." The thought left him unsettled. He had thought he had made his peace with the idea of going to war, but after his experience in the arena he was jumpy.

It was odd when he stopped to think about it. What was it about this attempt on his life that was different from the other attempts? Was it that they had used a beast to do it? The brazenness of the attempt? The betrayal? Yes. That was it. The fact that he had been welcomed, brought into the fold, and then betrayed.

Khan took a deep breath, let it out slowly. He was here to do right by the Inkidu whether someone wanted to kill him or not. He had made his choice and he was going to see it through.

Another knock on the door. This one more forceful. "Enter," he said, though he knew that was just a formality. He knew full well who it was. The door slid open and the door guard entered, followed by the Queen.

"Glad to see you're not dead," she said, looking Khan up and down.

"Despite someone's best efforts," Khan said. "I understand the Desert Demon was supposed to be drugged and its poison sacs removed. That didn't happen."

"But the spear worked," she said. "That's something."

"Yes. For all the good it did me. You have a traitor in your midst."

The Queen feigned a shocked expression. "No! You don't say! Of course I have a traitor. At least five of them. They all opted to kill themselves rather than reveal any information. I didn't even have them tortured. I'm sure there are more but I don't know who they are, yet."

"They don't want to go to war," Khan said. "If I die then I'm just another pretender."

"And their sure bet goes out the window," Bulls-Eye said.

"Oh, they want to go to war," the Queen said, "just not with me as their ruler. You are the only Champion I've backed. If you die they can say I was taken in by your roguish good looks and am unfit to lead. Were that to happen, a coup would quickly follow."

"I'm sorry," Khan said, suddenly flustered. "Roguish good looks?"

The Queen grinned at him. "Focus, Professor. We're talking about your life and my rule. There's only one thing we can do now."

"Yes, of course," Khan said. Focus. He had to focus. Did he really look roguish? He shook the thought away. "When do we leave?"

"In the morning. Once we engage Cyclone's troops this conspiracy won't dare move against us. Discrediting me is one thing, losing outright is entirely different. Until then, though, your life is in danger. I have a handful of soldiers I trust implicitly, but they're going to be occupied. Besides, you already have a Weather Witch and a crazy human to watch your back."

"I ain't that crazy," Bulls-Eye said.

"Duly noted," said the Queen. "You're still the best people for the job and I don't think I could separate you from his side, anyway. Since you didn't actually come with anything you shouldn't have much to pack."

"What's our strategy?" Khan said.

"Simple. We hit Cyclone where she'll feel it. Right in her city."

CHAPTER TWENTY-THREE
PREPARATIONS FOR WAR!

The mobilization of Queen Deena's troops left Khan slack-jawed. The palace had a lounge that looked down onto the military training grounds. From there Khan could see thousands of Inkidu soldiers with rayguns piling into immense troop transports. The vehicles were shaped like giant, wheeled insects bristling with weapons and clad in heavy armor.

Khan wondered how many of these soldiers would be returning. He quickly looked at Leandra and Bulls-Eye standing next to him, both lost in their own thoughts, and wondered how they would fare in the coming conflict.

"Am I doing the right thing?" Leandra said. "I'm sending an army against my own people. I thought I had come to terms with being a traitor, but now I don't know."

"You're trying to rid your world of a tyrant," Khan said. "One who has murdered thousands of innocents. If your people can see that, they'll lay down their arms."

"And if they can't?" she said. Khan had no answer for that. He suspected that no matter what Cyclone's people did the toll was going to be immense.

He wondered how they would reach their target. Once they were on the surface they were vulnerable. If they had to travel cross-country they could very well be picked off by Cyclone's rocketships. The Inkidu had already proven they could take down one of Cyclone's largest ships, but how would they fare against ten or twenty of them? There was only one way to do this and the Queen seemed to know this. Strike quickly and decisively. Hope for the best.

Khan hoped there was more to the plan than that.

Seeing the chaos of the troops from the palace was nothing compared to the insanity of being in the middle of it. They met Colonel Patrus at the palace entrance and even with his escort it took almost an hour to get to their transport.

Inside the giant vehicle wasn't much better. Though it was roomy, there were so many soldiers and so much equipment it quickly became cramped. Patrus found them seats and they buckled themselves in.

Once they were underway it was worse. The vehicles were designed for war, not comfort. They smelled of leaking fuel and close quarters. The vibrations from the engines threatened to shake Khan's teeth loose. He looked at his companions. Patrus read reports, Leandra looked worried. Bulls-Eye snored.

A few hours later the vehicle lurched to a stop, engines idle. "Here's where we get off," Patrus said. Khan picked his way past the soldiers and noticed they were the only ones exiting the vehicle. He asked Patrus why. "We're travelling in the flagship with the Queen. They're staying on the transport while it gets loaded."

"Loaded onto what?" Khan asked, stepping out of the vehicle. He stopped mid-step when he saw.

He had thought that the activity back in the Inkidu city was chaotic, but it was nothing compared to this. They had stopped at the shores of the Underground Ocean. Inkidu and K'kir soldiers crowded the beach, loading vehicles and supplies onto the K'kir fleet of submarines. So much commotion, so much noise.

Khan could see the similarities in the K'kir submarines to the Regent's escape sub that had brought them to the Inkidu's lands, but these were so much more. Where the Regent's sub was built for speed, these were built for battle. They were sleeker with heavy armor plating and were so much larger. Khan gawked at the immensity of the things. He watched transport after transport being lowered into the boats, each one disappearing into the cavernous cargo holds.

"This is how we're going to get past Cyclone's defenses," Patrus said. "Most of them, anyway. The Monatu have been harrying her borders with guerilla strikes. Cyclone has drawn off most of her troops from the city to deal with that. We'll come up as close to the city as we can and use that as a staging area for the strike. There's still a day's travel to reach it, but it will be much easier than trying to do it overland the whole way."

"Of course," Khan said, as they followed Patrus through the crowd. "Going overland all the way to Cyclone City would be suicide." Khan was heartened to hear that the K'kir and the Monatu had both joined with the Queen. If they were to win this she would need allies.

"That's why we're not doing it," Patrus said, giving Khan a wry smile. They stopped at the gangplank of a particularly ornate looking submarine. Like the others it was clearly built for war, but it was at least twice as large and painted with the royal seal of the K'kir.

"Permission to come aboard," Patrus yelled to the two K'kir guards at the top of the gangplank.

A familiar K'kir popped his head out of a nearby hatch and waved at them. "Yes, yes," the Regent said. "Come aboard. We've been waiting for you. War council, you know. We have much to discuss. Come on." He disappeared back inside the submarine.

"I'm glad the Regent was able to get safely back to his people," Khan said. They followed Patrus up the gangplank and into the submarine where they were escorted by guards to a conference room. The Queen and the Regent sat across from each other and against the far wall one of the K'kir viewing screens showed King Parsimal against a desert backdrop.

The Regent stood and grabbed Khan's hand, pumping it furiously. "So glad you found the Inkidu," he said. He turned to Bulls-Eye. "And even more happy that you didn't die."

"Not nearly as much as I am," Bulls-Eye said. "They took good care of me, your Highness. Thanks for getting me out of the palace in one piece."

"And you, young lady," the Regent said, turning to Leandra. "A Weather Witch. Well, I can understand why you kept it secret. I can't imagine your sister would have liked the competition. I'm glad to have you with us."

"Thank you, your Highness."

"I'm tearing up over here," Parsimal said over the view screen. "Really. This is very touching. Now are we going to have a war council? Because if not I'd really like to keep my people on the move. Some of us are actually fighting a battle out here."

"Oh, quit your whining, Parsimal," the Queen said. "We both know that if there was a threat you wouldn't have stopped moving. Quit grandstanding. Colonel Patrus, what's our situation?"

"We're almost loaded onto the K'kir boats," Patrus said. "We should be under way within the next two hours. Travel time is expected to be about two days."

"Excuse me," Khan said. "I understand that we'll be landing at a beach-head close to Cyclone City, but she has to at least suspect that we're on the move. Won't she have all possible landing points guarded?"

"Yes and no," the Queen said. "She's dedicated a sizable chunk of her army to pursue Parsimal's troops through the desert. Not enough to make this easy, but enough to make a difference. Good work on that, by the way, Parsimal."

"Hmph," he said. "Easy enough to do. Her armies are soft. They have numbers on their side, but not much else. And they don't know the terrain like we do."

"What about her rockets?" Khan asked.

Parsimal's face grew sour. "We're largely at a standstill on that front. Her initial attack on the city took out a considerable number of my fleet. We're using them as defensive air support and holding our own, but they have numbers on their side. If we lose many more we'll be switching our tactics and taking to the mountains."

"So there's that," the Queen said. "But you're right, Professor, she does have the openings to the Underground Ocean covered."

"So we're going to make our own," the Regent said. "We've identified several locations near Cyclone City where the ground above is relatively thin and close to the ocean's surface. We're going to blast through and deploy the Inkidu troops at that point."

"We'll still be about a day's travel from the city," the Queen said, "but the locations should be shielded well enough that by the time they notice it'll be too late."

"Fascinating," Khan said. "But what do we do when we get there?"

"Attack the city, of course," the Queen said.

"Just like that?" Khan said. "That's ludicrous. You'll be cut down in minutes."

"We expect about 60% casualties," Colonel Patrus said. "Cyclone has rocketships and the Alivons for air support. Though we have our own flying ships, they still outnumber us there. It's not ideal, but we should be able to breach the force field and take the city with the remaining soldiers."

"The Professor's right," Leandra said. "It won't work. The force field has multiple layers. Burn through one and another comes on-line to take its place. Then there are the defense cannons. You won't be able to take them all out. They'll burn through your soldiers."

"We know, but we don't have many options besides a frontal assault," the Queen said.

"The tunnels," Khan said. "Do they lead into the city itself? Particularly into the palace?"

"Yes," Leandra said. "They come up at several spots. But the Demon Dragon—"

"I done killed it," Bulls-Eye added, seeing the confusion on the assembled rulers' faces.

"There are a series of tunnels," Khan said, "that lead up into the city. We could go through there."

"We know about the tunnels," the Queen said. "But they're too small to move all of our troops through. Too much of a bottleneck. One strike at the right location and they'd all be killed."

"You don't need to send them all in," Leandra said. "The defense cannons and the force field are all controlled from the same location in the palace. You could send a small team in, take the control room, shut them down."

"What do you think, Colonel?" the Queen said.

"I think it might work. But we don't know where this control room is."

"I can draw you a map," Leandra said.

"I'd rather have a guide. Does anyone else know where it is?" He looked from Khan to Bulls-Eye.

"I can do it," Leandra said. "They don't know the city."

"You sure about this?" Bulls-Eye said. "Might be less dangerous staying outside."

"If I can bring down the defense cannons and make this quicker there will be less bloodshed all around."

"All right," he said. "I'll be right there with ya."

"So will I," Khan said.

"Oh, no you won't," the Queen said. "You're the Champion. The soldiers need to see you on the battlefield. There's no way you're going in there. Patrus, put together a team. We'll hold off the main assault until the Weather Witch gets those cannons down."

"Thank you, your majesty," Khan said. "This will work."

"I hope so," she said. "But if they fail we continue on with the original plan."

If they failed that meant they were dead. Khan left that thought unspoken and hoped he had not just condemned his friends to death.

CHAPTER TWENTY-FOUR
INTO THE DEN OF THE WEATHER WITCH!

Bulls-Eye sat on his bunk aboard the Regent's flagship flipping cards into his hat. He had gotten the deck from a K'kir cook who taught him a game very like poker earlier that night. He looked at the pile of coins and bills next to him and wondered what he was going to do with all the money he had won.

A soft knock on the door grabbed his attention. "Yeah?" he said. Leandra opened the door and peered inside.

"Hello," she said.

"Howdy."

Bulls-Eye hadn't seen much of her since they got underway. She was going over plans and maps with the Colonel, but he suspected she was avoiding him.

"May I come in?" she said.

"You still sore at me?"

"I—" She chewed her lip. "No. I was upset with myself."

"You got a funny way of yellin' at yourself, then." He picked up the pile of money off the bunk to make room for her and deposited it into his upended hat. "You wanna tell me about it?"

Leandra closed the door behind her and sat next to him. "I'm worried that I'll end up like my sister," she said.

"But you ain't her," he said.

She snapped her fingers and electricity sparked from them. "I'm getting more powerful," she said. "I can control it better. How do I know that this power won't make me like her?"

"Power don't work like that," Bulls-Eye said. "Sure, some folks get a taste of it and things go all pear-shaped, but that's because they already got a meanness in 'em. You ain't mean."

"I've betrayed my people and I'm sending troops against my own sister. How is that not mean?"

"You're doin' it to right wrongs, Leandra, not because you're tryin' to take over. Why, I don't think you even want to take her place as ruler, do you?"

"No," she said. "I'm terrified."

"Sure. And you should be. That ain't a job I could do. And it ain't gonna be easy. But that's exactly why you should do it, and why you ain't gonna turn into your sister. You don't want that power. You just wanna do the right thing."

"I hope you're right," she said.

"I am. And I'll be here to keep you on the straight and narrow." Bulls-Eye's heart hammered in his chest. Had he just said that?

Leandra smiled and took his hand. "I'd like that," she said. "Thank you." She leaned into him, exhausted. Bulls-Eye couldn't think of what to say, so he stayed silent and just enjoyed holding her hand.

Throughout the trip, as Bulls-Eye worked on the assault plan with Leandra and Colonel Patrus, Khan delivered radio address after radio address to the troops in the other submarines. Inspiring speeches that rivaled old FDR himself, and Bulls-Eye had no doubt that Khan had written those speeches himself. If things worked out and they got back home in one piece, Bulls-Eye was going to talk to him about running for office.

The submarines broke through the crust the next day with torpedoes launched from far enough away that the cave-ins left them unscathed.

Bulls-Eye could feel the submarine quake as the explosions traveled through the water. He hadn't been happy about being stuck in a big metal tube with the weight of all that water pressing down on him, but Leandra's presence and the focus demanded of their planning took his mind off the worst of it. Soon enough they were through and on solid ground and it was time to get moving.

"We're giving your team a headstart to get into position," Colonel Patrus said. Bulls-Eye stood with Leandra and a dozen Inkidu commandos in the submarine's briefing room. Instead of the heavy plate armor worn by the other Inkidu soldiers, the commandos wore thick leather armor. What they lacked in protection they made up for in stealth.

"You can move faster than we can," Patrus continued, "and once we begin offloading troops and equipment it won't be long before Cyclone's people spot us. We'll be at their gates before she'll be able to bring the brunt of her forces to bear, so we think she'll fall back to defend the city. But if they spot you coming you won't get very far."

He handed Bulls-Eye a small radio with a red button and light on its front. "When we're in position we'll signal you to begin. This light will come on. Once you've secured the control room, hit the button. That will be our signal to begin the assault."

"We'll have it all wrapped up in a bow for ya," Bulls-Eye said, slipping the radio into his pocket.

"As long as it's done quickly. After we give our signal, you won't have much time to bring down that forcefield and shut down those guns. Then you place the charges and blow up the control room. Any questions?"

The team had been over the plan a dozen times in the last two days. If anyone had questions now, Bulls-Eye thought, they were in big trouble. "All right, then," Patrus said. "Good luck."

Bulls-Eye and Leandra filed out of the briefing room with the commandos to see Khan waiting for them. "Perfesser," Bulls-Eye said. "Ain't you supposed to be givin' rousin' speeches to the troops?"

"I don't think I could rouse anyone," Khan said. "I know you're going to be heading out soon and I wanted to say goodbye before you went."

"You're makin' it sound all final like," Bulls-Eye said. "Ain't a one of us gonna get hurt out there. Ya hear?"

"Agreed," Khan said. "I'll let you two get to it. God speed and good luck."

"And you, Perfesser," Bulls-Eye said.

They left Khan in the corridor, and Bulls-Eye wondered if he would ever see him again.

It felt too easy. Avoiding the patrols was a snap. Even hiding the transport and getting into the tunnels beneath the city had been simple. The assault team wound their way through the caverns to the passage that would take them inside the palace without opposition. The feeling that things were going too well nagged at Bulls-Eye. As they rounded a corner he realized he was right.

"Cave in?" Bulls-Eye said, looking at the pile of rubble blocking their path. "Was there an earthquake?"

The commando's leader examined the blockage and shook his head. "Deliberate. They blew the passage from above."

"Can we climb it?" Leandra said.

"We're going to have to," the commando leader said. "It's going to take us hours to get up there, though. And there's no telling if the passage will be blocked off when we get there."

"I don't think we're gonna have time for that," Bulls-Eye said, pulling the radio Patrus had given him from his pocket. The light on its front was blinking on and off as it began beeping. "Clock's tickin'. We got ourselves an hour to figure this out and get up there."

"The gravity chutes," Leandra said. She turned to the commando. "Cyclone has pits scattered throughout the palace that all lead down here. Some of them have trapdoors but most are open pits. She uses them to throw prisoners down. They all lead here. We might be able to get up one of those."

"Won't we have the same problem as climbin' up?" Bulls-Eye said.

"They have force fields built into them to slow the prisoners. She didn't want them dying from the fall. She wanted them to be eaten. If we can reverse them we can use them to ride up into the palace."

"Is there one near the control room?" Bulls-Eye said.

"There's one in every room of the palace."

"Your sister's got issues."

"Tell me about it. Come on."

It didn't take long to find the gravity chutes in the cavern ceiling. They yawned above them, the lights ringing its length glowing a dim blue. They hummed quietly. After a few minutes of matching the locations against Leandra's hand-drawn map they were reasonably sure they had the right one. The commandos fanned out looking for a control panel, or an equipment box.

After kicking over a rock and seeing a series of cables poking up from the dirt, Bulls-Eye followed them to a rock nearby that proved to be hollow. He found a hidden catch that popped the front of the rock open on hinges revealing wires and blinking vacuum tubes.

The commandos clustered around the equipment, looking it over, arguing about which cables to re-route, which switches to throw. They cut and spliced wires, swapped vacuum tubes. At the flipping of the switch, the humming of the gravity chute changed pitch and the lights went from blue to green.

"Did it work?" Leandra said.

"Only one way to find out," Bulls-Eye said and before Leandra could stop him he stepped into the space beneath the chute. He felt a gentle tug at first and then he shot up into the air at blinding speed. He grabbed hold of his Stetson to keep it on his head and in a moment he found himself hovering in a room of the palace.

A room filled to bursting with Thavasian soldiers. They stared at him, slack-jawed.

"Howdy," he said, drawing his guns and firing wildly into the crowd. He dove out of the chute's gravity field and tucked into a roll, coming up to fire more shots. Soldiers dropped, some ran to grab their weapons. Bulls-Eye felled two that ran toward a button on the wall that he figured had to be an alarm.

With the soldiers focused on him, they didn't notice the Inkidu commandos come up behind them. Within seconds the fight was over.

"Well, we're up," Bulls-Eye said. "Now let's go find that control room."

CHAPTER TWENTY-FIVE
WAR AND BETRAYAL!

Cyclone's forces spotted the caravan of Inkidu soldiers late in the day. There were a few half-hearted rocketship bombardments, some minor attacks by winged Alivon scouts. The caravan returned fire, but kept going.

"They're testing our strength," the Queen said. She, Khan and Colonel Patrus stood on the observation deck atop a transport in the middle of the caravan. For the most part there had been little to do but continue traveling. The Queen had ordered returning fire, but didn't want to show their strength too quickly. The result had been one of the rockets downed, another sent on its way and over a dozen Alivon scouts taken out.

"The attacks are going to get more intense as we get closer," Khan said. "How long before we're at the staging site?"

"At this speed, no more than a couple of hours," Colonel Patrus said. "But we can stage from anywhere at this point should we have to. Once we deploy we'll be moving more quickly."

Khan felt a change in the air. The temperature seemed to drop quickly. His ears popped. He knew this feeling. Had felt this before in the desert.

Cyclone.

He turned to warn Patrus and the Queen but they were already moving. "Deploy the disruptors!" Patrus yelled into his radio as the Queen strode to the front of the observation deck and struck a pose. It was as if she was daring Cyclone's storms to seek her out.

"Are you mad?" Khan asked, running to her. "We've got to get inside. You'll be killed once Cyclone lets her storm loose. I watched it tear through desert. It laid waste to everything in its path."

"You forget, Professor," she said. "I've seen it before. Many times. Colonel?"

"Almost there," he said. "Only half of the disruptors are in place. Another minute."

Khan watched the sky darken on the horizon. Thick clouds congealed out of nothing and lightning shot through them like brilliant threads of flame.

Below them the transport vehicles deployed struts with spikes that dug deep into the ground to hold them in place. After seeing the fury that Cyclone could unleash Khan couldn't believe that they would hold.

As the struts were locking in place, Khan could see strange antennae popping up from trap doors on the hulls of the transports, each topped with a large crystal that began to emit a deep, throbbing hum.

"Wish us luck, Professor," the Queen said. "We've only tried this in a laboratory before. Oh, and you might want to hang onto something."

The winds picked up and soon they were a howling gale. They tore up dirt from the desert, turning it into thick sheets of impenetrable sand. Khan squinted, but there was no way to see through the all-enveloping dust.

Any moment now, Khan knew, the lightning would strike and it would all be over. The hum of the Inkidu devices grew and soon they were louder than the hurricane force winds. Khan clapped his hands over his ears as they rose in pitch.

With a sudden burst of sound louder than any thunderclap, the devices fired bright, green beams of light into the air. They met the cloud cover and even through the haze of dust and grit Khan could see them tangle with the arcs of lightning high above.

It was like watching sea serpents fight. The beams from the Inkidu devices twisted and surrounded the lightning, changing the hellish, red sky into a deep, sea green. The beams sliced through the cloud cover and in minutes there was nothing left but a clear sky and a heavy lattice of green light in a dome above the Inkidu troops.

"You know, I wasn't entirely sure that would work," the Queen said.

"What just happened?" Khan said.

"We've nullified Cyclone's powers. Out here on the battlefield, at least. Patrus, how long before the ionization effect wears off?"

"If we shut it down now, at least six hours," the Colonel said.

"Excellent," the Queen said. "That's one pain in the butt out of the way. We stage from here. Any closer and we'll be contending with the city's guns before we deploy. Send the signal to the strike team and start the countdown. We launch the attack in an hour."

"What if the guns aren't down?" Khan said.

"Then this is going to be a much bloodier war than you'd hoped."

Khan stood on the top of the Queen's transport, looking out over the troops, the Queen and Patrus by his side. The Queen gave Patrus orders, who relayed them through the radio.

Troops passed ammunition, loaded guns on vehicles. Khan watched soldiers unload a series of circular platforms with two seats each and cannons mounted to the sides.

"What are those?" Khan asked the Queen.

"Gyro-platforms," she said. "We'll be using them against the Alivons and Cyclone's rockets."

Khan watched pilots belt into a dozen of them and start them up. Sparks erupted underneath and they floated into the air with a sound like an electric razor. Amid all the preparations for war, watching these soldiers get ready for a battle they might not return from, Khan was hit with a sudden feeling of uselessness. What was he doing here? What purpose did he have in all this? He was supposed to be their Prophecy come to life. And all he could do was stand there and watch.

No, he thought. There was something he could do. "I need to speak with the troops," he said.

"Patrus," the Queen said, "patch him into the loudspeakers."

Patrus gave Khan a sidelong look. "Everyone is a little busy," he said. "Your Majesty."

"Nonsense," the Queen said. She stared Patrus down for his sudden insubordination and he quickly relented. He handed the radio to Khan, and pressed a button. A squeal of feedback burst from speaker on every troop transport.

"Champion," Patrus said, his voice a hint of contempt that Khan hadn't noticed before. "You're on."

"Thank you." Khan thought a moment and then thumbed the talk button and spoke.

"Warriors of the Inkidu," he said. "For many years you have endured much, the attacks upon your people, the privations, the horrors. Today that ends. Today you rise up against your enemies. Today, your skill, your hope, your dreams of a better future will be realized. Today you will make them rue the day they dared, yes, DARED to attack you! You will crush them beneath your feet, lay waste to their lands. You will tear them to pieces with your teeth and feast upon their entrails! Today, you shall devour their very souls and send them STRAIGHT TO HELL!"

Khan finished, his breath coming in ragged gasps, his mind filled with visions of fire and conquest. Slowly, in the yawning silence, Khan came back to himself. What had he said? What had he done? Had he taken his one chance to be of use to these people and thrown it away?

A cheer erupted from the soldiers assembled below, chanting "Khan! Khan! Khan!" until it was nothing but a roar, a terrible sound that promised vengeance upon Princess Cyclone.

"Good job," the Queen said at his shoulder. "You're much better at this than I think you realize."

Khan felt himself blush. "I— You see— There's—," he said.

"You really need to let yourself go sometimes," the Queen said. "You don't stammer quite so much." She took the radio from his hand, thumbed the button.

"My people," she said into the microphone and the crowd went silent. "You have heard the words of your Champion, now hear mine. You have trained for this day for many years. You have sacrificed so much to reach this point. Go forth and take back what is yours! Onward! To victory!"

The Queen grasped Khan's hand and raised it with her own for everyone to see. Every soldier, every officer, every mechanic, loader, cook and driver cheered.

Bulls-Eye kicked the control room door in, guns drawn, and quickly took stock. Eight guards, twelve technicians manning stations with large viewscreens, dotted around the room. They looked up from their displays, surprise freezing them in place.

That wouldn't last long, though, and Bulls-Eye didn't give them a chance. He dropped three guards in less than a second with a flurry of stun shots, and rolled out of the way to draw fire. The technicians were screaming, trying to hide beneath their stations.

As the guards focused on him, Leandra stepped into the room. Lightning crackled between her fingers and with a flick of her wrist, she sent bolts of electricity into the remaining guards. They stood a brief moment, jerking and suspended in a web of lightning, before falling to the ground, smoking and unconscious.

"Secure the door," the commando leader said, bringing his troops into the room. "Round up the technicians." He gave the Priestess a sour look. "It would be easier if you'd let us kill them."

"Whether you like it or not, these are my people. I would avoid unnecessary bloodshed."

"Fair enough," he said. He turned to his soldiers who had already tied up the guards and were working on the technicians. "Let's get these guns and that forcefield down. Now."

The Inkidu commandos went about their work with efficiency. It didn't take them long before they had the door barricaded and the city's defenses under their control.

"We're good to go," the commando leader said.

Bulls-Eye thumbed the switch on his radio to signal the troops that the defenses were down. The light on its front blinked red.

"Well, that's that," Bulls-Eye said.

"All right, everyone," the leader said, opening his backpack. "Let's get these charges in place and—"

The control room door blew open with a sound like thunder, filling the room with smoke. The edges of the frame glowed white hot. Thavasian soldiers poured through the opening only to fall as the commandos unloaded their rayguns. The Thavasian soldiers on the other side of the door gave as good as they got. Five commandos dropped in the first volley. Bulls-Eye fired blindly through the opening, his vision obscured by the smoke rapidly filling the room.

The Thavasian soldiers stopped firing. A moment passed with nothing but the sound of Inkidu rayguns. And then lightning filled the room. Arcs of electricity danced through the control room in a devastating chain. Commandos fell, others stood long enough to keep firing their weapons even as the lightning wrapped around them, setting them ablaze. Not even Cyclone's own people, the technicians and guards, were safe from the onslaught.

Leandra threw herself against Bulls-Eye and unleashed her power in a protective net, narrowly keeping him from the same fate. The invading lightning cascaded off of her shield.

"We've got to get out of here," she said. "I'm not strong enough to fight my sister." Beads of sweat broke out along her forehead and Bulls-Eye could see that protecting them was taking a toll on her already.

Bulls-Eye looked around frantically for any exit. There was just the one door and there were no windows. His eyes fell on a large grate near the floor.

"Down here," he said, pulling her toward the grate. They knelt near the ground. She held her shield up to protect him as he yanked the cover off, revealing a large vent. It was low, but wide enough for both of them to crawl through side by side.

When he had the cover off, he backed into it, and she followed. Her shield slipped a little and a stray streak of lightning bounced around, striking the radio in Bulls-Eye's hand and burning a hole through his hat. He yanked it off his head and frowned at the smoldering hole.

"Sorry," she said.

"Like I ain't never got a bullet-hole in a hat before. Least I still got a head."

Once she was inside with him, he pulled the cover back until it clicked in place. They crawled backward through the duct, Leandra keeping her shield in place until they were far enough that Cyclone's lightning attack no longer reached them. They waited, listening. Soon they heard bootsteps and then a voice they both dreaded.

"Ugh," Cyclone said. "The stink of burning traitors. Get these guns back on."

"And the force-field, your highness?" one of her soldiers said.

"We'll wait," she said. "We don't want them thinking we have control just yet."

Bulls-Eye checked the radio in his hand. Smoke drifted lazily from it where the lightning had struck it. The red light on its front blinked, sputtered, and died. He clicked the button a few times, but nothing happened.

Bulls-Eye and Leandra looked at each other, the same thought in their minds. They had no way to signal the army outside of what had happened. If they didn't get those guns turned back off, Khan and the troops outside were all going to die.

"Ready to lead from the front, Champion?" the Queen said.

"Excuse me?" Khan said. Below him he watched as the Inkidu vehicles lurched into motion, the gyroplatforms took to the skies. Thousands of Inkidu troops on the move, making the ground thunder, the skies darken.

"You didn't think this was going to be all fancy speeches did you?"

"Well, there was that bit with the gladiatorial combat, but I had hoped, yes."

"The arena's fun and all, I suppose, but this is war." She slapped him on the back hard enough to almost knock him over. "The people need to know you're with them."

"Did you get the signal that the guns were down?"

"Not yet. If the commandos come through we'll press our advantage. And if they don't—"

"We'll die. And this will all be for nothing."

"There are more things to contend with than just those guns," the Queen said.

"They'll chew up your troops."

"This is war, Professor, not school. Not theory. This is the blood and the smoke and the fire. Whether they bring those guns down or not we will take losses. It's what happens in war. We knew what we were going up against. Do I want to lose my warriors? No. Will I let them die to save their people? A thousand times, yes."

Khan sighed and hung his head. He knew she was right. Whether the guns came down or not the Inkidu were going to fight. A sense of unease settled into the pit of Khan's stomach.

"I don't like it any more than you, Khan. Less. These are my people. I wept for them when they died at Cyclone's hands years ago. I will weep for those who fall today. But I will be damned if I let them die without fighting."

"What do you need me to do?"

"Be visible. Be a symbol." She showed him a grin full of ferocity. "And if you can grab a gun and kill a few enemy soldiers even better."

The troops thundered across the plains toward Cyclone City and Khan watched as the city gates opened and disgorged a horde of silver clad soldiers. Rocketships and Alivon soldiers lifted off from the city as the Inkidu gyro-platforms sped up to intercept them.

They met with a clash of fire. Bolts of gunfire erupted from each side. The gyroplatforms zipped among the slower, more bulky rockets, hammering them. Rockets fell, gyroplatforms exploded, Alivon soldiers plummeted from the sky. The sound was deafening.

"We'll be engaging the ground troops in a few minutes, Your Highness," Colonel Patrus yelled. His voice was swallowed up by the battle overhead.

"How long before we're in range of the guns?" she asked.

"About ten minutes."

"And have you received the signal that they've been shut down?"

"Not yet," he said. He showed her the radio he held in his hand. "I don't think—" Suddenly the bulb on the radio lit up with a bright, red glow.

"I stand corrected. The guns are down, Your Highness."

"And the force field?"

Patrus looked through his binoculars at the city in the distance. Even without his own binoculars Khan could see that the telltale glow of the city's forcefield had vanished.

"It's off."

"Excellent. We now have a clear line into the city. Looks like your friends came through, Professor."

The Inkidu and Cyclone forces hammered at each other. Khan watched from the top of his transport, his heart hammering in his chest. He cringed every time he saw an Inkidu warrior engage, cried out when one went down, cheered when one brought low a Thavasian soldier.

The Queen fired into the air with wild abandon, bringing down flying Alivon soldiers like they were ducks during hunting season. Every few seconds she would aim down at the battle raging beneath them and pop off a few shots at the Thavasians engaged against her own armies on the ground.

Khan, on the other hand, tried shooting down Alivon warriors with a raygun as they swooped in, but his aim was so bad he didn't hit a thing.

The Inkidu were berserker warriors fighting for their homes, survival and revenge. They swarmed over Cyclone's soldiers like a massive tidal wave. A boiling sea of blue, gorilla vengeance. For every loss they took, Cyclone's soldiers took five. They advanced inexorably toward the city.

It was terrible to watch, but even amongst all the carnage, Khan couldn't help but feel proud of these people. He wasn't just a political pawn or a figurehead for them to latch their hopes onto. They would win this battle. They would win this war. And he had played a part in their victory.

And then the city's defense turrets kicked in.

Guns along the walls of the city sprang to life. They twisted in their mounts to bear down on the battle approaching the city and spewed fiery death across the land. Khan watched helpless as fire blasted indiscriminately through the battlefield, taking out both Inkidu and Cyclone soldiers and leaving behind smoking craters. The machines tracked anything that moved, chewed up huge swaths of the ground, blasting Inkidu vehicles to pieces.

"I thought those guns were down," the Queen said, growling.

If the guns were back then Bulls-Eye and Leandra were likely dead, a thought Khan let linger for just a moment before pushing it aside. There was no time for mourning now.

It was then that he knew that these were his people.

"It doesn't matter," Khan said, shocked at the words coming from his mouth. But he knew they were true. "We have to press ahead."

"A change of heart, Professor?" Colonel Patrus said.

"It's too late to turn back. We have to move forward. If we don't press on we'll never recover enough strength to try again."

"Exactly my thinking," the Queen said. She turned to Colonel Patrus. "I want you to—"

"No, I don't think I'll be taking any more orders from you," Patrus said. He leveled his gun at her chest.

"What are you doing?" the Queen said, her voice dripping acid. "Treason, Patrus?"

"I'm saving our people, Your Highness. You've gotten us this far but I'm afraid your time is over. Don't worry, you and your Champion will be remembered for your valiant, but ultimately fruitless fight against the enemy."

"I'll eat your heart, you traitor," she said and launched herself at Patrus. Patrus pulled the trigger, but the Queen dodged and the shot flew over her shoulder. She barreled into him, but he twisted and threw her to the side. He raised his pistol to finish her off.

Khan snapped. His vision went red and all he could hear was the blood rushing through his veins. Thought, doubt, and fear disappeared to be replaced by an all-encompassing rage.

Khan launched himself at Patrus, tearing the gun out of his hand. The Colonel beat his fists against Khan but nothing could deter the rage that seethed through Khan's veins. Khan tore into him with an uppercut, and then followed with a hammer fist that drove the Colonel to the floor. Khan punched him over and over again, the Colonel's defenses useless against the onslaught.

"Khan!" the Queen yelled. "Don't kill him."

Khan paused, recognizing her voice but he couldn't make out the words. His mind was a chaotic mess of broken, rage-fueled thoughts.

"It's all right, Khan. Let him live. I have questions—" Before she could finish her sentence a blast of gunfire arced down from one of the city's cannons and hit the transport.

The blast blew out the treads, sending shredded steel high into the air. The transport bucked, rocked to one side, tilted violently. The Queen was thrown against the edge. Khan leapt to her, panic cutting through the anger, but it was too late. She toppled over the side, disappearing into the fire and smoke below.

Khan leaned over the side, searching for her but it was no use. There was too much smoke and fire was already beginning to crawl up the side of the transport. He pulled himself up, prepared to leap but stopped when he heard Patrus' laughter.

"Do it. Throw yourself over the side, Champion. Make my life easier. With both of you gone I'll lead this battle to victory."

Khan turned, thought slowly coming back to him. The Colonel was lying on his side, broken and bloody. His breath came out in short gasps. Khan was horrified at what he had done to him.

"I don't think you'll live long enough," Khan said. A sickening thought came to him. If Khan went over the side to search for the Queen there would be no one here to give orders to the troops.

And the Inkidu would be slaughtered.

Khan struggled against it, but he knew what he had to do. Knew what she would want him to do. And he hated himself for it.

Khan stepped past the dying Colonel to the radio. Someone had to win this war, and he was the only one left to do it.

"You switched the beasts in the arena," Khan said, as he checked over the radio. It had taken a little damage from the cannons, but not much. He thumbed the talk button a few times to make sure it worked.

"My job was to be as trusted as I could," Patrus said. He coughed up blood. "And when you didn't die in the arena I was to shadow you and look for a convenient opportunity to kill you."

"You should have waited longer," Khan said. He thumbed the button, hoped he knew what he was doing, that no one would question him. For a moment he wondered if his progenitor, Gorilla Khan, felt like this. If he had ever had doubts.

Probably not. But still, here was Khan. In command of an invading army. Just like the ape that had come before him.

"This is Khan to the gyros," he said. "Break off from the rockets. Hit those defense cannons. At least three on each one. They can't hit all of you."

"They'll never follow you," Patrus said, quietly and then stared as a long string of affirmatives called in through the radio.

In the sky the gyros broke off their attack and headed out toward the defense cannons. It left the battle being waged on the ground without air cover, but Khan hoped that the pilots in the rocketships had more concerns about killing their own men on the ground than the people manning those cannons.

"I don't think anyone's listening to you, anymore, Colonel," Khan said and began shouting orders into the radio.

CHAPTER TWENTY-SIX
BATTLE OF THE WEATHER WITCHES!

"We can't just sit here," Bulls-Eye said. "Them cannons ain't gonna shut off by themselves."

"And how do you expect us to survive against Cyclone?" Leandra said. "She almost killed you last time."

"Like I don't know that. This time we got surprise on our side and we got you."

"I can't take her on. She's too powerful."

"How do you know that? You said yourself that you've gotten more power and you're controllin' it better. And you kept us alive when everybody else was gettin' all electrified. We get in there, we hit 'em fast and we get them guns back."

"We'll never survive."

"I ain't gonna lie to ya," Bulls-Eye said. "I don't think we're gonna get outta this alive no how. Don't matter if we go after them guns or not."

Leandra fell silent, deep in thought. "All right," she said. "You go after the soldiers. I'll take care of my sister."

They crawled their way back to the vent grating and listened. Targets were being called out, kills counted. Bulls-Eye squinted to see through the grate, but he couldn't see anything useful. An occasional boot, but that was all. From the voices there were at least six people in the room, possibly more. But if Cyclone was among them he couldn't hear her.

"She in there?" he whispered.

"I don't know."

"All right. You get behind me. I'll turn around here, kick the grate out and you shove me. When I get out I'll start blastin'."

"That's a terrible plan."

"You got yourself a better one?" he asked.

"No."

"Then hush up and get behind me."

Leandra did what he asked, giving him the room he needed to maneuver into place. Bulls-Eye pressed his boots against the grate, drew his guns and kicked.

The grate popped out and Leandra shoved him hard. He slid the rest of the way out of the vent and came up with both guns blazing. Thavasian soldiers dropped before they could even go for their guns, falling over their consoles.

Leandra slid out of the vent. By that time Bulls-Eye had taken out all the soldiers before they even had a chance to look surprised. There was no sign of Cyclone.

"You know how to shut them guns off?" Bulls-Eye said.

"How about like this?" Leandra said. She shot arcs of lightning from her fingertips at the nearest console until it began to smoke.

"Well, heck, if we're gonna do it that way, let's do it right." Bulls-Eye knelt down and rolled over the body of the fallen commando leader, his skin and fur patchy and scorched black from gunfire, and picked up the satchel of explosives.

"I was wondering when you were going to show your face," Cyclone said. "Traitor." She stood at the door, glowing from the electricity that danced along her skin and fed into the silver filigree crown atop her head.

"Sister," Leandra said. Lightning sprang from her fingers and flowed up her arms.

"I see you've found new power," Cyclone said. "Too bad it happened when you weren't here. I could have trained you. Taught you how to use it properly."

"You mean kill me. After you murdered everyone else you think I could ever trust you?"

"It didn't have to be that way. They didn't have to defy me and you know it. I saved you because I knew you had power."

Leandra let loose a burst of lightning at her sister. The arcs were met with Cyclone's own lightning bolts. Their powers tangled, fighting for the upper hand. Leandra struggled, but held her own. Cyclone grimaced from the effort.

Bulls-Eye ducked behind a console and watched as the two Weather Witches battled. Stray lightning coursed through the room, shattering consoles, burning gaping pits through the walls.

Leandra was struggling, and though Cyclone was clearly feeling the strain, he had no doubt that she was more powerful. He popped up from cover and fired a flurry of bolts at her.

They hit the arcs of electricity passing between the two Weather Witches and fizzled. There was too much power there for his shots to get through. They didn't even get her attention. He ducked back down as lightning arced overhead. His guns were useless, but he had to help Leandra somehow.

He had an idea. It was crazy and stupid, and the only way they were going to survive would be if he had his timing down right. And got really, really lucky.

He crawled to a spot where he could get a better shot, and one where he could get to Leandra as quickly as possible. Bulls-Eye stood quickly, yelling, "Hey, crazy lightnin' lady! Catch!" and threw the commando's satchel of explosives at Cyclone's head.

The moment the satchel left his hand he launched himself at Leandra, tackling her. They slid along the floor behind one of the consoles as Cyclone's lightning and the satchel met.

The blast was deafening. The console took the brunt, but shock waves hammered at Bulls-Eye like an angry mule. Smoke filled the room and heat washed over him. He tried to hold on, but unconsciousness swept up and claimed him.

The cannons fell silent. The gyroplatform attack had been working, but they had only managed to take down about a third of the cannons. But then one second they were blasting merrily away and the next they were frozen in place.

Khan had been directing troops through the radio atop his blazing transport for the last ten minutes, ordering them to attack the Cyclone army ground vehicles. Next to the defense cannons those were the biggest threat. He had been right about the hesitance of the Thavasian rocket pilots to take out their own people, but the ground vehicles didn't seem to share the same concern. They had a clearer line of sight and better accuracy. The Inkidu were doing reasonably well against them, but not well enough. But now the city's cannons were out of the game. Whether it was temporary or not Khan couldn't tell, but he knew an opportunity when he saw one.

"All gyros break off from the cannons and get on those ground vehicles. Squadrons two and four hit those rockets." A litany of Rogers and Affirmatives came over the radio and he watched as the platforms zipped down to the field or further up into the sky.

And through it all he had kept the army moving closer and closer to the walls. Now it was time to press the advantage even further. "Ground commanders, I want that gate down now."

Beneath him the soldiers broke off and swarmed the gates. They tore through the Cyclone soldiers like they were paper. In minutes they were at the wall, setting charges to blow open the gates.

And then something even stranger than the guns going silent happened. The gates opened.

"Hold off," Khan said into the radio. "Do not engage." Not until he knew what was going on, at least. He looked through his binoculars at the slowly opening gates. Were more troops coming out? Was this another one of Cyclone's devastating weapons?

When the gates finally opened Khan's jaw dropped. Thavasian citizens, thousands of them, crowded the gates. And they were all waving white flags.

"What's going on down there?" Khan said. He watched several of the Inkidu soldiers slowly approach and speak with members of the crowd.

"They want to surrender, sir," said a voice over the radio. "They say Cyclone's dead."

Above him the few remaining rockets began to land and the Alivon warriors, perhaps sensing that the tide had turned against them, disengaged and flew off in droves. The remaining Cyclone soldiers on the battlefield all laid down their weapons.

"My god," Khan said. "We've won."

CHAPTER TWENTY-SEVEN
VICTORY!

The battlefield was a nightmare of torched bodies, wrecked vehicles. The burning stink of death filled the air. The Martian sands were soaked red and green with the blood of the fallen. Khan wandered through the wreckage of the field looking for survivors, looking for the Queen.

The army was still securing the city. Though most of the soldiers and civilians had surrendered, there were still holdouts. At last report they had taken ninety percent of the city and he had crews working to clear debris in the palace. From what he had heard the control room had exploded with Cyclone in it. Of Bulls-Eye, Leandra, and the commandos, though, there was no word.

His search team, one of many, was fifty strong and they followed him unquestioningly through the debris of the battlefield. Even the generals who had been under the Queen's command were listening to him. He had told them as soon the fighting had ended what had happened to the Queen. He had assumed that as soon as the battle was over the generals would stand together and assume command of the army. But no one did.

His left arm was bandaged. One of the medics had outfitted him with a sling and told him he needed to keep the arm immobile, but once the doctors were out of sight he threw it away.

He wondered if there was some sort of line of succession he hadn't been aware of that somehow put him in charge. He hoped not. A ruler's life was an unhappy and often short one. One conqueror ape in the family was enough, thank you very much.

He told himself that that was cause of his urgency, the panic that filled him even now after the fighting was done. But a part of him knew that it was a lie.

They had been searching for the better part of three hours now and there had been no sign of the Queen. They were concentrating on the site where the transport had been hit. If she had fallen to her death then and there they should have found her. Not finding her body had actually given Khan hope.

The sun was beginning to dip toward the horizon and he ordered that lights be distributed to the team. He wouldn't let something as minor as a lack of light stop the search. He would find her. End of story.

As the hours wound on and Mars' twin moons rose his hope faded. He clung to the fact that there had been no sign of her to keep him going, but even that was beginning to falter.

As they neared the far edge of the battle one of his search team cried out in alarm. Khan rushed toward the sound, pushing everyone out of his way. Was she alive? "Did you find her?" Khan asked. "Is she all right?"

Dozens of soldiers surrounded the wreck of a fallen rocket, all working to get a section of one of its wings up off the ground. The soldiers heaved the piece up and others scurried beneath it, coming out a moment later dragging Queen Deena along with them. The soldiers let the rocket's wing down once she was clear.

Khan loped forward. The Queen was covered in dirt, soot, and small cuts. Patches of her fur had been burned away. One of the medics popped a vial of smelling salts under her nose and her eyes fluttered open and locked on Khan's.

"We won," she said.

"We did," he said. He wanted to grab her, wanted to lift her high and spin her around, he was so happy. But she was royalty and his staunch British manners wouldn't allow for such a display. A thousand things popped into his head to say, and after a moment he settled on a safe, "How are you feeling?"

"Like I was blown up, thrown into a battle and had to fight for my life. You?"

"Like I was betrayed by a trusted advisor and had to win a war all by myself," Khan said. "I'm glad you're all right."

She smiled at him. "Likewise. I watched you for a while; saw the change in the attacks. You did well. Patrus?"

"In custody. He'll live." Though Khan had expected more treachery from him, the Colonel had fallen unconscious. He was locked up and under guard in the back of a transport.

"Good. I'll deal with him later."

"What happened to you?" Khan said.

"There was no point in getting back to the transport. You were doing fine. So I joined the fight. Or it joined me. It's all a bit of a blur." She tilted her head toward the fallen rocketship. "Took that one down myself."

"How?"

"Good looks and tenacity," she said. She shook away the soldiers checking her wounds. "I'm fine. Just let me stand up."

"You're not fine," Khan said. "You're injured."

"Yes, but now that I'm back you're not in charge anymore so everyone has to listen to me," she said. She stood on unsteady feet, held tight to Khan's hand.

"Yes, about that," he said. "Why were they listening to me?"

"You're the Champion," she said.

"But what about your generals? What about your advisors?"

"Oh," she said, a wide grin spreading across her face. "Didn't I tell you? The Champion is also the Royal Consort. They have to listen to you. Now let's get into the city and see where things stand."

Khan stared, dumb-founded as she barked orders and marched, regally, if with a slight limp, toward Cyclone City.

"I was sure we was goners, Perfesser," Bulls-Eye said, shifting his weight on his crutches. He had a cast on his left leg and a bandage covered one eye. The doctors weren't sure if he would lose the eye, but the leg would heal just fine. It had been a clean break. Leandra stood not far off speaking with the Queen. Though slightly bruised with some scratches, she appeared none the worse for wear.

"We couldn't have done this without you," Khan said.

"Aw, heck, Perfesser, you'd have done just fine without us." He pointed to the bandage covering his eye. "Heck, I kinda wish ya had."

Khan had been so occupied with the recovery efforts on the battlefield that it had been more than a day before he got the news that Bulls-Eye and Leandra were all right.

A frown crossed Khan's face. He had been hearing troubling rumors since he had gotten to the palace. "Did they find any sign of Cyclone's body?"

Bulls-Eye shook his head. "And that's got me worried. So far we got that news under wraps, but if word gets out this whole thing could blow up. We don't know who's still loyal to Cyclone." Khan knew of the sporadic fighting still happening within the city. Amazingly, many of the Cyclone soldiers and civilians had joined up with the Inkidu troops to take the city. The Weather Witch had had few friends.

"Perhaps the explosion vaporized her?" Khan said, hope in his voice.

"And left me and Leandra in one piece? Not hardly." Bulls-Eye cast a glance back at the new ruler of Cyclone City. "You think they'll follow her?"

"I don't know," Khan said. "I think there's a good chance of it. The people know her. They know what she's done to free them of Cyclone."

"I hope so. I don't want to see no harm come to her. That reminds me. I been wantin' to ask you somethin'."

"Of course," Khan said.

"Well," Bulls-Eye said, "it's like this—"

Before Bulls-Eye could finish his sentence a soldier ran into the hallway demanding to see the Queen. Khan watched with dread as the soldier frantically relayed information to her. They were too far away for Khan to hear their words, but the soldier kept pointing at him and Bulls-Eye.

"Oh, what have we gotten ourselves into this time," Khan said.

A few minutes of this and the Queen dismissed the soldier who ran back toward the entrance to the palace, throwing worried glances at Khan.

The Queen and Leandra approached. The Queen's face was grim, Leandra's creased with worry.

"Who wants to kill us now?" Bulls-Eye asked them.

"No one," the Queen said, an odd expression on her face. "We have," she paused, looking for the word, "guests," she said, finally.

"That sounds ominous," Khan said.

"Well, I'm not crazy about it," she said, "though you might feel differently. Come with me, they're in the courtyard."

"I'm telling you, it's not possible," Edison said, running a hand nervously through his thinning hair. He sat in the back seat of the boxy Chevy Carryall, occasionally pulling out a small, metallic box, pressing a button on it and frowning when the little light on the top glowed green.

"I'm sure there's a perfectly reasonable explanation for it, Edison," Benjamin said. He stood leaning against the hood of the car parked in the elaborate courtyard of an enormous palace watching the crowd of armored, blue-furred gorillas surrounding them. They were polite, though heavily armed. And though none of the Earthlings could understand a word they said, they had made it clear that the trio was not going anywhere.

Edison, Amelia and he had encountered them a few hours after entering the portal that Edison's machine had created and coming out in desert wasteland of shifting, red sands. They had several days' worth of gas and provisions and didn't really know what they would run into, or how long it would take to find any sign of Khan and Bulls-Eye.

The patrol of blue gorillas quickly surrounded them, gibbering at them in a language Benjamin had never heard before. After half an hour of trying it was clear that all of their attempts at communication were failing. They were beginning to become hostile.

Until Benjamin had mentioned Professor Khan.

"Yes, there is an explanation," Edison said. "Everything I've been working on for the past years has been completely and totally wrong." He shook the device. Pushed the button. Growling at it when the light went green again.

The blue gorillas, clearly a military patrol of some sort, had loaded the Carryall into the cargo bay of some sort of armored personnel carrier with an open top and drove them through a scene of utter devastation. Clearly there had been a battle. Recently, too. Some of the bodies and vehicles littering the sands were still on fire.

"So you got some of the details wrong," Amelia said. "Buck up, Doc, you're on Mars." She lay on the hood of the Carryall, her arms propped up behind her head.

The transport had driven through the gates of a huge, walled city, the turrets on the walls still smoking from the battle. The buildings were of a grandeur he had never seen before. All polished brass, enormous rivets, walls decorated with ridiculous images of lightning bolts and stylized hurricanes. In all, it was rather hideous.

Benjamin wasn't sure if the blue gorillas had been the attackers or the defenders, but it was clear that they had been the victors.

"But that's just it. This can't be Mars," Edison said, waving his little box around. "This says there's air here. Real air. Almost Earth normal. The temperature. The light. The fact that there's life here. It's all wrong."

Benjamin felt bad for the doctor. He had explained that all of his calculations showed that this was indeed Mars, at least in location. But the readings he had gotten back through his instruments had shown something altogether different.

As Benjamin understood it, in Edison's time Mars had been partially explored and had proven to be a barren, airless, lifeless rock. And though this place certainly counted as barren, lifeless it most certainly wasn't.

"I thought I'd invented time travel," Edison muttered, scowling at the green light on his box yet again. "But no, I had to go and invent dimensional travel. And I didn't even know it. I'm a failure."

When they had come through the portal he had insisted that they wear thick, bulky suits with self-contained breathing apparatuses. After Edison's little box light had turned green indicating that the atmosphere was breathable they had shed the suits, though Edison still insisted on wearing his.

"Heads up," Amelia said. She hopped off the hood of the car. "Somebody's coming."

Benjamin looked up to see the crowd of warrior gorillas parting, snapping to attention. Soon the sea of blue fur gave way and he smiled when he saw who it was.

"Profesor Khan," he said. "We've been looking for you."

It had been an eventful evening.

Khan stepped into his room and sat on the bed. It had been the room of some departmental minister who ran away once the gates were breached. Whether to join the resistance fighters still controlling parts of the city or to hide out hoping he wouldn't be killed either by the Inkidu or his own people, Khan didn't know.

But the bed was comfortable, if a little small for his frame, and after the last several days he was more than happy to lie down in it.

The reunion with the other Centurions had been a shock. Khan had wondered if he and Bulls-Eye would ever find a way home and now, here they were. He should have known his friends would find a way to help them.

And now he wasn't sure how he felt about that.

The first few minutes of the meeting had been tense. Without the aid of the translation bracelets that Khan and Bulls-Eye wore, the Centurions and the Inkidu hadn't been able to understand one another. Fortunately, when they had been captured someone had heard Benjamin say Khan's name, recognized them as looking like Bulls-Eye and brought them to the city.

Khan and Bulls-Eye translated for them until they were able to get translation bracelets of their own. Once they had those, things went much more smoothly.

The Queen decided that between the defeat of Cyclone's army and the arrival of the Earthlings, a victory feast would be held. Diplomats from the various kingdoms were in attendance, as were Leandra and some of Cyclone's ministers who helped organize the surrender.

Benjamin, a natural diplomat, got along famously with the Queen and by the end of the evening it seemed he was well on his way to setting up trade relations.

Amelia had spent her time talking with the soldiers and looking over the transports and rayguns. She proved to be quite a good shot with them.

Doctor Thomas, on the other hand, had spent the entire night looking at a strange box and gibbering, "All wrong," over and over again. He had finally been escorted to a room where he was, presumably, still doing it.

As for Bulls-Eye, he had disappeared as soon as the banquet was over. He had seemed tense, not at all himself. Khan had seen him speaking with Leandra at one point and neither one of them looked happy.

A knock sounded at the door. He opened it to see Bulls-Eye standing there, his hat in his hands.

"Hey, Perfesser. You got a minute to talk?"

"I do. Come in." Bulls-Eye stepped inside and Khan closed the door behind him. "What can I do for you?"

"You still plannin' on goin' home?" Bulls-Eye said.

The question surprised Khan. Was he? It hadn't occurred to him that there was an option. "Of course," he said. "Why wouldn't I?"

"Well, you know, the Queen and all. I see how she's been lookin' at you. She fancies ya."

If Khan could blush he would have been bright red. He stammered. "Bulls-Eye! Please. That's ridiculous." He hadn't let himself think about that since he had heard that he had somehow become the Queen's consort.

"Settle down, Perfesser. Ain't no harm in it. I's just checkin'. See, with the other Centurions here and Doc Thomas' portal device workin', we're a lot closer to gettin' home than we been."

"Yes," Khan said. "We leave at first light." He yawned. "And I would really like to get a nap in before we go." And to not dwell too much on the implications, he thought.

Bulls-Eye looked at his feet. "I ain't goin' with ya."

"I'm sorry?"

"Leandra's gotta have somebody help her out here and well, I'd just as soon be that feller. Whatta ya think?"

Khan knew the man cared for Leandra, and this was all far from over. Khan couldn't imagine that any of the races would simply let bygones be bygones. It was possible that his presence might do some good. Though he was certainly not a disinterested party, he wasn't a Martian. That might lend him at least the appearance of impartiality.

"I can't say I'm overly surprised," Khan said. "Are you sure this is what you want? Is it what she wants?"

"She asked me to stay," he said. "And I said I had to think about it. Well, I thought about it. But I wanted to see what you thought about it. Because I thought that if you thought that I thought—"

"I understand," Khan said, cutting him off before the poor man confused himself with recursive grammar. "I think you should stay. I think it would be good for you, and good for her people."

Bulls-Eye's face broke into a grin. "Thanks, Perfesser. I just needed to hear that. I'll let you get some sleep. I'll see you off in the mornin'."

Khan stayed awake for a long time after Bulls-Eye left, thinking about what the cowboy had said. The man had made a choice that doubtless could not have been easy. He wouldn't be trapped here, of course. Since Thomas had worked out the details of his portal it looked as though travel between the two worlds would be, well, not easy, but possible.

Bulls-Eye was giving himself up to a greater cause. He would be helping to forge a new nation out of the remains of an old one, one that had made enemies of an entire planet. Khan hoped his and Leandra's love for each other was strong enough to see them through.

And what of the Queen? He still wasn't sure about this consort business. Why hadn't she told him about it? Because he would have balked, that's why. She was as shrewd a leader as any he had ever met. Intelligent, regal, fierce, infuriating, beautiful.

Khan paused. Where had that come from? He was tired. That's what it was. Just tired. He needed rest. He lay down and fell into a fitful sleep.

Khan tied the last of the crates into the back of the Carryall and closed the door. Trinkets, mostly, a raygun or two, several books, a couple dozen translation bracelets. The courtyard had filled to witness their departure. It was still strange to him to have become such a powerful symbol for the Inkidu, a privilege he didn't feel he had earned.

"You know, we have people who could have done that for you," Leandra said, stepping away from the crowd.

"I know, but everyone's busy. Even you."

She smiled. "I wouldn't miss a chance to say good-bye. You made this happen."

"Poppycock," Khan said. "I was merely at the right place at the right time. Can't take responsibility for that." He paused, not sure how to proceed. "I spoke with Bulls-Eye last night."

Her smile grew. "I heard. Thank you. I know he was very worried about what you might say. He respects you."

"And I him. Will you be all right?"

"The city is a mess. All of the kingdoms want to take a piece of it for themselves. Old enemies are already starting to make their presence known. It will be hard, but we'll manage."

"I'm sure you will. Take care of yourself, young lady. And stay safe."

"And you, Professor." Leandra turned and rejoined the crowd. A moment later Khan saw Bulls-Eye join her and the two seemed right for each other. She was right, it would be hard. But they would meet the challenge together.

Together. The word struck a chord in him he couldn't quite identify. It was an alien concept. He had always been alone, always been the outsider. Even among the Centurions, though he was seen as a friend and colleague, he was always apart. But here, he was the Inkidu Champion. He was among people like him.

And then there was the Queen. The thought of her brought a hitch to his chest. He had been terrified when she had gone over the side of the transport. Had lost himself to his rage when Patrus betrayed her.

"Not thinking of sneaking away without saying good-bye to your Queen, are you, Champion?" the Queen said as she stepped away from her entourage.

Khan paused a moment before answering. He wanted to say something, but wasn't sure what it was. Confusion ran through his mind, a state he wasn't used to. "I wouldn't dare, your Highness," he said.

"You know, when I mentioned that the title of Champion also makes you my consort, I wasn't entirely truthful."

"Oh." An odd feeling swept over him. He felt oddly disappointed?

"Yes, in fact that was a bald-faced lie," she said.

"I see," Khan said. "Why?"

"Did I lie to you or why did the troops follow you?"

"Both."

"The troops followed you because they respect you, of course. Because you're the Champion, because you gave them hope."

"And the lie?"

"Because I wanted to fool you into thinking it was the truth. I do need a consort."

Khan stammered. "I— I don't know what to say."

The Queen smiled. "Say yes. Rule by my side. Help me rebuild my nation. Help forge a new world."

"I— I have obligations. On Earth." Did he? Or was he just saying that out of fear?

The Queen's smile fell a little. "I know, Khan. I'm asking a lot. You need to go home. You need to spend some time back on Earth."

"I can come back," Khan said, hopefully.

"No," she said. "Not the way you arrived, at least."

"What?" Khan said. "But the portal—"

"Is unstable. That funny little doctor friend of yours says that it's already beginning to break down. Another few days and it will close forever. Keeps going on about trans-dimensional stability and total protonic reversal. He says it's not impossible to create another one, but the more often he opens one, the more dangerous it becomes. We won't be ferrying tourists between our worlds any time soon. Messages, yes. But not people."

She leaned forward and gave Khan a kiss on the cheek. "You're not ready to leave Earth behind. I understand that. When you are, we'll find a way. But you have to be sure. I won't have you pining for Earth while you're here with me."

Khan watched her return to her entourage, too stunned to speak. A few minutes more of good-byes and the other Centurions joined him at the car.

"Good to go, Professor?" Benjamin said.

Was he? Was he ready to go back to Earth? To leave these people behind? True, he had things to attend to. The Centurions needed his help, a whole world devastated by his progenitor, Gorilla Khan, to help rebuild. Like the Queen's obligation to her kingdom, Khan had an obligation to Earth.

She caught Khan's eye, smiled at him, made shooing motions with her hands. She was right. He wasn't ready. Not for her, not for Mars.

But one day he would be.

PROFESSOR KHAN
WILL RETURN

IN

KING
KHAN

KING KHAN
SNEAK PEEK

It was after sunset when Khan and Bertie arrived at Central Station, well past business hours. Nonetheless, Bertie was able to procure the Wanderer W22 the Blinkersly solicitors arranged as well as a map of Los Angeles.

The long route to Anselme's home took them through a small part of the Sunset Strip, making Professor Khan's first glimpses of the city contradictory and unpleasant. There were squat stone office buildings that lacked the art deco charm of Manhattan. There were intersections with pleasant little houses on one side and desolate scrub lots on the other.

And there was the strip itself: filled with neon advertisements for gambling and music, along with more subtle suggestions for other, less legal entertainments.

"I say," Bertie chattered nervously. "Sin city, wot?"

He wasn't wrong, Khan knew. Los Angeles seemed haphazard, self-indulgent, and flimsy. It looked as if it had been created to indulge the moment, without care to the long-lasting effect.

And yet, while he was waiting on Bertie at the station, or when they waited at a red light, the locals did no more than glance at him, raise an eyebrow, then look away. He felt none of the hostility he had grown accustomed to in New York and on the train ride west. No one scowled. No one stared at him while muttering to a companion. No one hurried away at his approach. It was almost refreshing.

"I'm awfully glad that the locals are not giving us so many awful looks," Bertie said. Khan was surprised he'd noticed. "Much better than in Oklahoma; I thought those fellows were going to draw their six-shooters and OK Corral us! Do you remember those fellows, Professor? They were dressed as cowboys even though they weren't from Texas."

"Bertie, I'm pretty sure there are cowboys in places other than Texas."

"Possibly, Professor, but they don't seem proper cowboys if they're not from Texas. I'm simply goggled that you haven't been treated more warmly. I thought you were famous, sir."

"Fame isn't all it's put up to be, my boy."

"Quite," Bertie said. "I say! Perhaps they think you are a movie actor! Or that we are driving around the city in costume to promote a new film! Wouldn't that be exciting! Tell me, sir, did you see that cracker about the colossal ape fellow? The one where he climbed that building in New York to win the heart of a beautiful woman?"

"I walked out of that film, Bertie."

"Ah. Yes. I'm sure she wasn't his type. My goodness! Is that a woman of ill-repute just standing out on the corner?"

"I suspect not, Bertie." Khan checked his map. "Make a right at this corner, my boy."

He did. Like so much else about Los Angeles, it surprised them by changing rather suddenly. After a short block, the street began to wind up a steep hill and they found themselves almost lost among stands of trees.

Leveque's home wasn't far up the hill, but the trees were thick enough to obscure most of the garish light from the strip below. Bertie pulled off the narrow, winding road into a parking space in front of the house. "Pleasant-looking little place," Bertie said.

Professor Khan almost laughed. The house before them was a two-story Italian villa with a tall privacy hedge, a wrought-iron gate, and a bow window with leaded glass. It was a beautiful place, and should have been far outside the budget of a University professor.

The doorbell rang like chimes. Someone switched on a light above the lintel, and then, after a series of locks were thrown, the door swung open.

A young woman of about twenty-four stood in the entry, framed by the light behind her. Khan heard Bertie catch his breath; yes, he supposed she was pretty by human measures. Her blonde curls had been cut to show off her long, pale neck. She had Leveque's long, narrow nose but her blue eyes were large and expressive.

She was wearing a sleek, elegant dress. In black.

While Khan was considering his own gray tweed and Bertie's jaunty lemon yellow jacket and bowler, Bertie spoke up. "Pardon me, but we've come a long way to speak with Doctor Anselme Leveque."

She glanced back and forth between Khan and Bertie several times, then bared her teeth. "Is this supposed to be a joke? Am I supposed to be laughing? Are you bringing the circus to my house? Damn you!"

She slammed the door in their faces.

Bertie turned toward Khan with a bewildered expression. In all likelihood, no one had ever slammed a door on him before. "Does this mean we start back to England now, Professor?"

Khan laid his hand on Bertie's elbow and pulled him aside so he could reach the doorbell. When it rang again, the woman called through the door: "Go away!"

"I'm sorry to trouble you, but we have come all the way from England on a matter of some urgency about Doctor Leveque. I received a message saying he is in terrible danger." Khan had almost said *was in terrible danger*, but he corrected himself at the last moment. That black dress...

"One moment."

Khan and Bertie stood on the front steps, for quite a little while, waiting. At first, the professor thought the woman had gone to fetch a gun, but the delay was much too long for that. Finally, when the door swung open, the woman's cheeks were covered with tears. "What message?"

"Please let me take a moment to introduce myself. My name is Professor Khan. I corresponded with your father often over the last three years and I consider him my friend. This is Bertie Blinkersly, one of my students. We have come all the way from Oxford University to see him."

The woman sniffled. "Well he never mentioned you to me. Let me see the message."

Professor Khan reluctantly took the folded sheet of paper from his jacket pocket and handed it to her. She glanced at it, then gave it back. "He didn't write that note."

"Certainly not. However, I should mention that it wasn't delivered in an envelope. It was tied to this."

Professor Khan took the metal arrow from his breast pocket. The young woman stood utterly still, staring at it as if it were a ghost. Finally, she took a long look at Khan and Bertie. It was clear she recognized the arrow, just as it was clear she was not sure what to do.

"Come inside," she said finally.

"Gosh, it's about time," Bertie said. "I thought we were going to be turned away like peddlers."

She led them down a few steps into a sunken living room. The couches were low and flat, almost like beds, and the walls were dominated by more bay windows. How much were university professors paid in the United States?

Professor Khan gripped his hat nervously in both hands. The young woman's eyes were wide and glistening, but she would not look directly at him. Her lips were pressed tightly together. Khan thought she might start crying right in front of them, or pull a gun.

Bertie threw his hat carelessly onto the nearest sofa as though he owned the place. "Is Dr. Leveque at home? We've come an awfully long way to jabber at him."

"This isn't his home," the woman said. "It's mine."

"Oh!" Bertie suddenly seemed utterly flummoxed.

Professor Khan laid a hand on his arm to silence him. "In that case, forgive us for calling at this hour. I'm sure it must have been a shock to open the door and see me standing there."

She drew a cigarette from a case, then returned it unlit. "This is Los Angeles. It's not that late and you aren't that shocking. How long has it been since you saw Dr. Leveque?"

Khan noted the pause before she said the name. "You're Sylvia, aren't you? Anselme's daughter."

She began to drum her fingers irritably on the metal rim of the case. "That's not what I would call an answer to my question, is it?"

"Three years ago," Khan answered. "It was a convention in Salzburg. I thought I had been invited to deliver a paper, but in truth the attendees saw me as a circus performer. Your father was the only one who treated me with respect. We spent several hours in his room that first night enjoying a very fine brandy and discussing the most fascinating topics. He really was the most brilliant theoretical physicist I've ever met."

Sylvia's tone was colorless and flat. "All right, maybe he did mention you. He told me that your letters helped advance his work."

"Pish," the professor responded uncomfortably. "Tiny suggestions."

"But he didn't write that note," she insisted.

"No," Khan said. "Neither did I, although the handwriting is supposed to resemble my own. Obviously, your father would never use one of my letters to mimic my script, but someone who had access to them must have. That person was anxious for me to come here, to help him."

"Well he's dead." She tossed the case onto the end table as though it had disappointed her. "I'm sorry to say it so abruptly but the whole thing has been sudden. Everything is sudden. My father is dead."

Bertie took an impulsive step toward her. "You poor old thing—"

She froze him with a glance. "What did you call me?"

"Forgive my student," Professor Khan interjected. "It was not meant unkindly."

"I'd hate to see what he'd say to someone he didn't like. Look, I know you came a long way, but you're too late."

"My dear girl," Professor Khan said gently. "I'm so terribly sorry for the loss you've suffered. I wish there was something I could say to ease the loss of a man like your father. Truly, if there's anything I can do, please ask."

Sylvia was quiet a moment as she considered Khan's words. "You're actually a decent sort, aren't you? Boy, have you come to the wrong part of the world."

Professor Khan accepted the compliment with a nod. "I'm sorry to ask, but considering the circumstances. I feel I must. How did it happen? And when?"

Before she could answer, there was a heavy pounding at the front door.

Sylvia looked mildly alarmed for a moment, but she excused herself and slipped into the foyer. Bertie looked at the professor and said: "Not a bad looker, eh? If she stopped clipping her nails and put a splash of color on them—"

"Pick up your hat, Bertie." The boy had not mentioned Petunia once since the start of their trip, even though she was only an ocean and a continent away. Khan couldn't help but be sharp with him. It was such a short distance!

"Ah. Quite." He stroked the cloth and the yellow sleeve of his jacket, realizing too late that he was inappropriately dressed.

Professor Khan scanned the room again. There was a well-stocked bar but few bookshelves. Not what he would consider a comfortable home. At the back of the house was a large window that looked onto a deck, a smallish back yard, and the lights of another house on the far side of the fence. It would have been pleasant to sit out on that nice deck and talk in the cool evening breeze, but Anselme's daughter would not—could not, in fact—welcome him the way Anselme himself would have.

From out in the entryway, they heard a man's voice, smooth and assured. "Don't worry your pretty head about it, doll. I'm here."

Two men strode into the living room. Both wore dark blue double-breasted suits with wide-brimmed fedoras. The one in the lead was in his early thirties; good-looking the way movie-criminals were, with a pencil mustache and an expression that suggested everything he saw was his for the taking. The crease in his pants looked sharp enough to slice an orange.

The man beside him was shorter, older and fatter, with a pug face and beady, mistrustful eyes. His mouth curled downwards in a contemptuous frown that Khan sensed was a permanent fixture. The hairs on Khan's arms prickled; both had the look of evil men.

They took badges from their jacket pockets. "LAPD Homicide," the younger one said, smiling like a shark. "I'm Detective Waters and my partner is Detective Cross. Who are you?"

Khan answered quickly, before Bertie could open his mouth. "This is Bertie Blinkersly. My name is Professor Khan. We've—"

Waters rolled his eyes. "Off with the mask, wise guy."

Professor Khan grew warm. "It's not a mask. This is my true self."

Waters put his hands on his hips. "You wanna play games with me? Because I play rough."

"Jim," Sylvia cut in. "It's true. He's one of the talking apes you read about in the paper."

"Oh!" Waters's expression became amused for some reason. "Like that crew invaded New York a couple years back. You're one of them?"

The Professor's memory of the invasion was quite different from most, of course, but there was no denying it. "I—

"I say!" Bertie interjected. "Professor Khan was certainly not one of them. He fought on our side!"

Waters leaned forward even further. Khan was standing a couple of steps below him, giving the detective the illusion of physical supremacy. "Betrayed your own people, eh?"

Cross spit out the word "Traitor," with more venom than Khan had thought possible. Part of him marveled that humans would hold him in contempt because he'd risked his life to protect other humans, but they were going to bully him no matter what. It was their way.

"So, Mr. Monkey," Waters said. "Where were you four nights ago at about 10:30?"

"Is that the night Anselme was murdered?"

Waters stuck a toothpick in the corner of his mouth. "Who said anything about murder?"

"You're homicide detectives, aren't you?"

Waters jabbed his finger into Khan's lapel. "Don't get cute with me. Where were you?"

"Somewhere near Albany, NY," Khan answered calmly. "We only just arrived in this city about two hours ago. Bertie has our tickets."

"Why, of course!" Bertie stuffed his hand into his jacket.

Detective Cross came forward like a shot, much faster than anyone might have expected from someone his age and shape. He bounded off the top step and bowled into Bertie, striking him across the forehead with a blackjack.

The young man sprawled across the couch, ticket stubs flying into the air like wedding confetti.

"Bertie!" Khan shouted, stepping toward the boy, but Cross was already holding a gun in his other hand, and it was already pointing at the professor's belly.

Would it be worth taking a slug to tear off Cross's arm? If the detective planned to murder them in cold blood, he didn't see what choice—

"Now now," Waters said. His gun was drawn, too. Khan let his arms fall to the side. "Let's not get all excited. It's just that when my partner here sees someone stuff a hand under a jacket, he gets all anxious. Get it? Your pal there ain't what you call a savvy operator."

Khan looked between them. While Waters talked tough, it was Cross who would murder them both in cold blood and never lose a wink of sleep. "You're correct," Khan said. His voice sounded steadier than he felt. Bertie, his eyes wet and shining, stared up at Cross in astonishment. "He's led a sheltered life, but he's basically good-hearted."

Waters seemed to consider that the way Khan would consider a menu option. Sylvia stepped toward him. "Jim, they have one of my father's arrows."

Detective Waters turned a questioning look at Khan. He didn't wait for the inevitable question. "Someone shot it at me."

Waters rolled his eyes again, then holstered his revolver. He stepped down into the living room like a prizefighter heading into a fixed match. When he was just a few inches from Khan's face, he spoke very quietly.

"*Professor*, huh? Mr. Talking Monkey is a professor? Let me ask you, Monkey: Do you think you're better than me?"

"At what?" the Professor responded.

Bertie sat up, his hand over the growing lump on his head. Cross moved to the side, stepping up one stair for a better look out the window. His pudgy sneer had a tiny twist of confusion. "What the hell is that?"

They all turned to look out the front window. The ocean breezes made the trees shimmer in the faint light, but there was something else, too. Faint figures that seemed to bounce toward them.

The front door crashed open, and an Asian man hopped into the room, his arms stretched out in front of him. His face had the ghastly pallor of death.

"Jiangshi!" Bertie shouted. "By golly, it's a jiangshi!"

The front window shattered as more corpses hopped through.

TO BE CONTINUED
IN THE THRILLING NEW
PROFESSOR KHAN ADVENTURE

KING
KHAN

COMING SOON
FROM EVIL HAT PRODUCTIONS

SPIRIT OF THE CENTURY ™

Spirit of the Century™ is the pulp roleplaying game based on the award-winning Fate system that started it all. If you enjoyed *Dinocalypse Now* and you're looking to tell your own tales of adventure from the Century Club, this is the game for you.

Character creation can be done in just a few minutes or expanded to take up an evening. Adventure design is a snap with three methods for creating relevant, flavorful, player-focused stories at a moment's notice.

Spirit can be played as a fun pick-up game requiring little preparation or as a longer term game delivering evenings of entertainment. All you need to play are some friends, some dice, and the game book.

Pick up your copy of *Spirit of the Century*™ today at our website—or wherever roleplaying games are sold.

www.evilhat.com
ISBN 978-0-9771534-0-4
EHP2000 • US $30.00

MORE BOOKS FROM
SPIRIT OF THE CENTURY™
PRESENTS

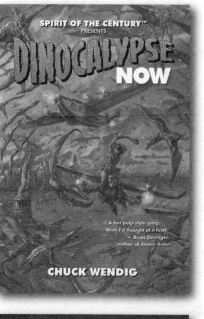

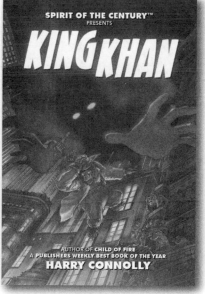

The *Spirit of the Century* adventure continues in these titles, available now or coming soon!

- *The Dinocalypse Trilogy* by Chuck Wendig: *Dinocalypse Now, Beyond Dinocalypse*, and *Dinocalypse Forever*
- *Khan of Mars* by Stephen Blackmoore
- *King Khan* by Harry Connolly
- *The Pharaoh of Hong Kong* by Brian Clevinger
- *Stone's Throe* by C.E. Murphy
- *Sally Slick and the Steel Syndicate* by Carrie Harris

RACE TO ADVENTURE!

THE SPIRIT OF THE CENTURY™ EXPLORATION GAME

Every year, a worldwide scavenger hunt brings together daring adventurers from all parts of the globe—members of the famed Century Club. Their adventures are filled with danger, excitement, and wonder! Centurions race to be the first to complete every mission, stamp their passports, and cross the Century Club finish line. Will this be your year to win?

Race to Adventure!™ is easy to learn and quick to play. Players take turns selecting exciting items to help them on their quest, like the Jet Pack, Zeppelin, or Lightning Gun! Then everyone moves and takes action at exotic locations.

Be the first player to collect every stamp on your passport, return to the Century Club, and declare victory!

EVIL HAT
PRODUCTIONS

ABOUT THE PUBLISHER

Evil Hat Productions believes that passion makes the best stuff—from games to novels and more. It's our passion that's made Evil Hat what it is today: an award-winning publisher of games and, now, fiction. We aim to give you the best of experiences—full of laughter, story-telling, and memorable moments—whether you're sitting down with a good book, rolling some dice, or playing a card.

We started, simply, as gamers, running games at small conventions under the Evil Hat banner, making face to face connections with some of the same people who've worked on these products. Player to player, gamer to gamer, we've passed our passion along to the gaming community that has already given us so many years of lasting entertainment.

Today, we are turning that passion into fiction based on the games we love. And, much like the games we make and play, we need and *want* you to be part of that process.

That's the Evil Hat mission, and we're happy to have you along on it.

You can find out more about us and the stuff we make at *www.evilhat.com*.

ABOUT THE AUTHOR

Stephen Blackmoore is the author of the novels *City Of The Lost* and *Dead Things* and his short stories have appeared in the magazines *Needle, Plots With Guns, Spinetingler, Thrilling Detective,* and *Shots* as well as the anthologies *Deadly Treats, Don't Read This Book* and *Uncage Me.*

He has also written essays on Los Angeles politics and crime for the website *LAVoice.org* (http://lavoice.org) and the *LA Noir* true crime blog (http://la-noir.blogspot.com).

He is a scintillating conversationalist but of only average height.